# BEYOND BRIGHTSIDE

## BOOK 2

### MARK TULLIUS

VINCERE
PRESS

Published by Vincere Press
65 Pine Ave., Ste 806
Long Beach, CA  90802

Beyond Brightside
Copyright © 2020 by Mark Tullius
All rights reserved.
For information about permission to reproduce selections
from this book, write to Permissions, Vincere Press, 65
Pine Avenue Ste. 806, Long Beach, CA 90802
Printed in the United States of America
First Edition
ISBN:  978-1-938475-59-7
Library of Congress: 2020913764

Cover design by Florencio Ares aresjun@gmail.com

To the Levesque family,
for the unconditional love and constant encouragement.
I'm forever grateful.

# AUTHOR'S NOTE

This book is the second book in the *Brightside* series (or the third if you count *Try Not to Die: In Brightside* which is a short segue between the two books told from the perspective of a female Thought Thief). If you haven't had the opportunity to read *Brightside*, I suggest you do that first. Brightside is free for newsletter subscribers at my website MarkTullius.com.

# Night 7

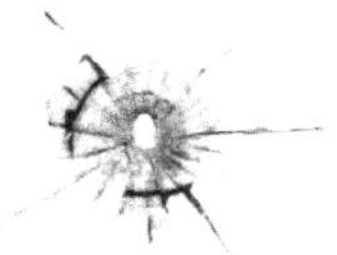

# CHAPTER ONE

In Brightside I counted by days, but since the escape it's been nothing but nights. It's nearly Night 7, the last bits of sunlight crawling through the cracked mud that patches together the warped pieces of plywood. The floor is a filthy strip of brown carpet covering dirty concrete, our roof a drooping blue tarp. This hanging black blanket is the only thing separating me from the rest of the shack.

Our shitter's an orange and black Home Depot bucket; a fifth of the five-gallon capacity is filled with my watery mess. The plastic edge is embedded in my legs and ass because I've been sitting here so long. I should be sleeping, but I'm too ashamed to face the person whose life I absolutely wrecked. I can't let her see me like this.

I assumed roaches would be the biggest problem under a bridge, but right now it's the flies. Dozens are buzzing between the bucket and my soiled clothes stuffed in the corner, but nearly as many are hovering above my left collarbone, the bloody bandage advertising a feast.

With the sling off, I can move my lower arm a bit, but the upper part is taped tight to my chest. Thanks to the oxy I can't feel my ankle much either, just a hot throb. My toes are the deep purple of overripe grapes because I'm terrible at taking advice, ignoring everyone who'd said we wrapped it too hard. But none of it matters. All I need the foot for is this one last night.

Beyond Brightside

From the other side of the blanket, she whispers my name. Her voice is sweet and innocent although I tore that away when I refused to take her no for an answer, a true American hero. "Joe," she says loud enough to hear over the traffic. "Please come back."

I say I will. *I'm almost done.* The syringe glistens in my palm. 5 cc. More than enough to end everything. *I need to say a prayer.*

Even when I was a kid, I thought praying was bullshit. Crazy how things change when the knowledge that you'll die one day solidifies into the understanding that the end could come any goddamn second.

It isn't just the Boots that want revenge. It's the whole fucking country, probably the world. They all saw the videos of what we did. According to the media, I'm a stone-cold killer, the most wanted man in America.

It's a long story and if you don't know about Brightside, I don't know where the hell you've been. It's where they stuck us, a beautiful prison for telepaths, a power so great it made our lives worthless.

That's the thing I need you to remember. They left us no choice. We had to get out of Brightside.

We did what we had to.

And there's one last thing left to do.

# Night 1

# CHAPTER TWO

The sun was still up when Day 100 became Night 1, the exact moment there was no turning back and simply saying sorry.

I'd been planning the escape for a long time, training my body and mind for what I imagined lay ahead. My escape was supposed to be sneaky, slipping away in the dark. After Sara, the beauty I shared an office with, turned down the offer, it was going to be just me all by myself. But then it became me and Rachel, someone to enjoy piña coladas with on the beach. Then Sharon, Brightside's shrink and undercover resistance ringleader, roped me into a master plan designed by my own father. On Day 99, I was left with no choice but to be their triggerman.

I'd still planned on Rachel being right there beside me, but she saw the lipstick, knew it was Sara's. When I said my final goodbye to Rachel, she had been dead for fifteen hours, stuffed in my closet. Her face was gone along with most of her skull, her Care Bears shirt drenched in blood.

With no sleep, a dead girlfriend, and a psychopath threatening to kill me, I went up to the rooftop of the tallest building in Brightside. From there, I took out one of their helicopters with a lucky shot and watched it crash on the Square below.

The Boots were already clearing the building so I hurried down to the fourth floor where I sold timeshares. That's when Wendell called me into the bathroom and saved me from that rookie Boot by thunking his head on the sink.

The burning helicopter was enough of a distraction that I was able to make it out of the building unnoticed and rendezvous with Sara, who got pulled back into the madness when that psychopath Wayne kidnapped her mentally disabled brother, Danny. We hurried up the mountain to the hidden mineshaft, but I twisted my ankle tripping over a root. As bad as it hurt, I could put pressure on it and we made it to the mine, where Wayne was waiting, the tip of his knife drawing blood from Danny's neck.

I tricked Wayne into trusting me and managed to get hold of the shotgun, but I was too much of a coward to pull the trigger. Wayne ripped the shotgun out of my hands and slammed me onto the rocks, used the Mossberg to crush my throat. Everything would've ended right there if it hadn't been for Danny attacking Wayne and Sheriff Melvin putting a bullet through his brain.

At first, I believed that if I'd left right then and gone down the shaft with Sara and everyone else, we would've gotten away without a hitch. Now I know that's not true. My going back to get Wendell's sixteen-year-old sister, Becky, slowed us down a bit, but they'd been waiting all along. Some of those fuckers knew what was going down. They fucking knew.

Agent Palmer knew. He was the one waiting for us with a sniper on the other side of the mine.

I'd just blown away three Boots on the 200-foot-high ledge and more were coming. The rope ladder was slick with ice, but I had control over my fear of heights, my will to live overriding everything else. I was halfway down when the sniper opened fire, missing my face by just inches before blasting the hole through my collarbone. Sheriff Melvin saved me again by taking out Palmer and the sniper. Sara and Danny waiting on the side of the Boot-splattered highway with Dad was the surprise. He was our driver.

They stuck me in the back of the moving van with forty others, leaving behind dozens more that couldn't fit. I hoped some of them would make it, but we've seen every one of their bodies on TV, their dead mugshots making you feel better, keeping all your dirty secrets safe.

# CHAPTER THREE

There were twenty too many of us in that truck, no room between our squished bodies, just dark thoughts to match the blackness. I was in shock but heard Becky's and Sara's thoughts along with everyone else's inside my six-foot radius. Most were scared, all of us delusional, hoping we'd just got through the worst of it.

Being more of a realist, I figured we were fucked but I tried my hardest to stay positive for the others. Sharon was up in front and didn't get to see it, but I think she'd have been proud of me. Even with the bullet through my collarbone and my mangled ankle, it was my delusion that brought calm to the van. I believed we were free.

But that shit only lasted like two seconds, Becky bringing back reality by thinking the cops were going to light up our vehicle, bullets blasting through the thin walls until we were all dead.

My mouth was parched, so I kept silent. *We'll make it. Palmer probably reported us, but he doesn't know where we're headed.*

It helped ease her mind. I told Becky that it was my dad driving. *He wouldn't have risked everything for nothing.*

The line seemed to work on her, but then I got to thinking about what she said, how we were all going to die in that box.

I tried to sit up and nearly screamed. Through clenched teeth, but loud as I could to be heard over the thrumming road, I asked "Who knows the plan?"

A man toward the front said, "None of us."

From somewhere close, Terrance said, "Yep, everything's compartmentalized."

A woman whose voice I didn't recognize said, "Only Sharon, and she's up front."

I asked about Demarius, Sharon's right-hand man.

Someone said Demarius didn't make it. "Ate a bullet in the park."

Carlos, my Brightside Travel boss, crawled over and said, "Hey, Joe, we're all proud of you."

I never thought I'd hear those words out of his mouth. I also never realized how meaningless words could be. I asked, "What do you know?"

"Some, but not much. You doing okay?"

I asked about guns and he said we had a couple. I asked what our contingency plan was if we got pulled over and reminded him, *We have to assume everyone's searching for this truck, or at the very least, something big enough to transport this many people.*

Carlos was just like the rest and didn't know shit.

*Think about how many men we've killed.* I wanted to be wrong but knew I wasn't. *They can't let us get away with this.*

Sheriff Melvin said, "I've got eight bullets on me. A small cache should be waiting at the drop off."

It was growing more difficult to speak so I directed my thoughts at Melvin. *Where's that?*

Melvin was all guesses. I called out for the other gunmen, but we hit a bump and I yelped from the blast of pain radiating from my shoulder.

Sara held me tighter and said, "Shush."

That just made things worse, had me feeling trapped with all that blood pooling on my lap.

Nervous like I'd never heard her, Sara said, "Is there anyone with medical experience in here? I don't know what to do."

No one said a word, but then Dr. Osaka, Brightside's vet, knelt beside me, put his hand on my forehead and wished me peace. He unbuttoned my shirt while Sara shined the flashlight she'd pulled from my pocket.

Osaka confirmed what I figured. "It's shattered but not bleeding badly. It'll need to be cleaned, but not while we're moving. Too dangerous."

Sara asked, "What can we do?"

Osaka placed gauze in Sara's hand and guided her to the hole. "Maintain pressure."

"Will he be okay?"

Osaka patted my head, but I could barely feel it, my hearing going the same way as my vision. It sounded like he was talking with a mouthful of cotton. "He'll have to be," he said. "He has no choice."


I woke to the tick of the truck's turn indicator as we eased off the freeway. I had no concept of time and asked, "How long has it been?"

Everyone agreed it was around thirty minutes, which meant we were either getting off the 190 west or M-90 south, either one giving us escape options. The truck slowed to a crawl but the turn up an incline bounced us all around, the pain whipping me awake.

My dad alerted us before raising the rear door, said we were safe and warned us not to shoot. The warehouse lights were dim, but it still took a second for my eyes to adjust, Dad standing in front of a bunch of strangers.

Everyone else's eyes must've started working too because they all rushed for the door. Someone knocked Sara into me and I screamed.

Dad yelled, "Stop!" He shouted it even louder and everyone froze in place. "Order! We have info and supplies, but we need order!"

Danny, Sara, and Becky formed a circle around me while the others cleared out. They were careful getting me down, but everything hurt, the noise so loud with everyone rushing about, hugging, crying, shouting. The voices blended with idling vehicles on either side. My head started throbbing and my hearing got fuzzy, sound coming in waves. They brought me to my dad, his dusty brown eyes sparkling behind his glasses, his hair so much grayer than it'd been three months before. I wanted to hug him, to say something, but all I could think was, *I feel sick.*

Always quick with an answer, Dad said, "Shock's wearing off is all." He ordered Danny and Becky to take me to the blue station wagon at the back of the warehouse.

My ankle was ballooning out my sock, a tenderness that couldn't be touched. I only had the one arm to hold on with, so Danny, who's built like an NFL lineman, took all my weight while Becky cleared a path through the reunions. Moving hurt like hell, but it helped me focus, kept away the nausea.

Becky, whose freckled face was scratched from being pulled through the trees during our escape, popped the rear door and cleared a space between all the bags and blankets. After a painful struggle getting my jacket off me, Becky placed it under my head for a pillow. She said, "You'll be okay."

Three loud claps echoed through the building, Dad's favorite call for attention. "Listen up," he said. "All Brightsiders need to follow whatever your Outsider tells you. We know what to do, where to avoid, how to act."

All I could see was the drab gray roof of the station wagon while a woman kept shouting for Tommy, demanding someone answer her.

Dad said something, but I couldn't listen because I was freaking out, afraid that I was about to die. I called for Danny then Becky, but neither was there. My eyelids were too heavy, my mouth parched. It was sad to think the gunmetal gray might be the last thing I'd see.

#

Father told me to wake up but my eyes wouldn't open.

He said it again. Even if I could, I wouldn't open them. I didn't want to go to school.

His hand went on my right shoulder. "Now."

Nearly every morning it was the same thing. Him shaking me awake all pissed off because Mom had stayed overnight at some friend's.

"Joe, wake up," Dad said, ripping me out of the past. "The morphine should take away some of the sting, but I don't want you jumping."

The lights were blinding and I'd been drained of all energy, the entire left side of my torso an angry throb. I mumbled, "Turn it off," and tried to shield my eyes, but that arm was in a sling and my right hand held tight by Danny, who was draped over the backseat, his usual smile hidden by an expression of concern.

Sara said sorry and moved the beam of light off my face, the gunmetal gray coming back.

"Keep the light right where it is, one hand on that shoulder," Dad told her. "Joe, you just breathe. And hold still."

I couldn't help but think of Dad's motto that I'd always thought was just talk. *Prepare for success but plan for disaster.*

His head hovered above the bullet hole. "We've got to get this clean," he said. "You'll be fine."

I closed my eyes and wished I'd just pass out.

Whether it was the morphine or Dad's skill, I didn't feel a thing. He pulled back out of sight and said, "Goddamn, you got lucky."

I kept my teeth clenched to speak. "Don't feel lucky."

Dad rummaged around in a bag by my head. The package he pulled out matched the gray roof. He tore off the top and said, "If that bullet hit two centimeters lower you would've bled out before you made the truck."

Danny squeezed my hand a little tighter and said, "It's okay. It's okay." For Becky's sake, he thought, *I'm keeping him brave.*

Dad's been out of the military for twenty-plus years but remembered the routine. "Alright soldier, we're almost done, but you've got to hold still." A red sweater appeared in front of my face. "Bite it."

Like a good boy, I chomped down without questioning, the scratchy wool rubbing the top of my mouth, my breath turning it into a furnace. *I'm ready.*

Dad jammed his finger into the wound, packing in the material with the gentleness of an enraged gorilla.

Danny shouted, "Oww! You're squeezing too hard."

I couldn't let go of Danny until Dad finished and patched me up with a bandage.

The gray roof grew dimmer until it blended with the black, into a crazy world where Dad said, "You did good."

# CHAPTER FOUR

A woman called my name, told me to wake. Her hand grabbed my leg and shook. "Joe. Get up. We need you."

My eyes opened but everything remained black. It was hard to breathe, something covering my mouth. For a second, I was back in first grade, that man's oily blue denim sleeve smashing my lips, his hand squeezing my throat.

My entire body shook. "Joe, please," the woman said, her hand rocking me hard. "Wake up."

My left hand couldn't move, but my right swiped at my face and threw off the itchy blue blanket, the gunmetal gray above. "Where am I?"

The sweet but scared voice said, "We're in the car headed to Mexico."

*Fuck.* Reality ripped off a layer of grogginess. It was Wendell's sister, Becky, leaning over the back seat in a bright orange sweatshirt. I asked, "My dad?"

From the front seat, sounding like she was about to snap, Sara said, "Joe, what do we do?"

Becky filled me in with rapid-fire thoughts, told me there were twenty cars between us and the high-powered lamps at the checkpoint.

I asked, "Do we have a gun?"

"I do," she said, crawling halfway into the back so she could help me sit up, the pain clearing the rest of the daze.

My head rested against the rear window, the headlights keeping away the darkness, everything too bright. I couldn't see Sara because of her headrest, but I found her eyes in the rearview. "Where's Sharon?"

Sara pointed two cars up at the black Audi. "Right there. What do I do? All I have is a bullshit ID that looks nothing like me."

Trying to sound confident like my father, I said, "They're rolling everyone through too quick to be checking licenses."

She said, "If we're going to try it, you better get back down."

There were nine cars between us and the checkpoint. Two Boots in blue jeans and black windbreakers stood there looking tough with arms crossed but not doing a thing. It was the guy in the middle of the cars with his colors reversed. He was waving people through, a thick silver brace wrapped around his neck, chin to chest. *Oh fuck.* "Look at the guy in the middle."

Sara said, "He's one of us."

I had never seen a Sentinel in practice but had heard about them on the news. Becky thought about them being used at all major functions in Los Angeles. Even some celebrities had acquired Thought Thieves of their own to help keep them safe from closet telepaths feeding off their fears.

The Audi's rear passenger door opened and the interior lights lit up Sharon's husband behind the wheel and their four-year-old daughter beside him. The girl threw herself over the front seat, arms stretched out, mouth wide with a piercing cry as her mother fled the car. Sharon ran for the dirt embankment, her daughter's sobs slicing through our closed windows.

I never cared for Sharon and she only tolerated me because she was my shrink and wanted to use me. We were all ordered to share every thought with her, but I kept it all inside. All the bad shit you box up and forget in order to protect yourself.

But even though we were not friends, I prayed Sharon would make it over the broken-down wooden fence at the bottom of the embankment and find a way back to her daughter.

The cry that'll never leave me didn't even earn Sharon's daughter a double take from either Boot. They just walked after Sharon with no sense of urgency, let her make it halfway down before they took aim and fired.

The gunshots jerked Danny awake and he screamed as Sharon did a final dance, crashing to the ground and tumbling into the fence, her face jammed in the hole where a board was missing.

The Boots turned back to the Audi. Sharon's husband stood beside the driver door, daughter shrieking in his arms, both with hands in the air. The Boots each fired two shots, the bodies falling to the highway.

Sara sat stunned so we shouted for her to punch it. She stomped on the gas and took us right, crushing the cones and jumping the curb to go down the embankment. The shoulder was blocked by vehicles, nothing but grass on the other side of the wooden fence. I hoped we were going fast enough and shouted, "Go through it!"

Danny acted like we were on a roller coaster, his hands on the roof. "Wooaaah!"

I had nothing to hold on to but was wedged in tight with bags and blankets, barely moving when the station wagon punched through the fence, chunks of board flying, our windshield smashing into a million-crack maze.

Sara kept her foot on the gas, sticking her head out the window so she could see. We were tearing through the back field of a park and were halfway to the playground when the clunking beneath us turned into a piercing grind and Sara threw on the brakes.

I pointed out the streetlights on the other side of the empty basketball courts and told Sara to keep going. There didn't seem to be anyone following, but I knew helicopters couldn't be far behind. I said, "We need a car."

The parking lot was empty, the neighborhood asleep, thick smoke rising from under us. There was the four-way stop to the right and the traffic light a couple of blocks down to the left. Sara asked how we're supposed to get a car. "Steal one?"

Becky spotted approaching headlights. She hoped it wasn't the Boots. Sara prayed it wasn't the cops. All I cared about was a vehicle.

This white kid looking straight out of college slowed his silver four-door Sentra for the stop sign. An old lady with glasses was close behind in a cherry red Cadillac.

I said, "Sara, block them."

Sara didn't hesitate and stepped on the gas.

I hated putting the second part on Becky, but she had the gun. "You got to jack one of their cars."

We flew through the intersection and Sara whipped the wheel hard, slid us sideways in front of the Sentra. Becky just sat there and watched the driver start yelling. I thought loud and hard to shake her awake. *Becky! The Boots are coming!*

Becky bolted out the door and aimed the gun at the guy, stood like she knew what she was doing.

The Cadillac burned rubber in reverse and sped away. Porch lights flicked on across the street.

Like she was auditioning to be the sweetest carjacker in the country, Becky said, "I'm so sorry, but we need your car." When the guy didn't move, she became a little more serious and said, "You can take our car. Please, I don't want to hurt you."

His hand came off the wheel and I was sure he was going for a gun. So was Becky, her finger hugging the trigger.

"Whoa, whoa, whoa!" The driver showed his hands. "I'm gonna unlock the door."

Becky lowered the gun. "Hurry up."

The back of the station wagon opened and Danny, who looked like a bodybuilder in his tight tank top, pulled me out, the movement aggravating the deep, dull pressure throbbing through my shoulder. Becky sat the driver on the sidewalk while the neighborhood came to life, porch lights popping on, angry voices yelling.

Danny stuffed us in the Sentra's back seat with a bunch of bags. Seatbelts were out of the question, but we had enough cushion to feel safe. Becky got in the passenger seat, loaded with gear. She was closing the door when some lady yelled, "I'm calling the cops!"

Sara asked, "Which way?"

I said, "The freeway. South."

Becky told her, "Straight. Just move."

Sara backed up, then zipped around the station wagon. Not wanting to get pulled over for something stupid, I said, "Don't go too fast."

Becky's heart was pounding, her palms sweaty. She wanted to throw the gun out the window. *I can't believe how close I came to shooting him.*

I thought, *But you didn't.*

I felt sick for sticking her in the situation, for the entire thing, but there was no time for remorse with Sara panicking about which way to go.

She asked, "Should I turn left at the light?"

Becky said, "We're too close to the checkpoint. I say go farther."

As a rule for all of us to remember, I said, "Don't stop if you see them coming, Sara. They're going to kill us."

Danny thought that made no sense. "But we're the good guys."

Becky asked Sara, "Where's that phone? We need a map."

"Sweatshirt. Right pocket."

Becky got the app working but didn't know what the single-digit number inside the bubbles that blinked about the map meant. She said, "There aren't any buttons so I can zoom in."

Sara asked, "Is there anything you can press? Those bubbles must be the safe houses."

Becky said, "How do I know which one to pick?"

I told Sara to take a left at the light. "The freeway's right there."

The blinker clicked on. Sara said, "Pick the closest one."

A cheery woman on the phone guided us onto the freeway, the southbound lanes nearly empty, the northbound a parking lot of red brake lights. Two helicopters thumped behind us, hovering over the checkpoint and park.

Becky said, "It's twelve minutes."

I said, "But what about Mexico?"

"Not in this car," Sara said. "Plus, your dad said that this makes for a good Plan B."

Back home Plan B stood for bullshit, but I kept that to myself. "Yeah, for how long?"

Sara said, "It'll give us time to think."

Becky said, "And plan."

Danny said, "And eat."

Mexico had been the plan. "What about a boat?"

Sara said, "If we somehow got our hands on one, what then?"

I can barely keep from barfing at sea and know nothing about sailing. I settled back with the bags and closed my eyes to stop the spinning. I concentrated on my breath and focused on good thoughts, let the morphine pull me back down.

I didn't remember falling asleep but the next thing I knew some strange woman said, "Get off the freeway in 600 feet."

Becky apologized for startling me and lowered the phone's volume. Speaking nice and calm, she guided Sara left at the light, right on a two-lane street, then another left just past the grocery store.

It looked like a decent neighborhood with at least one SUV in each driveway, the lawns neatly trimmed. After a few turns, Becky said to slow down. "It's that brown one on the left."

The small one-story could barely be seen behind the giant tree. Sara pulled over at the next house up and asked, "You're sure?"

"This is it," Becky said. "And there's nothing else to press so I guess we're supposed to go up and knock. Did Joe's dad say anything else?"

Sara said, "There should be a word on the screen upon arrival. Is there anything?"

"Here it is," Becky said. "Ghost."

"That's it." Speaking to Danny and me, Sara said, "Everyone got that? Just say ghost."

Becky asked about the car and reminded Sara that I couldn't walk.

In that extra slow drawl of his, Danny said, "I'll watch him."

Becky assured Sara we'd be okay. "I'll go with you to dump this and we'll run right back."

It was too late at night to be standing out on the sidewalk. I said, "Where should we wait? Someone's going to call the cops."

Sara pointed at the tree. "How about under there? I can't see anything from here."

We were out of options so they left us with half the bags and drove away. Danny set the bags beside the sidewalk while I did my best not to fall over or puke. As quietly as we could, I hobbled with Danny to the safe house. It was dark under the huge oak, but only until we took another step and motion detectors lit the yard.

I squinted, the light too bright for my dilated pupils. "Over there," I said, directing Danny to the door. We reached the first step just as the porchlight blinked on and a blue light appeared on the doorbell console. Sounding as scared as I felt, a man asked, "Who's there?"

Before I could say anything, Danny said, "Me and Joe."

I elbowed Danny's side and told him to say the password, hoping he'd remember what I'd already forgotten, my mind all mushy.

Danny put his mouth next to the console and whispered, "The password."

The guy said, "Off my property or I'm calling the cops."

I said, "Go ahead. Can't wait to tell them about your involvement."

He went silent so I kept on going. "Turn this light off before someone else calls it in. You'll be just as fucked as us."

The light snapped off and two locks disengaged. The door opened just enough for me to see the black semiautomatic gripped by chubby little fingers. It opened a bit more to reveal the rest of the middle-aged man, his Wallflowers T-shirt bulging over his baggy khaki cargo shorts. His voice cracked when he said, "I'm only equipped for one. And not some…"

I said, "Differently abled."

Danny smiled. "Plus Becky and Sara."

The guy shook his head, his cheeks jiggling. "What? No way."

I said, "Sorry, man, it'll just be the night."

He opened the door a little more so he could peek out, look up and down the street. "Who saw you?"

"No one, but if you don't let us in someone's going to."

The guy was scared, no ability to hide his thoughts. A hundred percent he didn't want to take us, but he knew I was dangerous. He stepped to the side and said, "Hurry up. Down that hall."

The living room had a scuffed hardwood floor and ugly furniture, in the hallway a worn green carpet. We stopped at the last doorway, but he scooted past us and stopped in front of the painting at the end of the hall, a dark ocean with a beaming lighthouse.

He turned to us, his face all serious like a substitute teacher on his first day of assignment. It was me being injured and no longer a threat. "Look, once you're in here, you aren't coming out. Not until I say it's clear." He kept the gun by his side, chastising himself for not just pulling it out and tossing us. "I don't know why you're running or where you're headed, I just know you can't stay. Especially with fucking four of you."

I nodded, didn't say a word, just looked him dead in the eyes, let him cook. This guy never dreamed of talking down to anyone even close to his pay grade. He'd also never been in a fight he'd won and was worrying about Danny and how strong he was.

He cleared his throat. "So you understand?" he asked, his confidence gone.

My eyes didn't leave his. They were right there waiting for him each time he looked away. "You swore you could be trusted," I said. "Can we trust you?"

He said, "Of course," and pressed a button on the bottom of the painting. A lock clicked and he pulled open the hidden door. He waved us into the small room that'd been added on, not much in it besides the small bed Danny helped lay me on.

I told Danny I wanted to sit up and wait for the girls, but that wasn't the truth. Now that there was a small sense of safety, that we had at least a few minutes to rest, the nausea was back, worse than before. Closing my eyes and taking big breaths were the only things keeping me from retching.

Danny remembered our bags were outside and went with the guy to collect them. They returned before I could pass out, Becky and Sara not far behind them.

I couldn't open my eyes, but I knew everyone was staring at me. Danny said, "He's sleepy."

Becky sat beside me and put a pillow under my left leg, said we needed to get some ice on it. She and Sara worked together to prop up my shoulder.

Clear as I could, with just about the most shame I've ever felt, I thought, *I am so sorry. To all of you.*

Sara held my face and told me to hush, tried not to think about how warm I was. "Let's all get some rest while we can."

Their worlds had been entirely different twelve hours ago, none of them facing death. *This isn't how I imagined it.*

Becky said, "We know."

Danny said, "We're okay."

Sara said, "We're alive."

My mind was a muddled fog of death, the darkness closing in, leaving me with nothing but bullets destroying faces and nearly blowing off heads.

I said, "For now."

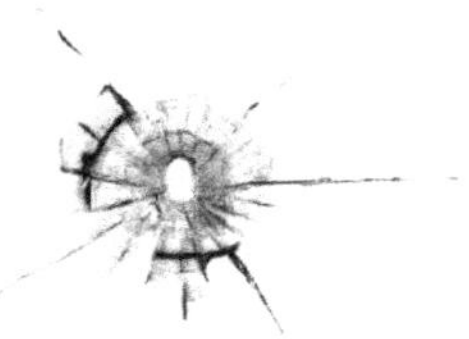

# Night 7

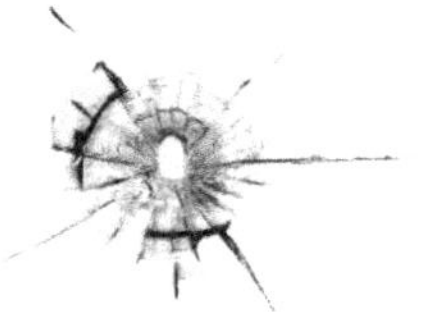

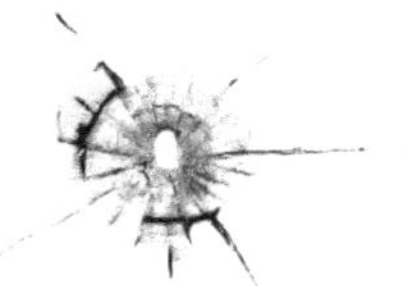

# CHAPTER FIVE

My concept of time is shot, but the sunlight's gone, the rumble of traffic turned down. Night 7 is now official. I feel like a piece of shit hiding in this corner, but I'm not so sure I can stand.

Careful not to push the plywood wall down, I use it to rise and steady myself. Even crouched over, my head's hitting the drooping tarp. The mirror stapled into the plywood is level with my shoulder. I'd promised myself I wouldn't look at it again, but it itches so damn bad it's taking all I have not to scrap it clean with a knife.

I set the syringe on the milk carton, put my phone beside it, flashlight on. The bandage is sticky, takes skin and pus with it as I peel it back from the wound, the raw stench worse than the nastiness floating in the bucket toilet. Now I know why everyone who's seen it makes a face that says I'm fucked. What should've healed up with antibiotics and a hospital stay has turned into the Eye of Sauron, yellow pus bubbling up between the black and red, a circle of angry raised skin surrounding it, dark red lines spreading the disease through my veins.

The bandage won't stay up so I just leave it, bend over to get my phone but rise with the syringe. I thought I could trust myself, but I'm no longer so sure. I don't know why it comes as such a surprise to me though, considering just seven days ago I had the shotgun under my chin thinking of joining Rachel, her half a head and my half a head completing each other.

Things would've been so much better if I hadn't been a coward and just pulled the trigger. All the things I wouldn't have seen, wouldn't have known, wouldn't have felt. All the sickness, all the suffering, fearing for our lives every second.

What I couldn't do then, I would now if I didn't have any responsibility. But maybe the most responsible thing would be sticking the needle in my neck and plunging it all the way down, but I've got to look myself in the eyes before I do what half the world wants me to.

My eyes are cold, no shine, can't ever go back from what they've seen. What the Boots have done. What we've done. So much death.

All I wanted was freedom, just didn't think this was the way I'd get it. Twenty-eight years old with nothing to show for it except a name people will forever despise.

I used to hear my dad telling me to pull the trigger, but that voice was all wrong. Now he's screaming at me to be a soldier, fulfill my mission until the end.

# Night 2

# CHAPTER SIX

Waking up on Night 2 was a slow climb out of a syrupy haze, no memory of where I was or if anyone was around. The air was warm on my stomach, cold on my crotch. I hoped I was dreaming.

Becky startled me when she said, "It's okay. We need to get you changed anyhow. It's not a big deal, Joe."

Sara agreed. *It's nothing.*

I wished the piss was my only problem because right then it was the pain, a red-hot pressure radiating from my left shoulder.

"Joe, look at us," Becky said. She was kneeling on a duffel bag piled in front of the barred window. "We look different, right? Come on, that's what we've got to do with you."

I couldn't remember what she'd been wearing before, but now she had on a tight pair of jeans and a black Misfits T-shirt. The big change was her hair, chopped short like a boy's, the brown now blond.

Danny's number 78 blue and white Giants' jersey swayed back and forth as he corralled a bug in the corner. He'd found a pencil and was doing that nervous thing, rubbing his thumb up and down the end of it. It's the same way he held that stick before plunging it in Wayne's cheek.

I shake the image and concentrate on Danny, struggling to see what's different. He looks at me over his shoulder and points to his jet-black hair.

"Oh yeah. And no hat," I said, keeping my thoughts to myself that with eyes too close and a smile too big, Danny's wasn't the kind of face you forget.

Sara sat on the corner of the bed dressed like she was going on a date in gray pants and a dark blue blouse that matched her eyes. It was nice to see she'd gotten over the tiny scars on her arms, but I wondered what they'd make Becky think. Sara's hair was how she usually had it in Brightside, pulled back in a ponytail, but I never imagined seeing a pink ribbon tied around it. Her attention was on the video playing on her phone, an earbud in one ear.

I thought of sitting up but said, "I can't do it. It hurts."

Danny groaned as he got up and came to my side. "You'll be okay."

My shoulder needed to be itched, but Danny grabbed my wrist and said, "Whoa, Joe."

I sat up and shouted at least five fucks.

All of them warned me to keep quiet.

I lowered my voice. "Goddamn it hurts." *Not just my shoulder. My whole body.*

Sara grimaced when she scooted over close enough to take hold of my arm in the sling. "You've been through a lot. We all have."

Becky kept watch out the window. "Feels like I had twelve jiu jitsu matches yesterday. Just the second-story fall alone."

Danny nodded, the cut on his neck a reminder of how close he'd come. "We'll feel better."

Sara held a small syringe and found a vein in my forearm. "This might sting."

The needle pierced my skin, a tiny prick compared to the throbbing pressure.

I apologized and promised I'd be quiet.

"It's fine," Sara said. "I should've done it before, but we didn't want to wake you."

"What time is it?"

Becky said, "A little after six."

"Can you see anything?"

"Nothing. Just this guy's backyard, twenty planes flying by every hour."

"Looking for us?"

Becky chuckled. "We're under a flight path to LAX. Everyone around here is."

Sara said, "But it's not just out there we need to worry about, Joe. It's everywhere."

"What do you mean?"

She unplugged the earbuds and held her phone so I could watch some dorky white guy in a black suit and purple tie, a huge American flag behind him.

Sara saw I didn't get it. *That's the White House. Their last press briefing.*

Trying to sound sincere while his eyes read a script, the guy said, "Let me start by saying our hearts go out to all the families of the victims of yesterday's tragic terrorist act. The assault on and the escape from Brightside will not be tolerated. It only solidifies our nation's commitment to removing Thought Thieves and converting them from threats into assets."

Some people clapped, but he held up his hand for silence. "Last night's attack was one of the worst acts of domestic terrorism in this great country's history. These rebels caused millions of dollars in damage and will cost us so much more for their recapture. But our president promises he will not spare a penny to see they face justice for taking the lives of 63 men and women sworn to watch over them."

The screen switched to the smiling face of a Boot in uniform, his name and rank below, along with his military experience and a list of family members he'd left behind. The screen stayed on for several seconds then switched to a new face. Another Boot. Another former soldier.

"In this heinous act of violence, these convicted telepaths poisoned their protectors, shot them point blank, and burned them alive. Those Thought Thieves still on the loose are America's top threat and we will not rest until they are accounted for."

The scene switched to the inside of a fancy office filled with important looking people in suits. The reporter said, "Last night, just hours after the attack, the president showed his support by signing the Beyond Brightside Act. This act gives the Secure Solidarity System jurisdiction everywhere there's a Thought Thief. Citizens are reminded to respect their authority just as you would any other form of law enforcement. Their success is crucial for all our safety."

Sara paused the video and pointed to the gray-haired man in the military uniform standing beside the president. "General Voltier. That creep came in on my interrogation, kept asking the same thing over and over."

I'd been in Brightside a month longer than Sara but had never seen him. "What was it?"

Sara hit play on the video and answered me. "What do you know of the Underground?"

The video went back to the slideshow of faces that'd never smile again, the suit still spouting his double talk. "Yesterday's cowardly terrorist attack underscores our need for vigilance as these Thought Thieves assault the homeland and its protectors. There has never been such a need for the careful vetting of all citizens, the call for honest, hardworking Americans like yourself to take a stand. Don't just comply, help. The American spirit will never be broken and those that seek to divide us will only bring us closer."

A list titled Approved Hashtags appeared on a black background.

"Support your country by using the approved hashtags such as #NoThoughtThieves when you share this and all other relevant posts. And remember, any lead that results in the apprehension of a Thought Thief will receive ten thousand dollars. The email and hotline are at the bottom of your screen. Every entry will be taken seriously."

I told Sara, "That's enough."

She put the phone away and said, "The border's been shut down. All family members of known Thought Thieves are being called in for questioning. The—"

I held up my good hand and sighed, "Holy shit," louder than I'd meant to. I couldn't let myself think about just how fucked we were. We were safe for the moment. "Where's what's-his-face? How's he been?"

"His name's Kevin." Sara pointed out the window. "He left a little before eight."

Becky said, "He looked dressed for work. Black slacks, white button-down."

Beyond Brightside

Sara said, "I'm afraid there's another video you need to see."

"Can I change first?"

Becky said, "I picked out your clothes and set them in the bathroom. Your dad said you should be an Army vet, especially with the injuries. Just act like they're old, you know, from the war."

The searing pain in my shoulder worsened when I moved, but I braced myself as Danny took hold of me. I wasn't ready when my left foot touched the ground, an angry ring of red around that ankle.

Sara said, "We've got to shave your head and darken your stubble."

Danny helped me into the bathroom then slid the slotted door closed behind him. Having only the one hand made things more difficult, but I was able to untie my sweats and let them fall to the floor. I peeled off my piss-soaked underwear and used the washcloth next to the stack of clothes. I scrubbed soap and water everywhere I could reach but still felt dirty after washing.

Sitting on the toilet was the only way to put on the clean underwear. I got dizzy and leaned back to clear my head. When I opened my eyes, the mirror scared the shit out of me. I was face to face with the most hated man in America.

The last two days had been the roughest of my life, my face showing all the signs. A scraped-up cheek, dark circles under sunken eyes, cold and black from all they'd seen. Shaving off my hair would help, but like Danny, you see my face, you probably won't forget it.

The sweatpants were my thin blue ones. I didn't know if it was Becky or Sara, but one of them was thoughtful enough to slit the bottom of the left leg so I could get it on over my foot more easily. They also slit the left side of my T-shirt so I could slip it over the sling.

Kevin's straight-edge razor lay next to the sink. I could've grabbed it and put an end to this whole mess, but I rationalized away the urge, telling myself I couldn't be selfish. It wasn't just me. I was responsible for bringing along all three of them. I had to be a good soldier and do my duty. Death would come without my hand in it.

# CHAPTER SEVEN

It was dark outside, but Becky was still at the window. The knife she'd gotten from Tommy, who'd died in the escape attempt, was folded beside her on the carpet. I'd wanted Danny to hold it since Becky had the gun, but Sara shot down that idea before I could speak it.

I was sitting on the bed, gripping the wooden handle of Wayne's knife, wishing some of that psychopath's energy would transfer to me. I don't know if it was the morphine, the gunshot, or maybe some of Wayne's madness, but my stomach was queasy, the room gently rolling.

Closing my eyes usually made things better, but this time I had a slow-motion movie on loop. A bullet blasting through the side of Wayne's head, the snow turning red.

"Shush," Sara said with a pat on my good shoulder.

Danny thought, *Screw Wayne*.

Sara didn't chastise her brother, just sat a little closer and handed me the phone. Becky stayed where she was because she'd already seen the video. Danny, who was crouched in the corner, covered his ears because he'd watched it as well.

The words on the bottom of the screen matched the voice over. "Warning, this video contains graphic content that may offend and upset audiences. Viewer discretion is advised."

The video cut to a beautiful shot of Brightside, the American flag slowly waving above the Square, the pine trees and small town so quaint and peaceful.

"Yesterday at 5 p.m. one of the most heinous acts of terrorism in American history took place at the Thought Thief Rehabilitation Center located in Brightside, California."

A photo of Sharon in her white pantsuit filled the screen. "This woman, Dr. Sharon Appleton, had been a trusted part of the Brightside community, acting as the resident psychiatrist. She abused this position of power and used it to mastermind the escape that culminated in the death of 63 agents and support personnel."

The screen went to a shaky video of someone walking down a dirt embankment, stopping at the bloody body crumpled against the wooden fence. Hands flipped the body onto its back, dirt clinging to Sharon's face, her lifeless eyes staring at the sky.

"Although she managed to evade detection for several hours, this criminal was apprehended in Southern California, attempting to escape with her family."

I shouted, "Where's the picture of her daughter? Show that!"

The video went to a split screen. The top half showed an open road speeding by at night. Below it was the same road, but with a car racing slightly ahead and to the left, red and blue lights swirling on top.

The reporter said, "These videos were taken from the dashcams of Secure Solidarity agents Gabriel Ortiz, on the top, and Michael Baylor, on the bottom, who were in hot pursuit of the escaped terrorists."

Beyond Brightside

Several blocks ahead, a car darted out of a warehouse driveway and turned right, the brake lights flashing red and releasing. A station wagon followed, swerving as the Boots closed in.

Both civilian vehicles turned right at the light, the station wagon nearly flipping. The videos slowed to a quarter speed. Ortiz up top showed no warning, but just as he was passing the warehouse, Baylor's screen was filled with a moving truck zooming out of the driveway, a tremendous jolt as it plowed through Ortiz's car, knocking it into a vicious roll, spinning over and over.

Baylor's car smashed into the back end of the truck, his windshield shattering, the car spinning until it slammed into the light post.

Ortiz was upside down. A low whimper came from his car. From the other, a man I guessed was Baylor said, "Oh God. My legs. Agent down."

Baylor's camera was useless with the window all cracks, but from the top we could see the truck's door open, the cab lighting up as two figures walked out. Ten feet from Ortiz's cam, I made out my dad, upside down, but determined, a semiautomatic in hand.

Ortiz, who was whining like my dog Lily after she'd been shot, said, "I can't move. Can't feel anything."

From out of the frame, but his voice loud enough to recognize, Dad said, "Good."

"What are you doing?"

"You picked the wrong side," Dad said. Three loud blasts rang out.

Baylor shouted, "Dispatch! Shots fired! Agents down!"

No one else said a word but three more blasts echoed. I'm guessing it was Sheriff Melvin.

Dad's driver's license filled the screen, his Ohio address there for everyone to see. The reporter said, "This cold-blooded killer is Hank Nolan, the Outsider who helped mastermind the assault on Brightside and our freedom. For the death of these two men and the aiding of the terrorists, he is now America's number two most wanted criminal."

The photo changed to my Brightside mug shot, the angriest I've ever looked, roughed up, ringing in my ears, wishing I'd been killed along with Lily. "The number one spot goes to his son, Joseph Nolan, the Brightsider responsible for setting the escape in motion."

The reporter said, "We don't have all the details yet, but here's what we know so far. Joseph Nolan, age 28, a liar, thief, and master manipulator, now a merciless murderer. Here he is in footage taken from yesterday's assault on Brightside."

I'd never noticed a camera on the flagpole, but that seemed like the only place the video could have come from, me on the rooftop firing the shotgun at the helicopter, watching it crash to the ground below.

The faces of three Boots filled the screen, a laundry list of humanizing facts listed below them. "We take a moment to hail these heroes who will never see their loved ones again. We pray for these victims and their families and we beg all of you honest citizens to help bring the Nolans and all remaining Thought Thieves to justice. If you love this country and what it stands for, share this video with the approved hashtags and report any suspicious activity to one of the contacts below."

Sara stopped the video, not a sound in the room.

I said, "I had to. I didn't have a choice."

Sara's eyes were cold, staring right through me. "Did your dad?"

"That was us in the station wagon," Becky reminded her. "He did that for us."

Sara thought that was bullshit, that he didn't have to murder them.

Not trying to justify it, but only to end it, I said, "We've all made hard decisions."

Sounding only seconds from losing it, Sara said, "So what do we do now?"

I knew we were fucked but tried sounding like a soldier. "We stick to the story, hope we never have to use it."

So Danny might not catch it, Sara thought, *You know they'll never give us a chance. It'll be just like Sharon.*

"Then we stay hidden."

Sara motioned at the locked door. "With this guy? We don't even know if he's coming back."

Danny got out of his corner, no trace of his usual smile. "He's not coming back?"

"Or what about a fire," Sara said all panicky, not even acknowledging him. "We'd burn alive in here."

"Stop it, Sara," I said a little meaner than I meant to. "There's not going to be a fire."

Becky pointed at the ceiling, a square hatch I hadn't noticed. "We can get out if we need to."

"If Kevin does return, he won't let us stay." Sara got off the bed and paced back and forth. "Jesus Christ, Joe. What did you do?"

Becky said, "Even if they keep the remaining Brightsiders alive, they'll just be slaves."

"We don't know that," Sara said, taking her time with each word to keep herself under control. "That's just speculation."

I hadn't seen Danny upset with Sara before, but his voice was raised, brow set for a debate. "It's not Joe's fault."

"Yes, it is, Danny. Don't be dumb."

Danny shouted, "I'm not dumb!"

"Let's drop this," I said, pausing because Sara's pacing was making me sick. "If Kevin doesn't come back in an hour, we go through the attic."

Sara stopped beside Becky and pointed at me. "You can't."

So Sara could stop trying to hide her thoughts, I said, "Yeah, I know I'm fucking useless."

"I can do it," Becky said as she got up from the window and moved to the other side of the bed. "I can get around and unlock the door. I saw the button he pushed."

I wasn't looking to be anyone's leader, but someone had to. I said, "One hour. Agreed?"

They all said fine, Sara sitting at the foot of the bed and staring at the wall.

Becky walked around the bed and asked me if she could check out Wayne's knife.

I'd forgotten I was even holding it. She took it and returned to the window. "How about I keep this for a while?"

I said, "You have Tommy's."

She nodded at my forearm, the thin line of red travelling down. The cut wasn't deep, but I didn't remember doing it. I said, "Yeah, you better."

Danny offered to clean the cut, but I needed to close my eyes and didn't want to be bothered. "It's not bad. I'll be fine."

I hadn't thought I dozed off, but I jerked awake when Becky said, "Headlights! Someone's here."

The engine turned off and Becky confirmed it was Kevin.

"He's got to have seen the videos," Sara said, her panic back. "He won't let us stay."

I said, "I want the gun then."

Sara shook her head. "You look like you're about to pass out."

"Good. Means I'm not a threat." I nodded at Becky. "He'll think she still has it."

The car door opened and shut. Heavy footsteps headed for the house, faster than I pictured Kevin moving.

Danny stood and held out his hand. "I could do it."

Like it was a fact, Sara said, "No, you can't."

Danny had been through enough. I gave him a big thumbs up and said, "I know you could."

Sara couldn't even look at me as she said my name, her tone disappointed.

"What? That's real. Danny saved me with a pencil because I was a coward." I motioned for Becky to give me the gun. "That's not happening again."

Becky slipped Tommy's knife into her pocket and moved to the false door, Wayne's knife in one hand, the gun in her other. She put her ear to the door and said, "He's inside."

I got that she didn't want to upset Sara, but I needed the gun. "Hand it here, Becky."

Sara gave a slight nod and Becky brought it over.

The gun was heavy so I rested my hand alongside my thigh. I had Danny cover it with the sheet and stand by the door. "Becky, wait in the bathroom."

She stood between me and the false door, the innocent lamb I was leading to slaughter. "You're not going to hurt him, are you?"

"I'll be careful."

"He's letting us stay," she said.

I nodded at the bathroom. *Go.*

Sara backed into the far corner and sat down, concentrating on the phone. No one said a word for the next minute.

Footsteps came down the hallway, but not fast like before. The lock disengaged and the door pulled open. Kevin still had on slacks, his shirt untucked and wrinkled, red tie hanging loose. I couldn't see the gun by his side, but I heard his silent mantra. *Stay calm. Do not fire.*

Sara said hi and gave a little wave.

Kevin didn't acknowledge her, just glanced around the room. He nodded at the bathroom and, with renewed confidence, said, "She almost done? I'm only saying this once."

The door muffled Becky a bit, but we all understood when she said, "I can hear you just fine."

All gruff and tough, he said, "Get in here."

I said, "Maybe she's shitting. We've only had protein bars to eat since you locked us in."

Becky said, "I'm not."

Kevin looked me in the eyes but could only hold it a second. "She's not."

"Well, it's still fucking rude."

Kevin leveled the gun at the bathroom door, an additional six inches of metal added onto the barrel. His finger was on the trigger, not resting on the guard.

I said, "Wow, you don't even know if you put it on right."

To me he said, "Get out," and started counting numbers to himself. He thought about all his bullets, how he had way more than he needed, how he had control of the situation.

I laughed and said, "No amount of bullets matter when the other guy is already aiming at your head."

Kevin froze and thought, *Oh fuck.* He considered calling my bluff.

My arm was shaking but I kept my voice calm when I told him, "I wouldn't. You know I'll pull the trigger."

Still facing the bathroom and sounding so sincere, the goddamn liar said, "I only want to talk. Remember, I'm helping you."

"Yeah. What were you going to tell us? And why are you so worried about the silencer and whether or not it'll work?"

He remained motionless but was looking at me from the corner of his eye. *Stop it.*

I told him some more that'd already slipped. "Just bought it, rushed to put it on. Afraid things might get ugly."

"That's not true."

"Then why think it?"

Loud as he could, he thought, *Seven. Seven. Seven.*

"Look, Kev, just like you, I only want to say things once. Put your gun on the table and step to your right."

Kevin obeyed and faced the bed. "I wasn't going to hurt anyone."

"I know, just had to make sure." I told Danny to give the gun to Sara and help our host into the far corner.

Kevin sounded a sniffle away from crying. "What are you going to do?"

I asked, "To you?"

He nodded.

"Not sure. Probably give you the same hospitality you gave us."

Becky came out of the bathroom. "We have money," she said. "We'll pay you."

Kevin shook his head. "I don't want your money. I saw the videos. I know who you are."

I asked, "Why the hell did you sign up to help others? Lock us up all day and come in here with your gun drawn. Why do that? You're no telepath."

"My brother Andrew was. Andrew Westmore. He was up there with you."

The others shook their heads. I said, "I don't think I knew any Andrews."

"He didn't last a week, just long enough for one letter." Kevin paused, thoughts of him and Andrew standing atop the Empire State Building talking about what that fall would be like. He cleared his throat and said, "He wrote he was going sky diving one last time. Told me not to be sad, to remember he was smiling the whole way down."

# CHAPTER EIGHT

We left Kevin locked up in the safe room, hands tied, mouth gagged. Turned out he was a screamer.

The four of us had made ourselves comfortable in his living room, which wasn't much bigger than where we'd been. Becky was too far away to hear her thoughts, on a stool she'd pulled beside the long bay window, our self-imposed sentry's head hidden under the drapes. Sara and I were on the couch, my left ankle propped two pillows high on the coffee table, ice bags packed in on either side of it.

Plates clanked in the kitchen, Danny putting together our second dinner. The first round had consisted of two peanut butter sandwiches, five pickles, four turkey slices, and six Ding Dongs.

I'd thought the big screen TV had all of Sara's attention, but her thought was for me. *He's doing his best.*

I said, "You know it's not like that."

Becky said, "Pause it."

I thought she meant us, but Sara knew she was talking about the video. The smiling face was Mark Wharton from Louisville, former soldier. There was no mention of a wife or kids, but the cute little Yorkie snuggled in his arms tugged at the heartstrings.

Becky pulled back from the curtain and asked, "You hear that?"

My first thought was football, the announcer blaring in a stadium.

Sara walked to the opposite side of the window and peeked out the drapes.

I could move around with the morphine, but everyone kept telling me it wasn't a good idea and I should stay still. From the couch I couldn't make out much more than someone mumbling over a loudspeaker. "What's he saying?"

Becky held up her finger for silence. After a few seconds, she said, "They're saying where to go if you want to become part of the Secure Solidarity System or turn in one of us. They're reminding everyone to cooperate with them to ensure their own safety."

Danny set the platter of food next to my pillows. Half a bag of Cheetos, three crumb donuts, and a handful of Saltines. He asked, "They on our street?"

Sara assured him they weren't. "The SSS broadcasts from cars. Sounds at least a few blocks away."

Speaking to them both, I said, "You don't think that's for us?"

Sara said, "There've been clips of this all over the news, Boots setting up camps in local parks. It's everywhere, at least throughout Southern California."

I told Danny, "See, it's not just us. They're everywhere."

He looked at me like I was the idiot. "That's good?"

Sara came back to the couch and thanked Danny for the food. When she hit play, the anchorman said, "As I'm sure many of you have seen, there has been a rash of people protesting what they consider the unethical treatment of Thought Thieves. Instead of going into all the legitimate reasons for his decision to outlaw telepathy and hunt down murderers, your president directs you to watch this video. In his words: 'To win any battle, you must first know your enemy and what they're capable of.'"

Like it finally sunk in, Danny sounded defeated when he said, "We're the enemy."

The anchorman said, "And remember to obey any order given by a Secure Solidarity agent. We can correct this problem and become stronger as a nation if all honest citizens unite. We must come together. Take pride in your country and do your part."

From behind the curtain, Becky said, "Do we really need to keep watching this stuff?"

Danny reached for the remote that was beside my leg pillows. "Yeah, put on something superhero. Go on Netflix."

"No," Sara said, loud enough to make Danny pull back his hand like he'd been slapped. "We've got to be prepared. Information is all we've got."

The next segment began with a twenty-something blond holding a red-cheeked baby boy. By the music you could tell it was going to be another sad one. Sara said she'd seen at least ten, each a brief highlight on a hero whose light had been snuffed out too early.

The woman sat in front of a piano, a row of family photos lined along the top of it. Her speech was clipped, her chin quivering, her hand constantly patting her boy's back. "My husband was a good man. Honest. Thoughtful. Caring. A proud father. And now he's gone."

The camera zoomed in on the 8 by 10 over her shoulder, the young couple beaming over their newborn. The guy had a mustache and looked kind of familiar, but I couldn't place him.

"The murderer of my husband faced justice and for that I am grateful. But not the madman who made him do it."

The only person I could think of forcing someone to kill was Sharon, kind of like what she did with me. But the video went to my Brightside Travel bathroom, an angle I'd never seen it from, high and wide, the camera tucked away in the corner. And there I was, backed up to the sink, shotgun pointed at her clean-shaven husband, the newbie I'd run into at Robert's earlier that day.

Becky gasped. "Is that Wendell?"

Yep, that was him, all 400 pounds pressed against the wall like a hippo hiding behind a haystack. The Boot couldn't see Wendell, all his focus on me.

The anchorman said, "Agent Jacobsen was responding to the helicopter crash that killed three of his coworkers, searching for Joe Nolan when he encountered him in this bathroom."

The video played, the sound quality perfect so everyone at home could hear Jacobsen order me to put down the gun.

Knowing he was going to fire, I followed his instructions and kicked the shotgun over. I told him, "I just want to get out of here."

Keeping his gun aimed at my chest, Jacobsen grabbed his walkie-talkie, nearly dropped it.

The video paused and the anchorman said, "The Thought Thief situation is much more dire than we feared. Although there have been countless cases of this happening around our country, this is the first time we've captured Thought Thief compulsion on camera. Of course, we can't hear it, but the Thought Thief in question verified that he'd been mind-controlled by Joseph Nolan, and that it wasn't the first time it happened."

I can't remember exactly what I was thinking in the bathroom, but I didn't command Wendell to do my will. "That's bullshit! They fucking shot him!"

The video played and Wendell inched forward. Jacobsen turned too late, Wendell smashing him into the paper towel dispenser while I fought for the gun and he tore at Wendell's face. Wendell brought Jacobsen off his feet and slammed him down, the Boot's head connecting with the rim of the sink, all fight gone as he slumped to the floor.

The camera zoomed in on Jacobsen's face, the left side of his head bulging. The shot faded to black as all his info appeared, including a website accepting donations for his son.

His wife came back with their boy, tears streaming down her cheeks. "Do not feel sorry for these people," she pleaded. A photo of Wendell filled the screen, a huge black hole where a bullet had shattered his cheek, both eyes swollen shut. "Hunt them down before they hurt someone else."

Becky looked away too late. I wish I hadn't seen it either. Seeing Wendell dead removed the ridiculous hope that he'd somehow gotten away. The morphine had been keeping me on the edge of nausea, but right then I had to rush to the bathroom.

Sara helped me to my feet and I limped down the hall, holding onto the wall for support. The others probably couldn't hear me, but I kept saying, "I didn't do it. I didn't force him."

I closed the bathroom door and sat on the toilet to take the weight off my ankle, pulled the trashcan over in case I got sick. Looking in the mirror helped a little. With the shaved head and darkened stubble, I looked less like that killer on the loose. The one who could control others with his mind.

That's probably where lots of the hatred comes from. It wasn't just about keeping telepaths away so secrets would stay safe. It was the overblown fear of being manipulated or controlled by someone else.

The ridiculousness of their claim didn't seem so crazy when I thought back to who I'd been. A salesman convincing people to buy .cars they shouldn't. A scumbag seducing women to sleep with him who otherwise wouldn't. A magician who never revealed his trick.

Maybe it wasn't Obi-Wan Kenobi-level mind-control, but I couldn't pretend it was all bullshit.

Once I felt like I could keep my food down, I hobbled to the sink and ran water over my head, the cold clearing my mind. I was drying off when Becky yelled, "It's no safer in here than out there!"

When I got to the living room, Becky was gone. "Did she really go outside?"

Sara was still on the couch, eyes focused on the screen, a rage boiling beneath. "I told her not to."

Danny pointed at the front door. "She wants to see if the car is there."

I said, "She shouldn't be out there by herself."

As if I didn't get it, Sara said, "She shouldn't be out there at all."

I limped to the front door. "Well, if we're going to go out, we can at least do it together."

"Don't be stupid, Joe. You can barely walk."

I didn't say screw you, but the thought slipped loud and clear as I changed direction for the dining room table.

Sara slammed the controller on the couch. "It's not just you anymore."

I grabbed the tape from our bag of medical supplies and sat down to wrap my ankle. "No shit."

"Do what you want then!" Sara said but only because that's what I was doing.

Danny saw me struggling with the tape, realizing there was no way I could wrap it myself. He came over and said, "I can do it."

I handed over the roll and raised my ankle so it rested on the chair beside me. "Thanks, but try to be careful."

Danny tried, but the morphine had largely worn off, the ankle so tender as he wrapped it front, back, and all around until he ran out. "Too much?"

"Feels solid." I gritted my teeth and forced myself to my feet. "Way better than before," I said as I tucked the gun into my waistband, the handle hidden under my sling.

Danny followed me to the front door and handed me Kevin's raincoat that'd been hanging on the wall. "Be careful."

"Always." I slipped on Kevin's sandals and Danny helped me with the coat. I told him, "I'll be right back."

The night was quiet, the street dark except under the low-intensity streetlight at the corner. I stepped off the porch, my eyes squinting in anticipation of the motion detector.

Becky startled me with her thought, *I turned it off.*

She was sitting with her back to the oak a few feet away. I asked if I could join her. She got up and said, "If you want."

I had meant sitting next to her, but I understood the need to get out. The fresh air felt good, the night hiding the fact that it was filthy.

Becky kept it slow so I could walk beside her. "The car's this way."

Nearly all of Kevin's neighbors had their lights on, but only a few had drapes drawn. "How far?"

"Huh? Oh, up here to the right a few blocks."

There wasn't much else I could say so I asked, "You okay?"

She huffed. "As if."

"What can I do?"

"I can't be in there," Becky said. "It's nothing personal, but I can't be around her."

"She's not that bad," I said. "I mean, she means well. Hell, she saved my life."

"And you saved hers." Becky blew out a breath and said, "It's not that. Other people's emotions make me sick. That's what happened when Wayne killed Sheila. It floored me and they were on the other side of a wall."

I'd never had anything like that happen to me, but I understood how we all experience things differently. "Sounds awful."

"And being around Sara's like standing next to a blaring fire alarm." Becky led us around the corner. "She's a mess."

I wasn't trying to hear Becky's thoughts, but it was clear there was something else. "So what's up?"

"I don't know." She sounded on the verge of tears, looked away so I'd stop staring. "It won't help."

"Is it about Wendell? I'm sorry you had…"

Becky went back to watching where we were headed, her gaze well down the sidewalk. "It's not that. Or at least, it's not all that. I never knew him that well. With ten years between us and different mothers, there wasn't a whole lot connecting us."

"But still."

"I know it sounds terrible and I feel like shit about him, but I think I feel even worse about the others."

"The ones we left?"

Becky stopped and made me face her, a teenager drowning in despair. "The ones we killed."

I looked away. "Don't do that," I told her. "It won't help."

"That doctor. Nurse Jennie. Fuck, who knows how many others."

"We all did some things we didn't want to."

She waited until I faced her. "Joe, I poisoned her. I looked her in the eyes and killed her along with all those others."

"And I blew a guy's head nearly all the way off."

"I keep seeing them," Becky said, the tears rolling. "I keep hearing her say 'let's roll.'"

I turned Becky's head so she was looking at me, held her chin until she stopped blaming herself so loudly. "I didn't want to kill anyone, but you know what? When those motherfuckers were about to shoot me but ended up splattered on the ground, I was happy it was them and not me."

"Yours weren't premeditated and in cold blood."

"The helicopter was." The blinds were raised on the house we were standing in front of. "Come on," I told her, shuffling ahead in my sandals so she would follow. "What's done is done and had to be done. We only go forward."

Becky caught up and took hold of my free hand, a reassuring squeeze that she could be strong. *Thanks for coming after me.*

*Of course. We're in this together.*

We had just crossed the street when she said, "The car's two blocks up." Two more steps and she stopped.

Kind of joking, I said, "What? Afraid I won't make it?"

*No, no, no,* she thought, squeezing my hand and directing me to look at the black town car blocking the next side street. Two Boots stood in front of it, full protective gear over their windbreakers, submachine guns slung over their shoulders. I didn't think they'd seen us.

Becky thought they did. *We keep going. The tall one's going to stop us either way.*

We were at least thirty feet away from them so I figured Becky was going off a hunch.

*No. They're stopping everyone. He's looking for a bonus.*

I hadn't considered how powerful her range might be but was grateful for the warning. We kept forward and she snuggled against me, taking some of the weight off my leg.

*I'm your girlfriend, remember?*

*I thought Sara was.* A hundred thoughts flew through my head; the loudest being how I was dressed and how young Becky looked. *Fuck, I don't think I'm ready for this.*

*Too late.*

The taller of the Boots said, "Hey," so loud we had to look. Halfway down the street behind him there were several Boot vehicles, two with their headlights lighting up a house.

Becky stopped to face him and silently warned me, *Don't look so suspicious.*

I would've laughed at her if my butthole wasn't puckered shut, trying to keep from shitting myself.

The tall guy didn't look the least bit friendly when he asked, "Where you two headed?"

Becky didn't even seem phased, actually sounded excited when she said, "Del Norte. Best tacos in town."

He said, "We're doing our best keeping it safe, but it'd be wise to get inside."

Becky said, "Sorry, I didn't realize we shouldn't be out."

The shorter one with the goatee said, "Haven't watched the news?"

A loud pop echoed out behind them, then two more. I'd hoped it was a car backfiring, but some Boot over the radio said, "All clear. Threat neutralized."

Becky's arm was wrapped around my waist, probably the only thing keeping me from hobbling away as fast as I could. Real slow like she was thinking it over, she turned us back the way we came from. "We'll stick with delivery."

I didn't have to hear their thoughts to know they were less likely to hurt an ass kisser. I said, "Thank you, officers."

The tall one corrected me. "Agents."

I kept walking and said, "Sorry. My bad."

"Hey, how'd you hurt your arm?"

I thought about pushing Becky to safety and going for my gun even though there was no way I could hit them from that far.

Becky thought, *The war. Turn around and tell him.*

I pivoted toward him and motioned to my arm. "Iraq. Never use it again."

Becky thought, *Oh shit. He doesn't believe you.*

The Boot started another question when this guy walking down our sidewalk said, "Frank. What the hell you two doing? I texted you to say we'd cancelled our plans."

I silently asked Becky if she knew him.

*Hopefully a friend.* Speaking to the stranger, Becky said, "Dang, I didn't see it."

The guy, a light-skinned Hispanic with a dark flat-top, looked like a fit fifty-something. He nodded at the Boots and sounded amused when he asked us, "You didn't know about all this?"

She shook her head. "Been in bed most the day."

What she was hinting at made me cringe on the inside. *They're gonna arrest me for statutory rape.*

Becky ignored me and focused on the stranger who was waving us toward him. "Come on," he said. "I'll drive you home. I'm right around the corner."

The Boot said, "And who are you?"

The stranger squared up, perfect posture, nothing but authority when he asked the Boot, "Where did you serve?"

The Boot's chest puffed a little. "Army."

The stranger's face showed no emotion. "Yeah, but *where?*"

The Boot glanced at his partner before answering, "Mostly Fort Irwin and Fort Hood."

"Anywhere people actually shot back at you?"

The Boot didn't answer. "You?"

The man came close to a smile. "Well, I didn't get a purple heart for doing laundry. Just seems like they would've taught you some respect for your superior."

The Boot cleared his throat. "I'm sorry, sir. I didn't know."

"That's alright. I'm glad we have dependable men watching over us." He pulled out a cigarette and took his time lighting it, his dark eyes never leaving the Boot. "But I do believe I've proven I'm quite capable of taking care of myself and my friends."

The Boot nodded. "Have a good night, sir."

The vet nodded back, blew out a huge cloud of smoke. "You two as well."

Becky turned me in the right direction and we followed the vet around the corner. He kept thinking, *Stay silent. Do not talk.*

*Who are you?* I asked.

*I'm Tone.*

Becky asked, *But how do you know us?*

He flicked the lit cigarette to the gutter. *The Boots aren't the only ones looking for you.*

We were about halfway down the street, no longer able to see flashing lights, but I kept it quiet. *The Underground?*

*Don't get too happy, son. There ain't much of us and you can't count on me saving your ass again.*

There wasn't much to say about that, my thoughts turning to my ankle, wondering how much farther I could go, how it was going to feel when the drugs wore off.

At the end of the block Tone checked both ways then took us right. He thought, *You'll need to watch your own backs.*

We made another right. I didn't realize it, but Becky thought, *This is our street.*

Two doors south of Kevin's house, Tone pointed at the windowless white van parked next to us. *This is me.*

I asked how long he'd been there.

*Off and on.* Tone checked over his shoulder to make sure we hadn't been followed. *I don't know what more I can tell you. They're after all of us, especially you four. If his house is safe, I suggest you don't leave it.*

I thought, *It should be safe, unless the system gets compromised.*

Becky said, "Or if they start checking families of everyone who'd been in Brightside. This guy lost a brother there."

Tone said, "Stay low. If you do need to split, find me by the riverbed off Washington and Soto. Look for my van by the entrance. There's a community down there."

# Night 3

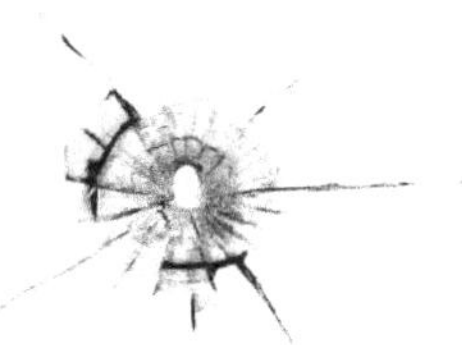

# CHAPTER NINE

The clock on the nightstand said ten after seven. Kevin's bed was king-sized, my torso and bum ankle propped up with his pillows. I had tried getting up a few times during the day but didn't see the point. My entire body ached when the morphine wore off, and we were down to six syringes. If I stayed asleep I was giving myself a chance to heal, as well as a break from the constant awfulness and fear.

I sat up all the way with a long sigh, the smell of moldy bread hitting me hard. At first I thought it was my breath because I'd only brushed with toothpaste on my finger, taking pride that even though I was able to kill innocent people I drew the line at not using another man's toothbrush. The smell was all wrong though, a putrid foulness coming from my shoulder. We'd been so caught up with everything else that we hadn't changed the bandages that were now yellowing around the edges.

The walk the night before had been a bad idea, my ankle a hot throb when I lowered my feet off the bed. Becky had left me four Advils on the nightstand next to the water. I popped them, hoping they would ease the sting until I got my fix.

Melvin's silver .38 lay at the foot of the bed, Sara keeping hold of Kevin's. The holster was too big even on the last hole, but my baggy sweats held it up. Danny's extra-tight tape job enabled me to walk but didn't do shit for the pain. The hallway was empty, the safe room door closed. I headed left for the living room and froze at the loud boom, popped the holster's strap.

The happiest I'd heard him in a while, Danny said, "Hah, got you!"

Danny was on the couch with Becky, each with an Xbox controller. He was still wearing the Giants jersey, but Becky had changed into black leggings and a baggy blue sweatshirt I assumed was Kevin's. Becky gave me a weak smile and asked, "How you feeling?"

"Probably about as good as I look," I said, the cottonmouth so intense I could barely understand myself.

Sara sat at the dining room table, her hair down and disheveled, the ribbon gone. She'd changed into a white top, a black skirt that stopped right above the huge bruise on her shin she got saving my ass on the roof. She was holding the phone she had charging in the wall. Three full duffel bags were on top of the table beside the medical supply bag we'd restocked from Kevin's bathroom. She looked up from the phone and said, "It keeps getting worse."

I continued past her into the kitchen. "How? They going to kill us twice?"

"I'm serious, Joe." Sara stood in the doorway, dark circles under her eyes, paler than I remembered. "This is so much bigger than Brightside."

I filled a cup of water from the sink, figured it didn't matter that it wasn't filtered. "I thought you didn't believe any of that."

"It's all the videos. People keep posting clips of neighbors being raided by the Boots, but the footage disappears within minutes."

I finished the water and took the vodka from the freezer. "Same as what they did with all the videos Sharon released."

"Exactly." Sara watched me take off the cap, pour an inch of vodka into the cup, then screw back the cap all one-handed. She asked, "You think that's a good idea?"

I chugged it down, the fire in my throat making me take a second to speak. "This isn't what's going to kill me."

Sara crossed her arms. "So what's the plan? We can't stay here."

I rarely woke in a good mood back home and right then I was weak and groggy and getting irritated. "You got somewhere better? I told you what Tone said." I left the vodka on the counter and opened the fridge. "We lay low. Don't leave until we have to."

"Well, I think we have to."

"Someone might spot us in the car." I pulled a package of ham from the middle drawer. "Not to mention, I don't know where the hell we can go. I suppose we can vote on it though."

Sara shook her head. *You think their votes should count the same?*

I did but wasn't about to get into it with her. I peeled off half the ham and took a huge bite. *What's the rush? If they haven't come here yet, maybe they won't come at all.*

"Maybe." Sara took a blue phone from her back pocket and held it up. "But we can't keep Kevin tied up forever. He's already had six different people try to get hold of him, the same number calling once an hour now."

I swallowed the ham and washed it down with water. "Probably just his work."

"We don't know that. Maybe he told someone about us. How about when his friends stop by to check on him? How do we handle that?"

"Well, I'm guessing he doesn't have many of those. Doesn't seem very sociable."

"Joe, enough of this," Sara said, her spite so strong I had to look. "Everything's a goddamn game to you."

"Then you go fucking ask him. You forget you can hear his thoughts?"

She just stood there so I kept going. "Ask him who he told. Ask him who the fuck keeps calling. Ask him if we should run and hide."

Sara turned her back on me and returned to the dining room table. "Do what you want, Joe, but Danny and I aren't staying."

I bit off another chunk of ham, chewed it while thinking of what to say. "I'm sorry."

She ignored me, set Kevin's phone on the table and disappeared back into hers. The thought of turning ourselves in and begging for mercy slipped from her mind, but I ignored it, not ready to get into that argument.

I left the ham on the counter and grabbed Kevin's phone. "Fine, I'll do it. I'll have him record a new message on his outgoing, say he's taking off a few personal days to recharge."

"What makes you think he'll do it?"

I limped into the living room. "Danny, I need to borrow you. Bring the knife."

"Why?" Becky said all concerned. "Kevin's tied up."

"Seeing something sharp has a way of convincing people to do what you want."

Danny paused the game and picked Wayne's knife off the table, carried it like he might bury it in someone's skull, his thumb gliding up and down the last inch of handle.

I pointed at him. "Tell me you're not going to tell the truth if he's the one asking."

Becky stayed on the couch and shook her head. "I guess."

When we got halfway down the hallway, I asked Danny, "When was the last time you checked on him?"

"When you told me to."

"You haven't seen him since last night?"

"No. During your nap you kept shouting for me to shut him up."

I didn't remember doing that at all but let it slide. I pushed the button below the painting and, loud so Kevin could hear me, I said, "Back away from the door."

I pulled it open, ready for him to come rushing out. Kevin didn't seem the hero type, but people are prone to panic and do dumb shit when cornered.

Still behind me, Danny said, "It's okay, Joe. He's not coming."

Kevin took up the entire bed, hands behind his back, lying on his side. I said, "Wake up. We have some questions."

He didn't say anything so I called him an asshole and shook his arm, a cold piece of unmoving flesh. I said, "Oh shit," and searched for a heartbeat. "He's dead."

Danny asked, "Can I go finish my game?"

Surprised he didn't care, I told Danny to hold on. "What'd he look like when you came in here?"

Danny took up the doorway, looked right at me. "All mad and red."

"What was he making all the noise over?"

"For us to let him go. Could barely breathe."

I wanted to let Danny return to his game but had to ask, "How'd you get him quiet?"

Danny's eyes pierced through any shield I might have up. *He was going to get us busted.*

I tried to keep my thought curious and not an attack. *What'd you do?*

Danny's eyes didn't leave mine. *Pushed him on the bed. Pinched his nose.*

*On purpose? You killed him?*

To prove he'd been paying attention, Danny thought, *It was him or us.*

*Holy shit, Danny. I'm sorry I told you to come in.*

He shook his head. *We tell Sara it was an accident. I made a boo-boo.*

I didn't have time to feel sick because I just realized Becky was behind him in the hallway.

She turned tail and said, "That's it. I'm out of here."

# CHAPTER TEN

The backdoor slammed shut before I even hit the kitchen. Sara was at the sink looking out the window. She asked, "What the hell's going on?"

Danny, who was right on my heels, said, "An accident."

Sara said, "She just got in Kevin's car."

I headed for the door. "Who gave her the keys? Can she even drive?"

We all heard the car turn on, but Sara still said, "She started it!"

The knob slipped out of my hand and Danny bumped my back, my shoulder slamming into the door, making me shout, "Fuck!"

Danny said he was sorry, but I just pushed open the door and told him to wait. I didn't bother answering Sara, who was asking what I was going to do.

Kevin drove a blue Prius, its taillights lit red. I limped down the steps, the concrete cold on my feet, and got behind the car, waving my arm to make sure she saw me.

Becky rolled down her window. "Move, Joe."

She was obviously upset but I wasn't afraid of her running me over. "Only if I can come in."

The locks popped up. It took me five seconds to ease into the passenger seat. "So, where we headed?"

Becky had been thinking of ways to convince me to let her go. "You're coming? What about them?"

Melvin's .38 was still holstered on my hip. "They've got Kevin's gun. They'll be fine." I hesitated, wondered if I'd missed something. "Are we not coming back?"

"Your guess is as good as mine."

"You can drive?"

She looked the youngest I'd yet to see her, confidence shook. Becky blew out her breath. "I have my permit."

"Well, that's safer than me with one arm and not knowing the area."

Becky used the rearview mirror to see Sara and Danny standing at the backdoor. *I've got to go.*

No arguing would change Becky's mind, and I was just as responsible for her as I was for Sara and Danny. I told her, "So get us out of here."

Becky stepped on the gas harder than I expected, and my body fell forward, my good arm crunching on the glove box. While I bit back the curses, Becky shouted out the window like she was talking to her parents. "We'll be back."

"You ever drive at night?"

Becky stopped the car at the end of the driveway and looked both ways before backing out. "Once."

Instead of my usual fear, I was beyond caring, just wanted her to have a good ride. "Cool. Not really any different than the day."

"Except the whole being darker part."

It was good to see her lighten up a little. Driving around with two sticks up our ass wasn't going to help us be any less conspicuous.

*Two?* Becky chuckled and came to a complete stop at the corner, put on her turn signal. *Each?*

I asked her, "So do we have a plan or we just joyriding?"

"Can't really call it a plan, per se." Becky zipped out into the street and kept to the left lane. "You looking for cops?"

"Guessing if I see one, it'll already be too late. Just drive cool."

"If we do get spotted, what'd you want me to do? Go for it, right?"

I leaned over so I could see our speed. "For sure. Just remember we're not outrunning anyone in this thing."

The more we drove, the more I relaxed, a break from the never-ending worry that men with guns were going to break down Kevin's door. I sat back and pretended I was back home, the streets not looking so different from Columbus after dark.

We'd been driving about ten minutes when Becky turned into a school's parking lot. Most of the lot was empty, a cluster of cars parked closest to the huge building with lights shining out the second-story windows. "Basketball game," Becky said.

"This your high school?"

"Used to be." Becky backed into a stall in the last row so we could see everything.

The gymnasium and the rest of the campus were separated from the parking lot by a chain-link fence topped with razor wire. The pedestrian gates by the gym were open, but all the rest appeared locked. The few people walking around looked like parents. "You think this is a good idea? You're not worried anyone might recognize you?"

She flipped the back of her hair. "Even if I hadn't changed this, I'd be fine. I tend to blend in."

"A valuable skill."

Her eyes were back on the gym. Sort of to herself, she said, "It's hard to let anyone close when you know what they really think of you."

*Ain't that the goddamn truth.*

There was a small booth with lights on beside the entrance to the gym. At first, I thought it was for tickets, but Becky said, "Nope. Telepath check-in booth. Students can stop by to volunteer, apply, or turn someone in."

"You're serious?"

She stretched an imaginary banner above the dashboard. Sounding like she was narrating the trailer for an action-packed movie, she said, "Creating a better country rests on our youth."

I pointed at the booth. "Is that what happened to you? You know who turned you in?"

"Wasn't at school. It was this dumb bitch at jiu jitsu who couldn't handle me always subbing her."

"Subbing her?"

"Submitting. You know, armbar, heel hook, chokehold. Stuff like that."

I'd seen a couple UFCs but didn't know the first thing about fighting. "That's nuts. I can't imagine you doing that."

"Why?" She cocked her head to the side, flashed a fake smile. "Because I'm so sweet?"

"That's probably part of it. Seems like a tough-guy thing."

"What about you? Someone from work?"

"That's what I figured at first. Then I thought it might've been my mom or the girl I'd been dating."

Becky didn't talk, just waited.

A cloud darkened the moon. "My dad," I said, the words still hard to speak.

"Whoa. That's heavy." Her forehead crinkled. "Hold on. Then why'd he come to the rescue?"

"He got it in his head I'd make some kind of secret weapon, a tool the other telepaths could use to escape. I was his sacrificial lamb."

"So he was right."

"I guess, sort of, but it sure as hell would've been nice if someone had told me."

I hadn't noticed them before, but there was a kid sitting on the hood of a car, kissing the girl standing between his legs.

Becky thumbed a quick beat on the wheel and said, "Joe, can I ask you something? I don't want you to get mad though."

I had a bad habit of getting defensive but was usually able to avoid it when I knew it was coming. "Go for it."

Becky took her hands off the wheel and looked at me. "I get it if you don't want to talk about her, but I need to know about Rachel."

My face must've done something weird because Becky asked if I was okay. I cleared my throat and tried to ditch the image of Rachel's lower jaw lying on the bed. "I didn't think I'd hear her name again."

"They ran a whole news segment on her, told people not to watch it if they were sensitive."

"You did?"

"Sara had it on. They ran a bunch of photos: Rachel with her family, her graduating from college, looking professional and happy in Brightside."

"What'd they say?"

"They had videos too. You and her at Oscar's. At the bar." Becky checked out her window. "In your bed."

"Video?"

"They said she was your girlfriend."

"Well, she kind of was."

"But then you found out she was a double agent and—"

"A double agent!"

"Shush." Becky glanced all around, made sure no one was staring. "That's just what they said. They said you found out about it and you killed her."

"That's fucking ridiculous. She was going to escape with me. It was supposed to be me and her."

"You're sure she wasn't working with them?"

"They nearly lobotomized her in the Cabin." I didn't think it was possible she had tricked me and wouldn't consider the possibility. "All she wanted was out of there."

Becky swallowed, didn't want to say it. "They showed her body, said you left her in your closet."

"Those sick motherfuckers. They put that on TV?"

"Along with a warning because they care." She rolled her eyes.

"You know that's all bullshit. Rachel blew her brains out. We'd had a fight..."

Becky said, "I believe you. I just had to make absolutely sure you aren't the psycho they're making you out to be."

The memories were less than a hundred hours old but more than I could handle, tears of guilt and frustration falling.

"I'm sorry." Becky looked out her window. "I shouldn't have asked."

I did my best to pull it together. *It's not your fault. None of this is.* "It's all mine."

She faced me with teary eyes but her voice strong. "No, it's not. It's every piece of crap who voted against us. It's every coward who didn't take a stand."

"I brought you."

She held onto the seat with her right hand, the left squeezing the wheel. "You think any of this is fair or just?"

I shook my head, unsure of what I really believed, if maybe we were as evil as they made us out to be.

She eased back into her seat, blew out the rest of the steam still inside her. "But here's the thing, Joe. This is what I don't get. They knew."

"What?"

"About the escape."

"That doesn't make any sense."

"They had cameras in all our rooms," she said, trying to not think of me and Rachel "They knew all of this was going to happen. They had all our footage, probably heard everything we ever said."

I said, "If they knew, why didn't they stop us? They would have seen my shotgun."

Becky thought about it and said, "Unless they didn't watch the videos until after the escape, but I don't buy that."

I didn't either. "No, they would've been watching."

"So that means they let us go," Becky said, helping me think.

I searched for a reason she was wrong but couldn't find one. "Shit, even Palmer, he was just there waiting for me. You guys were already in the truck, but he didn't care."

"I don't know," Becky said. "It's crazy."

"Why let us escape?"

"My dad always says follow the money. If you ever want to find out why someone did something, see what they had to gain from it."

"All we're doing is costing them money."

The gym's buzzer sounded and we both jumped.

Becky said, "Let's get out of here before the crowd leaves."

I was busy trying to understand why the Boots would give us any chance to escape. "We're nothing to them. Why let a prisoner go?"

Becky took us left out of the driveway. "One more stop, okay?"

I didn't care where we went. This whole thing was so screwed up, nothing really mattered.

# CHAPTER ELEVEN

Neither of us said a word for the next five minutes, Becky focusing on the road, me on anything other than Rachel, restarting a hundred times because that's where my mind kept going.

The things she said. *I love you. I hate you. Do you wish I was her?*

The way she smelled. Piña colada, vodka soda, blood, bleach.

The way she felt. Warm. Wet. Dripping off the ceiling. Fucking Rachel.

Becky stopped at the red light. "She loved you. I overheard her thoughts at the deli."

I thought Becky was saying it just to be nice, but she said, "No, she came in for lunch, all happy because she'd just seen you. I didn't know who you were, only your name, but there was no denying her feelings."

I wasn't sure whether that made me feel better or worse. If Rachel hated me, I could hate her back, blame all of this on her. If she hadn't blown off her head, maybe I wouldn't have gone through with all this craziness. I could've been back in Brightside living a seminormal life, making everyone around me bitter.

Becky turned left on the green. *You've got to stop it. You're right.* "Thanks, Becky. You're a good kid."

"I'm not a kid," she said, the shortest she'd been with me.

I didn't react, just calmly said, "It's just a saying."

"It's fine." Becky took a deep breath and blew it out. "Alright, here we go."

I hadn't been paying attention to our surroundings. We were driving down a quiet residential street, not all that different from Kevin's. "Where?"

"This is my street."

"Hold on. Your house?"

She nodded and said, "I need to go by. I need to make sure they're okay."

"The Boots have to be watching it." There was no one outside, not a soul on either sidewalk. "You're just as wanted as me."

"Not quite. I barely made the top ten." Trying to keep it light, she said, "Total discrimination. Females aren't nearly as dangerous as male counterparts."

The added stress was making me nauseous, my forehead clammy. "This isn't smart."

Becky came to a complete stop at the sign. "They won't be looking for this vehicle, and no way would they think I'd be this dumb."

I drew my gun from the holster, felt a bit better with it in hand. "I vote no, but if you have to, you have to."

"It's the fourth one on the left," she said, my input meaningless. "The blue single-story."

I said, "It's nice," because it was and I didn't want to overdo it.

"That's not our car."

The only things in the driveway were a black Toyota 4x4 truck and a bunch of cardboard boxes. I said, "Keep driving."

Becky took her foot off the gas and craned her neck toward the house. "Someone's in there."

I saw him too. Solid build, buzz cut, dark tattoos down both arms, about my age. "You don't know him?"

"Never seen him." She turned left at the corner. "That was a Boot."

"He had on a tank top."

She made a left down a dark alley. "So?"

"So I've never seen a Boot not in uniform."

Becky cut our speed in half and coasted to a stop beside a wooden fence.

"What are you doing?"

Becky turned off the car and put us in darkness. "No one ever drives down here."

"Then should we?"

"We're not." She took out the keys and stuffed them in her pocket. "See?"

"This is suicide."

Becky turned to face me, her young, pretty face full of pain. "Anything we do is suicide."

*Good point.* "So what are you going to do?"

She rolled up the sleeves of her sweatshirt. "See why that asshole's in my house."

"Your dad have any weapons in there? How much would that suck if he shot us by accident."

Becky shook her head. "Hates them. Said all the NRA were psychopathic pricks."

"You got a plan? We knocking?"

"Don't know yet." Becky slipped out of the car and came around to my side to help me out. "You don't have to come."

The cold concrete reminded me I wasn't wearing shoes. I leaned against the fence. "I'm fine. Didn't get my shot today so I've got the pain keeping me sharp," I said, more of an exaggeration than a lie.

"Alright," she whispered. "Follow me but don't do anything dumb. My mom and dad might be in there."

I promised I'd do my best but we both knew that didn't mean much.

Becky reached over the top of the gate and unlatched it. The backyard wasn't much more than a small square of dead grass, a shed, and two trashcans.

Becky kept heading for the backdoor but got a little defensive. *Yards cost extra in Southern California.*

On the porch there was a miniature ceramic snowman she'd made in fifth grade. Under it was a gold key with a green plastic key tag resembling a tiny Ping Pong paddle.

*Shhh.* Becky knelt beside the door and listened for sounds and thoughts. She whispered, "I'm not getting anything. Probably no one in the kitchen or living room."

She was about to stick the key in the lock when I asked her about the knife. *Think you should carry it?*

She shook her head and thought she should leave it in her pocket. *Probably end up stabbing myself.*

A weak meowing came from our right. I didn't see anything, but Becky hurried to the corner of the house, staying low beneath the windows.

There was no way I could crouch down like that so I stayed where I was. *What are you doing?*

So soft I could barely hear her, Becky said, "Oh my God, Mellow. What happened?"

Becky was on her knees, a few feet from the far window. What I thought had been a dirty towel yowled when she picked it off the grass. "Oh no, baby. What'd they do?"

I leaned against the porch railing, aimed the gun at the door. *Becky, that guy's going to hear you.*

She crept back, a dirty white cat with brown paws crying in her arms, dried blood on the right side of its head. *His leg's hurt. He's not supposed to be out here.*

*I'm sorry, but we can't help him right now.*

Becky glanced over her shoulder. *I bet someone tossed him out my window.*

All I wanted was to not go in that house. *We can leave now, bring him with us.*

Becky shook her head and shushed the cat, set him down gently by the stairs. She whispered in his ear, "I'll be right back for you. I'll get you food."

Mellow meowed back but didn't move. Becky set her ear against the door then stood, slid the key in the lock.

I asked, *You're sure about this?*

She turned to me, face hardened, ready for battle. *That asshole's gonna pay.*

# CHAPTER TWELVE

The door creaked open. The kitchen light was on, two pizza boxes and a case of empty beer bottles stacked beside the trashcan.

Becky slipped Tommy's knife from her back pocket and pulled out the small blade. *My parents don't drink.*

I steadied my breath and followed her in, holding back the pain with a grimace. The tile was cold and sticky like it hadn't been washed in a while, the air-conditioning rattling overhead. *Maybe they moved.*

*In two weeks? No way, especially not without Mellow.* Becky crept forward like a trained assassin, the knife aimed down but ready to thrust. *Around this corner's the living room. There's three bedrooms and two bathrooms past it down the hall.*

Becky froze and held up her hand. *He's in the living room.*

A TV turned on with an ad for premature ejaculation. I asked her, *Can you tell what he's doing?*

She remained motionless, narrowed her eyes as she concentrated. *Laughing at the guy in the commercial, thinking he'd fuck the shit out of the actress.* Becky eased forward, keeping close to the counter, the doorway just a few feet away. She pointed at the living room table, a black Boot windbreaker draped over the chair.

The commercial switched to Channel Nine News, a man saying, "The Headhunter strikes again with another viral photo."

The reporter kept talking but the Boot watching said, "Holy shit, that motherfucker got another one." Even louder, he said. "Goddamn, you've got to see this."

I asked, *Is he talking to your parents?"*

Becky shook her head and crept to the very edge of the doorway. *Doubt it.*

The TV went silent. "Come on," the guy shouted. "Hurry up!"

I asked, *You want the gun? He might be armed.*

She didn't bother answering me, peeked her head around the corner.

I stepped forward but Becky pulled back so quick it knocked me off balance, my knee banging into the cabinet.

"I thought you were in the bathroom," the Boot said. "Grab me a beer while you're there, will you."

A muffled female voice said, "What'd you say?"

*Oh shit.* Becky thought, *You get the girl,* and took off around the corner.

I couldn't move like Becky but did my best. By the time I turned the corner she was nearly to the back of the couch where the big guy was sitting. He whipped his head toward Becky only for her to wrap her arm around his neck and slam him into the couch.

The guy tried punching her with his right hand, but the shot was weak and Becky had her body turned so it glanced off her shoulder. His other hand pulled on her wrist, looking like he might break her grip until she slid the knife under his chin.

"Don't move," she said.

I couldn't see the woman because the hallway door was closed, but I heard her say, "What the hell's going on?"

The door swung open and revealed a tall blond with a fake tan, something silver in her hand.

There was no time for hesitation, my finger squeezing the trigger, the bullet blasting her back into the hall where she crumpled to the carpet.

The guy grabbed hold of the knife's blade and twisted it out of Becky's grasp, dropped it on the cushion as blood streamed from his hand. With her choking arm, Becky grabbed hold of her other bicep and put that hand behind the guy's head, pushing down so hard his face went purple.

I hobbled to the hallway to kick away the woman's gun only to see it was a framed photo of her and the Boot at Disneyland. I hoped she hadn't wasted money on an annual pass, the exit wound in her back saying this had been her last ride.

The Boot had two handfuls of Becky's hair, the veins popping out on his forearms. She took the pain and squeezed harder, silently screamed at me to help. *But don't shoot!*

I got between the couch and TV, aimed the gun at his groin so there wouldn't be an accident. "Hold still!"

His eyes were glassy, cheeks bulging, but he brought up both hands.

Becky eased off the choke. *Close the drapes.*

The Boot coughed hard as I made my way over to the window. Becky warned him not to yell.

There didn't seem to be anyone looking around outside, the community already accustomed to gunshots going off. I closed the drapes and noticed the pile of cardboard moving boxes by the front door. Behind the boxes, leaning against the wall, was a large painting of a cityscape, which had most likely been taken down for the Raiders' poster hanging above the leather recliner.

With her arm still tight around his throat and ready to squeeze, Becky asked, "What's your name?"

His voice was all scratchy, barely above a whisper. "Where's Debbie?"

Becky constricted and he gagged. She said, "Your name."

It took him a second. "Brendan."

The image frozen on the TV made it hard for me to breathe. My first thought was Rachel, but that didn't make sense because this woman's face was still intact. Then my mind went to Krystal, the guy in black fatigues and a Rambo headband holding her fiery red hair, her emerald green eyes open but unseeing. His other hand was holding a bloody machete, only strings of flesh dangling beneath her chin.

At the bottom of the photo, typed in big bold letters, it said, "STAY OUT OF MY HEAD OR I'LL TAKE YOURS."

I fell to my knees, didn't notice any pain, my eyes glued to the screen.

Becky was only a few feet away, but sounded over a hundred when she said, "Joe, what are you doing?"

I dropped the gun on the floor, ran my hand where my hair had been, squeezed my head as hard as I could. "No!"

"Joe! Keep it together."

*I'd just talked to her three days ago. She was fine.*

*What are you talking about? We got to deal with this guy. Cops might be coming.*

Brendan said, "Let me go."

The noise I was making scared both of us. *The TV*, I told her. *They fucking killed my mom.*

Becky moved her head to the side of Brendan's. *Oh my God. Are you sure?*

I couldn't talk, couldn't think, couldn't look at the TV. The gun was in front of me, felt perfect in my hand.

*I'm so sorry, Joe, but I need to find where my parents are. Don't do anything rash.*

It wasn't easy but I got to my feet. Brendan begged Becky to release him. He swore he wouldn't call it in.

Becky said, "Where are the people who lived here?"

"Gone."

"Gone where?"

I shuffled to the couch, paused at the corner.

"Don't know. Probably a holding center."

"Were you here when they took them?"

Brendan said no, but we both knew he was lying.

"What about the cat?"

"Fuck the—"

Becky squeezed and Brendan's hands shot up, his left connecting with her face. She buried her head against his neck and applied more pressure, his face darkening again, both his hands yanking on her forearm, blood everywhere.

Sounding nothing like a sweet sixteen-year-old, she said, "Last chance, motherfucker. How do I find them?"

Brendan tried to talk but nothing came out. Becky shouted at him to think it.

His thoughts were erratic and scrambled, his brain short on oxygen.

I said, "He's worthless."

Becky yelled at him. "How do we get people out?"

Brendan's arms fell by his sides, his eyes closed.

I told her, "He's asleep."

Becky kept squeezing. *I know.*

I understood what she was doing and why. We didn't need a witness, someone to call the Boots. A wet *schlop* came from underneath him, his pants darkening as the smell of shit hit us.

Hoping it would help her cope, I said, *He had it coming.*

# CHAPTER THIRTEEN

Becky sat against the back of the couch, staring at her forearms, her left smeared with blood from fingertips to her elbow, her blond hair streaked red. I peeked through the drapes to make sure no one was coming. I stayed there so she was out of my range and I couldn't hear her thoughts.

The only sound in the house was the ticking of the bulky grandfather clock in the corner. The thing looked ancient and didn't go with the Raiders' poster.

"It was my great-grandma's, then my grandma's," Becky said, her voice hollow like part of it had been scraped away. "We got it two years ago when she died."

I'd forgotten Becky's range was stronger than mine, a reminder to stay more positive. It wasn't just me I had to worry about.

Becky studied her hands, her face showing no emotion. I knew it sounded stupid but I had to say something. "Are you okay?"

She looked up, her lip cut, a bruise taking shape on her cheek. A simple fact, she said, "We'll never be okay."

I couldn't argue that but needed to get her focused so we could get out of there in case a neighbor called it in. "I'm sorry."

She shook her head, took her gaze to the floor.

The TV was still on, my mother's head frozen in air for all to see, the motherfucker with the machete grinning like he'd just done the world a favor. This was the news. The glorification of a suspected Thought Thief being decapitated. Open season on us all.

Becky said, "Turn it off."

I had no idea where the remote was, but figured it had to be near Brendan. Now that the adrenaline dump was over, my ankle was tender each step, my shoulder a deep throb. Brendan was hunched over like he was trying to sniff his shit soaking into the cushion. I holstered my gun, scooped up Tommy's knife and wiped the blade on the couch. The remote rested on the coffee table. I clicked off the TV and set the remote back down, my fingerprints all over it.

Becky's thoughts were spiraling in self-hatred and fear. I went around to her side and said, "Before we do anything, how about I help clean you up?"

She said, "Why bother?"

"Because you look like you just stepped out of a horror film."

She couldn't take her eyes off her hands. "It's pointless, Joe. This whole thing is so fucking pointless."

"I know it feels that way, but we got to keep trying. That's all we got left."

That set her off, the tears finally falling, the tough girl gone. *Nothing's left.*

It'd be a bitch getting back up and the cops could barge in any minute, but I got down on my knees and eased back against the couch beside her. *I'm sorry, Becky. Sorry for everything.*

She was thinking about her parents, how she'd caused them to lose everything. Through her sobs, she said, "I don't even know if they're alive."

"Then let's find out."

"How?"

"I don't know. We'll need a plan. We'll find out where they took them and go there."

"That's ridiculous."

"Like you said, pretty much anything we do is suicide." I gave it a second to sink in and said, "But I say we go out fighting. Fuck these motherfuckers."

Becky wiped her face with the back of her arm, the blood and tear mixture marking her like an Indian princess in war paint. With a bit of a smile, she said, "I love your eloquence."

"Thanks. That was my major in community college."

"So how do we find out where they went? This dick's not talking."

"Neither's his girlfriend, but we'll figure it out. First things first. Let's clean you up."

Becky nodded and got to her feet, helped me to mine. She kept hold of my hand and walked toward the hallway. "We can use my bathroom."

We skirted around Debbie's body and entered the last door on the right. Becky huffed and said, "It used to be my bathroom."

There was a cardboard box on the counter full of lotions, shampoos, and pill bottles, a black trash bag beside it. The medicine cabinet was ajar, only a few items in it. I said, "I think we interrupted her redecorating."

Becky opened the far drawer and slammed it shut. In the next drawer she found a washcloth. "They couldn't even put shit in the right place."

"Do you want me to help?"

She faced the mirror, her tears back. *I can do it.*

I was tempted to go through the bottles and see if I could find some pain pills or at least some Advil, but now wasn't the time. I left the bathroom and closed the door behind me.

It didn't feel right exploring the house that'd been hers so I went back down the hall, stopping beside Debbie. I wondered if they'd make a sappy commercial for her or if only Brendan would be eulogized.

Debbie was innocent but now she was dead. Wrong place, wrong time. Wrong boyfriend. Wrong guy breaking into her dwelling and blasting her for holding a photo.

I took the fuzzy black blanket from the back of the recliner and covered her up, thought that might help Becky. There was another blanket in the pile of stuff by the door. I took it to the couch and laid Brendan onto his side, noticed the large tattoo on his right arm, the same military insignia I'd seen on several Fallen Heroes eulogy clips. Two pistols crossed at the top. A sword and key crossed in front of an ax and the scales of justice. The words encircling it. Assist. Protect. Defend.

I took out Kevin's phone and snapped a photo, not trusting my memory.

I'd turned the recliner so it faced the front door, left the gun on my lap. I hadn't checked the time but thought it'd been about ten minutes before the bathroom door creaked open.

Becky walked out from the hallway, all the blood washed away, looking like her new old self. She placed an orange pill bottle in my hand but kept hold of it. "Only one every four hours."

I tried to see what the prescription was, but Becky wasn't letting go.

She waited until I looked her in her eyes, the whites so red from crying. "Promise me."

She needed to know I wasn't going to be leaving her. I said, "Yeah, yeah, for sure. Just one."

Becky released the bottle. "I need time in my room."

"How long?"

"I don't know. I'm going to gather stuff, try to figure things out."

I said, "Sure thing," but couldn't stop from worrying about the Boots breaking down the door.

"They would've already responded if they were coming tonight. You can relax. How about you search the house?"

"You sure?"

She waved her arms at everything. "Except my bedroom and those boxes, all of this is their stuff. Plus, it doesn't matter either way. Take anything you think we might need."

Sara and Danny were on my mind, but I forced that thought down until Becky closed the hallway door behind her. She was in no shape to consider them.

I eased out of the recliner, set the gun on the armrest, went over to the boxes by the front door. I dumped a huge pile of women's clothing out of the biggest one and took it into the kitchen.

Before I began the scavenger hunt, I set the box on the kitchen table and popped open the pill bottle, took out one of the white Vicodin that'd been prescribed to Peter Glynn. I found a bottle of Jack in the cupboard to wash the pill down and take off some of the sting, warming my throat and stomach.

I glanced around the kitchen, tried to imagine what we could use. I don't know if Becky expected me to pack for long-term survival camping out in the mountains or useful stuff to get through the night. There was quite a big difference between surviving one day, ten, or one hundred.

The drawers were pretty empty except for utensils. We were already set on knives with Tommy's and Wayne's, but I threw in a sharp steak knife just in case. From the cupboard I grabbed a bag of beef jerky, a couple cans of soup, and a box of Clif bars, figured that could get us through a few days.

I set the bottle of Jack beside the box in case we had room and Becky wouldn't judge me. Trying to carry the box around with one hand seemed like a bad idea so I left it on the table and headed for the hallway.

The first door led to the master bedroom, the light brown bedsheets clashing with the bright blue paint. Everything else in the room looked as if it were Brendan's, his clothes filling the entire dresser. Although he was a good deal bigger than me, I grabbed a couple of his T-shirts and sweatpants, a bunch of underwear.

Debbie's big brown purse sat on the nightstand. I went through it and pulled out $55, a debit card, and the tiny slip of paper with the four-digit PIN she'd hidden behind it.

The next room had been Wendell's, although, judging by the Nickelback posters covering the walls, he hadn't stepped in the room for over a decade.

## Beyond Brightside

In Brightside, I'd always considered Wendell a lot older than me, but that was probably because he was the size of two adults. At 26, he was two years younger, and, thanks to me, he wouldn't see 27.

The bed was bumpy, sunken in the middle. I sat on it to catch my breath and pull my shit together. Wendell was the one who had called me into the bathroom. I didn't force him to kill that Boot. Yeah, I know there was no way Wendell could've known what was going to happen or that I was the one causing all the chaos, but what still amazes me is that he wanted to help.

I don't know how many terrible thoughts I had about Wendell in Brightside, or how many he picked up on, but it was enough for him to know I was a piece of shit. I hadn't meant any of those thoughts to be hurtful or overheard, and none of them were intentional, but I couldn't deny them.

Wendell's help seemed like forgiveness, something I sorely needed to do for myself. I'd failed him in life by not being a friend, but at least I made good on my promise to save Becky, albeit a promise that completely ruined her life. And her parents.'

I could wallow in self-hatred and second-guessing the entire night, but I wanted to get out the second Becky said she was ready. I wasn't expecting to find anything in the dresser other than shirts the size of bedsheets, but none of the drawers had clothes in them. The bottom one had two boxes of photos and letters, most of them of Brendan in uniform, the desert behind him. The rest were selfies of Debbie sent to brighten his day.

There wasn't anything in the middle drawers, but I hit the jackpot with the top one. A fully loaded duty belt with handcuffs, keys, flashlight, taser, pepper spray, baton, radio, disposable gloves, and two magazines. The only thing missing was the pistol.

The belt was heavier than I'd imagined it would be, and I had to sit back down on the bed to put it around my waist and replace the holster I had on.

# CHAPTER FOURTEEN

It had just turned nine o'clock when I dropped the last batch of items into the box on the kitchen table. Brendan's blue jeans were baggy on me but didn't look ridiculous. I slipped his windbreaker on my good arm and shrugged it over the sling, tucked the front in. I doubted it'd fool anyone but perhaps I could pull it off.

The Vicodin had taken away some of the soreness, but all the walking around the house had made my ankle angry, Danny's tape job coming loose. Using scissors, I cut several lengths of the silver duct tape and secured that foot so it could barely move. I tried it out by walking over to the fridge, pulling out a Coke so I could make a real drink.

If I hadn't made the promise to Becky, I would've taken another pill, but seeing how there was no lying to one another, I slipped the bottle into the windbreaker and settled for the whiskey. When I set my empty glass beside the sink, there was a noise by the backdoor.

Everything stopped, my hand drawing the 9mm Glock I'd found in the living room. The low scratching sound came again from the door. I eased forward, kept the gun steady, aiming a foot up and over from the knob.

There was another scratch followed by the tiniest cry. Shit, we'd both completely forgotten about Mellow.

So I wouldn't spook the little guy, I eased open the door and took my time getting to a knee. The backyard was empty except for Mellow mewing on the top stair, no need for my gun. I holstered it and let him have at my hand, mushing his face against my fingers.

There wasn't much chance of not hurting his leg with only the one hand to pick him up, but I couldn't leave him on the porch. I laid my hand flat and slid it under his body, raised him up with a whimper.

I didn't see anywhere soft to lay Mellow, so I took him into the living room and set him on the recliner, told him I'd be right back. There wasn't any cat food in the kitchen, but I put together a bowl of broken-up hamburger and a slice of cheese I got from the fridge. Mellow devoured the food, licking the bowl clean.

When he was finished, Mellow cuddled on my lap, snoring for twenty minutes. I thought of getting up to refill my empty glass on the TV tray but didn't want to be shitfaced in front of Becky. And I could imagine Sara now, bitching at me for my irresponsibility, how I always disregard everyone else's safety and only think of myself.

It was ten minutes past ten, a full three hours since we'd left Sara and Danny. Every time my mind went to those two, I bent it back to Mellow or Becky or the next unlucky motherfucker who would cross my path. I didn't want to put my worries and responsibilities on Becky, but the thought of our friends freaking out on their own with Kevin dead in the safe room made me sick.

The last thing I wanted was for Becky to think I was choosing Sara and Danny over her, but I needed to know if she was planning on spending the night. At first, I'd thought that'd be crazy, but the later it got, the more dangerous it'd be for us to drive around when there was no traffic.

As carefully as could be, I eased Mellow onto the recliner, managed to get up without waking him. Outside Becky's door, I called her name, asked if I could come in.

She didn't answer.

I rapped my knuckle on the door. "Becky, can we talk?"

Again no answer.

I did it louder, three solid knocks, wondered whether she was asleep or just avoiding me. I gave it a few seconds, then opened the door. The light was on so I walked inside, made it two steps when suddenly she burst off her bed, the short sword she'd been sharpening slicing toward my head.

I threw myself back, caught the doorknob with my hip, the blade barely whizzing by my face.

Becky's mouth dropped, then the sword, the metal bouncing off the carpet. She ripped out her earbuds and screamed, "What in the world were you thinking?"

The pain killed any politeness. "I knocked! What the hell were you thinking?"

Becky held out her hand, motioned at me as a whole. *Look at yourself*

I turned to the mirror above her desk, saw I was still wearing the windbreaker and decked out like a Boot. "Oh shit, I'm sorry. I found all his stuff, figured it could help."

"Help give me a heart attack. Jesus, Joe." Becky picked up the katana and sat back on the bed, took the sharpening stone along the blade which was about the length of her arm. "Just wish you'd warned me."

The tops of her desk and dresser were covered with trophies, her walls with medals and ribbons, photos of her looking like a superhero in a brightly colored skin-tight suit. Becky saw where I was looking. "Rashguard and spats. What we wear instead of a gi."

I didn't know what a gi was, but nodded anyway, trying to count the medals.

"Forty-three." Sounding beaten, Becky said, "And this is what I've got to show for it. My whole life comes down to a bunch of worthless medals."

"Well, not that it's much consolation but it's a thousand times cooler than any shit I've ever done." I could see she didn't believe me. "Seriously. Come on, you're a fucking badass. Most kids your age haven't done a damn thing."

The kid remark rubbed her the wrong way, but Becky just told me. "Forget I said anything."

"So what's the deal?" I motioned at her sword. "You planning on going all ninja on me?"

She ran the stone down the blade one last time and set it on the bed. "I won it last year. Never used it, just thought it couldn't hurt."

"We came a little too close to proving that wrong."

Becky gave a quick smile, both hands holding the bed, her eyes on mine. "So what'd you want?"

I hated being put on the spot and went with the good news first. I pointed at my belt and said, "So besides all the gear on here, we got an extra gun and a good amount of ammo."

She nodded. "You realize we can't win a showdown?"

"Yeah, I know, but it could help us escape. We got the radio too and can listen in. I'm even thinking we go Star Wars on them."

"How much did you drink?"

"Not much."

"Star Wars?"

"I'm just saying we got a disguise. Become stormtroopers like Luke and Han. Maybe it'll get us in somewhere. You know, so we can find your parents."

Becky hadn't seen that coming. "Are you serious? You'll do that with me?"

"Of course."

Her face softened. "Thanks, Joe."

"I also took care of Mellow. Got him keeping me company in the living room."

"Oh, I totally forgot," she said, beating herself up until I told her to knock it off. "I'm going to get him."

"Just a sec, alright?"

"What?"

"Sara and Danny."

"What about them?" she said, back to business.

"That's the thing. I don't know what to do about them. I wish I could call and tell them something, but I don't even know what to say."

"What do you want to tell them?"

"I don't know. I guess that we're okay." I studied her eyes, looked for a reaction when I said, "That we'd see them tomorrow when it's safe to go back."

"So what happened to finding my parents?"

"Well, I'd rather have help."

Becky shook her head, disappointed I believed that. "Sara would never allow it."

"So we don't go back?"

Becky wanted to say yes, but said, "I want to stay here but I know we shouldn't. At least for the night? You give me that and we go back for them tomorrow, see if they want to join us."

I agreed. "But I don't know how to get hold of them."

Becky reached into her back pocket and pulled out a folded piece of paper. She handed it over with Kevin's phone and said, "Sara's number."


Not counting Brendan, I had the living room all to myself. Becky had scooped up Mellow, giving me privacy so I could make my call.

The number I wanted to call wasn't the one on the paper. The number I punched wasn't Sara's. I wanted to hit dial, but there'd be no one to answer it—Dad who-knows-where and Mom headless because of us.

I didn't watch the rest of the news, so I wasn't sure if they mentioned my mother's name or if Sara would even catch it if they did. But I guessed she would, and she'd be worried sick, hoping I hadn't seen it, worried I might call it quits.

I erased Mom's number and typed in Sara's. The phone rang four times and I was about to hang up when it clicked on. She didn't say anything so I checked if it was her. "Sara?"

Like there was someone standing outside her door, Sara whispered, "What are you doing? Where are you?"

"About fifteen, twenty minutes away, but we can't get back there. Not tonight."

She gasped. "What?"

"I'm sorry."

More of an accusation than a question, she asked, "You know what happened?"

"To Kevin?"

"Yes to Kevin."

"Danny said it was an accident."

"He did it because of you," she said, her hatred coming through loud and clear.

I didn't say a word, wasn't sure I even could.

In the background, Danny shouted. "Not Joe's fault."

There was a loud blast down the street followed by two more. I nearly dropped the phone, realized I'd stopped breathing.

"Joe, you okay?"

I cleared my throat, made sure I could talk. "Sorry. I'm here."

Back on the attack, Sara said, "You abandoned us. We couldn't leave if we wanted to."

"I'm sorry, but neither one of us is in any shape to be driving."

"That's why I said not to go."

"I had to."

"Have you been drinking?"

"Some bad shit went down," I said, my finger ready to end the call. "We'll be back tomorrow."

"Yeah, let's just hope Danny and I are still here, right?"

I ignored her remark. "We got more supplies, another gun."

She humphed. "Like that'll help."

I was tired of everything I said getting shot down. "Well it's better than fucking nothing."

Sara didn't say anything.

I didn't either and just hung up. She could hit redial if she wanted to, but I wasn't holding my breath. I'd chosen sides and she hadn't won.

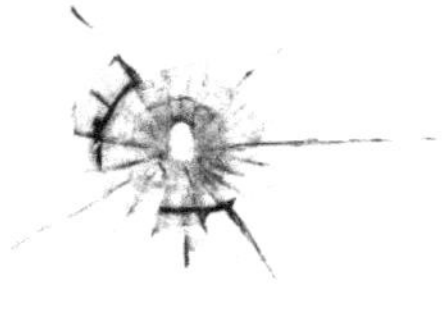

# Night 4

# CHAPTER FIFTEEN

"Joe, wake up." A hand nudged my good arm. "I want to leave as soon as it gets dark."

It took me a second to open my eyes and remember where I was, the smell of Brendan's shit bringing me right back.

Becky stood beside the recliner in a zippered black hoodie, Kevin's holster and Melvin's .38 just showing beneath it. "You could've slept in one of the beds."

I cleared my throat and motioned at the front door. "I wanted to be ready."

"Well, I appreciate it." Becky picked up the Vicodin, tried to hide she was counting pills. "How are you doing with these?"

"Make me all itchy but they help. Would you mind getting another one for me?"

She handed me a pill and waited until I swallowed it. "I'm impressed," she said. "You kept your promise."

The Glock rested on the armrest. I put it in the holster and said, "Yeah, you'd be surprised what I'm capable of."

"It's almost five o'clock so I'm guessing we have about thirty minutes before we can move."

I pushed off the recliner, winced when I put weight on my bad foot.

"Jesus, Joe, your toes shouldn't be that color."

"Danny's taping got too loose so I had to use the duct tape."

"Well, we've got to redo it."

I shrugged her off. "At our next stop. I need it to walk."

Becky walked over to the front window and peeked past the drapes. "Did you hear any of the gunshots today? Sounded like they were just down the street?"

"Nah, I was out." There were two backpacks on the table beside the box I'd packed. "You watch the news? Any developments?"

She let the drape go and shook her head. "Didn't bother. It's just the same stuff over and over about how awful we are."

"It'd make me hate myself if I didn't already."

"So I've done a lot of thinking."

"Our destination?"

"And what to do with these guys," she said, nodding at the blanket covering Brendan. "I can only imagine how much evidence we've left."

"I don't think two more counts of murder are going to make a difference."

"Yeah, but if they know we were here, it'll only help them track us."

"I suppose."

Becky steeled her face and said, "So we burn it down. Help me get them into my parents' room and we'll torch it."

"You sure?"

"My parents will never get the house back, but who knows, maybe there's a chance they can get the insurance money."

I wondered if her parents were still alive but smashed that thought down. "Let's do it."

Becky walked over to Brendan and tossed his blanket aside. She grabbed hold of his wrists and pulled him off the couch, his heavy body hitting the floor with a loud thud.

I picked up his left leg to help, but two steps in and we realized I'd be better suited as a cheerleader.

Becky slid Brendan into the hallway, past Debbie, and next to her parents' bed. While she struggled getting his limp body on the mattress, I uncovered Debbie. I bent over and wiped the hair from her face, as if giving her a little dignity in death made it okay that I killed her.

From the bedroom, Becky said, "Eww, that's so gross."

I didn't want to ask what it was, figured it probably had something to do with the snail trail of shit sliming the floor. I grabbed Debbie's wrist to see if I could pull her on my own, but when I started tugging, there was a loud buzz beneath her.

Debbie's hand fell to the floor as I went for my gun. I was shaking when I realized it was just a phone in her back pocket.

The iPhone looked brand new in its shiny purple case. I couldn't unlock the phone to check the three unread texts until I used Debbie's fingerprint to swipe it open. I scrolled through the settings and disabled all the security.

The sun was minutes from going down and I had Sara's number on Kevin's phone, waiting for Becky to finish a final run through the house. I'd told Sara we'd call when we were leaving.

It still made me sick to think we'd left those two alone, and not just alone but with a dead body. And even though it was Danny who did the killing, Kevin's blood was on my hands. I was the leader of the pack, the one showing them it was fine to kill anyone who crossed us, intentionally or not.

Becky came out of the hallway with two duffel bags. "I've been doing more thinking."

"Yeah?"

"We should take his truck. If we need to go off-roading again, I'd rather be in that than the Prius."

Our escape from the freeway and through the park wasn't exactly what I'd call off-roading, but I got her point. "Plus, we'll have more room in the back for whatever we want to take."

She held up the bags. "I got all my important gear. There's just one more bag and the box in the kitchen."

I set down the phone and slipped my foot into Brendan's right boot, a good fit with the three pairs of socks. The left was snug with just one sock thanks to all the swelling. "You give much thought to where we should head?"

Becky set her stuff by the front door. "We'll find another safe house somewhere. Hell, we'll find a cave to live in if we have to."

I said, "We have friends here."

She looked at me sideways. "The Underground?"

"Yeah."

"Look, I'm glad Tone was watching out for us, but like he said, he's just one guy and we can't rely on him. Doesn't exactly inspire confidence."

I'd already decided I wouldn't fight Becky on any decision. Everything came with a risk, and her say was more important than mine. I nodded and said, "I get it. The keys are on the table. Anything you need to get from Kevin's car?"

She shook her head. "Just need the gasoline from the garage. Be right back."

I held up the phone. "It's fine if I call her?"

Becky headed for the kitchen. "Tell them they've got 15 minutes."

The backdoor closed and I hit dial. I expected Sara to answer on the first ring. Then the second. For sure by the third. Fourth. Fifth.

It went to the default voicemail, a computerized woman saying to please leave a message.

I hung up and redialed. Five rings, no answer.

The possible reasons rattled around my brain. Sara was dead. Danny was dead. She had it on vibrate, set it somewhere she couldn't hear. Maybe she was in the bathroom. She had to be okay.

The backdoor closed, the lock turned. The smell of gasoline hit me before Becky turned the corner with the can in one hand, a long lighter in her other.

She stopped. "What's wrong?"

I shook my head and redialed. "She hasn't picked up."

"Put it down."

It rang twice. "What? I'm supposed to call. She's probably just in the bathroom or something."

Becky shook her head. "She wouldn't do that."

My finger was ready to cut off the message, but then the phone clicked on.

Sara didn't say anything so I asked, "Are you there?"

Becky's eyes got big. *Joe, hang it up.*

I stopped talking but gave it another second until Becky thought, *Now!*

"That wasn't her." She snatched the phone from me and said, "We've got to go."

"You don't know that."

"Yeah, well, neither do you." She disappeared down the hallway. "Get everything by the door. We're out of here."

We hadn't discussed Mellow so I was happy to see him lying in a carrier balanced on the gym bag Becky brought out from the hallway, her sheathed sword sticking out the top.

I asked, "Will it spread? Think it's big enough?"

Becky nodded. "We gotta go."

I pointed to the box on the kitchen table. "I couldn't get that one, but I can take your bag."

Becky set down her bag and scooped up the box. She started saying something but cut herself short, held up one finger. *Not a word.*

The smoke drifted around the corner from down the hall, a fine stream of gray heading for the open window.

She pointed toward the backdoor, other hand on her holster. *There's at least two of them. Just entered the yard.*

*Cops?*

*Boots.*

We each had a gun but wouldn't win if we went down that path. They'd surround us if we took too long.

Becky was quiet on the outside but freaking out as she fumbled with her jacket and holster, trying to get the .38.

I got an idea but didn't like it. "Shit," I said, moving to the backdoor. "It's the only way."

"What're you doing?"

I tucked in the front of the windbreaker so it covered my sling and slipped on Brendan's hat. "It's our only chance. You hide in the living room and surprise them. Use the gun as a last resort."

She nodded and backed up.

I went silent, couldn't hear anything but Mellow's sad mewing. *Tell me what you can. You think either of them knows Brendan, what he looks like?*

Knowing I couldn't hear her thoughts from that range, Becky whispered, "I can't tell. I'd give another name, say Brendan's down."

I put the gun in my weak hand so I could turn the knob. Praying the Boots would be slow to shoot, I opened the door and yelled like I knew them. "Agent Patterson's down and I'm hit! They're in the back room and there's a fire!"

I kept all my focus on the kitchen, switching hands and aiming at the doorway, imagining Becky popping around the corner and opening fire, paying me back for what I'd done to her. I must've been convincing because neither of them blew me away.

The first Boot looked like he should still be in college, ready to follow orders. I told him, "The big guy in the back's got a knife, did in my shoulder. There's been no gunfire."

He said, "Yes sir," and slipped past me.

The second guy stopped beside me, but never took his eyes off his partner who was halfway across the kitchen, nearly to Mellow. I tried to imagine where Becky was hiding, and thought as loud as I could, *They're coming about six feet apart!*

My entire body was shaking, sweat dripping off my chin. The smoke swirled thick, the crackle of flames covering the Boots creeping forward, the first guy nearly to the doorway.

He took another step and there was a flash of silver, a foot of metal ripping through the back of his neck. His gun fell to the ground, both hands clutching the sword only for it to flay them when Becky jerked it back out before she retreated around the corner.

The second Boot yelled, "Garner!" and aimed his weapon as his partner fell face first, thudding off the table and onto the carpet.

I closed the distance, afraid I'd miss at anything other than point blank range. I was three feet back when he said, "I'll cover you."

I didn't know if this was standard protocol or if he was just scared. I aimed at his head and tried squeezing the trigger, but couldn't do it, not with him just standing there not seeing it coming. That was worse than cheating. I told him, "You go."

He glanced back, looked down my barrel. He swiveled toward me and Becky swung around the corner. Either he heard Becky or saw my eyes, because he spun back to her.

I couldn't shoot with Becky rushing right at us, sword above her shoulder. It was too close to tell who was going to win the race. I put everything I had into my leap forward, slamming the butt of the Glock at his head.

The thunk rippled all the way up my arm. He collapsed to the floor and I tripped on top of him, coming down hard on my injured shoulder, screaming on impact.

*Shush!* Becky stepped on the Boot's submachine gun and slid it behind her. *Get up, Joe. We've got to leave.*

I rolled on to my side, right into a spreading puddle of blood, felt the warmth through the windbreaker.

Becky used the dishtowel to wipe off her blade. "Grab their guns and let's go. More'll be here any second."

I couldn't get up without her help, but once I was on my feet, I powered after her, biting down the pain. With two guns in hand and one in my holster, I followed Becky out the door, smoke pouring above our heads.

# CHAPTER SIXTEEN

I couldn't tell if Becky was reading my mind, but she was doing a perfect impression of me, drumming the wheel with her thumbs as we waited for the light to go green. *Oh fuck, oh fuck, oh fuck.* We were only two blocks from her parents' house, the flames licking the night in the rearview. Sirens headed right for us.

Everything hurt too much to speak, my jaw clenched tight, the deep throb in my shoulder now a rapid drumbeat, knives piercing my foot. *Sounds like firetrucks,* I told her. *We'll be okay.*

She sounded dazed when she said, "I can't believe any of this."

*You're telling me. It's like we stepped into* Kill Bill.

Thinking she had no business being behind the wheel, she said, "Like a nightmare."

*For sure, but let's take control of the dream, direct it how we want.*

Becky huffed, kept thumbing the wheel. "All I want is for it to all go back to how it was before Brightside. Maybe it wasn't great, but Jesus Christ, Joe, everyone's trying to kill us."

*Trying,* I reminded her. *Not succeeding.*

I pointed out the green light as a terrible thought hit me. I had no idea where we were or where we were headed. *You remember how to get there? I can try Kevin's phone, look at recent destinations on his maps.*

A few blocks up, flashing red lights zoomed toward us. Becky turned left in front of them and said, "I got it. My old jiu jitsu studio was close to Kevin's and I remember his street."

I kept my eyes on the side mirror, relieved when fire trucks sped past, no cops or Boots in sight.

Becky said, "Maybe you should set that down with the others."

I'd forgotten the submachine gun in my lap, my finger resting inside the trigger guard, a sin my father would never forgive. I said sorry and double-checked the safety, set it by my feet beside the others, covered them with the Raider's sweatshirt from the backseat.

We turned right at the next light, left a few blocks later, silent the whole time. "Joe, I need to know what you plan on doing once we get there." Becky checked her mirrors. "What happens if Sara says they decide not to come with us?"

The constant pain was becoming tolerable enough to talk more easily. "They'll come."

"They might not even be there."

"Then the choice will be easy."

"I don't think it will." She gave me a sad smile. "You're too nice. You'll want to wait for them."

"No. I promise," I said, drilling it into my head, Becky comes first. "But what should we tell them? Where we headed?"

"We find a safe house until we know what's going on with my parents. After that, we'll get out of Los Angeles County, maybe California."

It was hard to think critically, and I was going along with whatever she wanted. "We'll need Sara's phone for the safe house."

"If she doesn't come with, I'll trade her for Kevin's. All she cares about is watching the goddamn news."

"Yeah, but I get it."

Becky rolled to a stop at the red light. She looked right at me. "Can you leave her? Can you leave Danny?"

"If I have to." I didn't want to point it out but needed her to understand. "I already did it once."

Becky could barely hold back the tears. "I'm sorry. I don't want to do this by myself."

If my arm wasn't immobilized, I would've reached out to comfort her. As solemnly as I could, I swore, "You won't have to."

The light changed and she took us through the intersection, made a right just past the grocery store. She asked, "Remember this?"

We could have been anywhere, any city, any state. "Not at all."

"Just a few blocks away." Becky started saying something about the neighborhood when we slammed into a pothole, the jolt making me scream.

"I'm so sorry. I didn't see it."

*Motherfucker. Goddamn, someone just shoot me.*

"Take another pill."

*I need to give it time.* The deep ache made me think, *I'm going to puke.*

"Take it, Joe. My dad would have to do up to three when his back got really bad."

Becky wasn't testing me, just wanted to help. I took the bottle from my pocket and asked her to open it at the next stop sign. We didn't have anything to drink, the pack of bottled water left on Brendan's table with the other box I'd packed.

Becky shook out a pill and handed it over with the bottle. It was rough getting the chalky pill down with only saliva, but I managed. She said, "Two blocks up."

I grabbed a submachine gun, flicked off the safety. *Cross your fingers.*

Kevin's street was the next one on the right. Becky pulled over a half block away and put the car in park. "I've got a super bad feeling, Joe. Sara would've called back by now if they were there."

I checked the phone in case the ringer was off, but there were no missed calls or texts. "Only one way to find out."

"I'll park and run out, ring once." Becky's eyes stayed on the rearview. "You don't leave the car. Cool?"

I was a useless liability who could barely even move. "Makes sense."

*Joe?*

I didn't know why she got silent, but I could hear her fear. I wanted to turn, to see what was worrying her, but she said not to before I moved.

*There's a car back there with Boots in it. I can see the driver.*

*Can he see you?*

*They're facing the other way. Doesn't look like he noticed, but we drove right past them.*

*So what do we do?*

Becky blew out a big breath. *Shit. Keep going I guess. Yeah, we can't just sit here.*

She flicked on her turn signal and eased into the street. She clicked the blinker to the right, started turning on Kevin's street.

A pair of bright headlights flashed on and blinded us as a vehicle that'd been parked on the opposite side of the street crossed the center divider and headed right for us.

Becky jerked the wheel to the left way too hard, and I slammed against the door. She overcorrected to stop our ass end from flying into the oncoming lane and stomped on the gas.

I bit my tongue and checked the side mirror, the headlights turning toward us and giving chase. *They're coming.*

*I see that.* Panicked, afraid she was going to kill us in a crash, she said, "What do I do?"

The headlights were getting closer, but I kept calm, the gun in my hand reminding me we had an out, one way or another. "Slow us down. Can't look guilty."

*We are guilty!*

The headlights flashed twice. My vision was a little blurry, the light all I could see behind us. *What's he doing?*

Becky checked her mirror. "The driver's got his hand out the window."

I waited for gunshots, considered trying to turn and fire out the window, but I wasn't going anywhere strapped in.

Becky was back to focusing on the street and whipped a right at the next corner. The large white van followed right behind.

"He's waving," I said. "He's pointing toward the curb."

"You said don't pull over."

I buried my fear to keep her calm. "I didn't have the disguise or the firepower."

Becky slowed and put on her blinker. "Why isn't he using a siren?"

Something wasn't right with me, my vision going dark, my heart thudding against my chest.

"Should I do it?" Becky asked.

I pulled it together and said, "Up there where there's more space so he can't box us in. Keep it in drive."

She did what I said, both hands gripping the wheel tightly, her gaze straight ahead, the van's headlights lighting the street as it crept forward.

I had the Raider sweatshirt over the gun, my body turned so my uniform showed. *Don't lean forward. I got this but get ready to punch it just in case.*

The van rolled to a stop a few feet from her door, its window down. Tone was not looking very happy behind the wheel. To me, he said, "Aim that somewhere else. What the fuck's wrong with you two?"

Becky kept her voice low but allowed herself to look over. "You scared us."

Tone checked his mirror to make sure the street was empty. "Grab your shit and get out of there."

Becky said, "What?"

I didn't have to hear his thoughts to know what that stare meant. *Don't ask questions. Follow orders.*

That snapped Becky out of it. She told me, "You worry about yourself and the guns. I'll get the rest."

Taking care of myself wasn't as easy as I thought it'd be, my balance shaky on the street, making juggling the guns with one hand that much harder. The van's side door slid back, revealing dull gray paneling and a wooden futon with a blue cushion.

Tone said, "Get in."

Becky slid in the biggest box and helped me inside.

I sat on the futon and leaned back, my head resting against the paneling, my breath so shallow it scared me.

Becky tossed in two more bags and her sword. She sat beside me, Mellow crying in his carrier on her lap. "Should I lock it?"

Tone sounded tiny, a football field away. "Toss the keys. Same with any electronics you got from the safe house."

Becky obeyed with no hesitation. Dad would've been proud, the keys banging off Brendan's window and clanging to the street. She pulled Kevin's phone from my pocket and threw it out.

The door slid shut, the lock engaged, and we sped off. Becky took my hand and squeezed. "You okay?"

I couldn't even pretend I was remotely close to okay, my head feeling like it was wrapped tight in cotton. *I need to lie down.*

She scooted over and helped me onto my back, placed my head on her lap. "Deep breaths, Joe. You'll be okay."

It felt like she was lying, but I concentrated on breathing, on not throwing up all over her.

Tone said, "Everything cool?"

My eyes were closed, and I couldn't tell if she was talking or thinking, my processing slow and scrambled. She sounded just as scared as I was. *He's sweating real bad. Shit, I think he's bleeding.*

The sweat poured off me, and not just from my face like normal. *I don't think the blood's mine.*

Tone said, "He's probably in shock."

Becky's voice was full of fear. "What do I do?"

"Turn his head if he's going to puke. You can use that blanket to cover him up," Tone said, his voice dimming, nearly drowned out by the rising thrum in my ears. "I'll pull over soon as we're out of this area. He'll be okay."


By the age of six I was used to Mom not showing to pick me up. And in first grade it was no longer required.

It wasn't snowing that day, but it was cold, both hands buried in my pockets. It was down to me and Stephen, plus two other kids, when Stephen's father pulled up, his mother in the back seat.

Stephen was the only friend I'd had, but back then I had no idea he was cursed like me. He said, "I can ask them to take you home."

I wanted to say yes, but I'd get my ass spanked red if Mom pulled up and I wasn't there. "Thanks, but I better stay."

Stephen got in the front seat, his little hand popping up quick for a wave goodbye.

I didn't know how long I'd been waiting, but I knew it was safe to leave after the other two kids got picked up. It wasn't that far to walk and I'd done it a bunch. Even had my own key.

My imagination back then was all G.I. Joes and Star Wars, and that shit went on hyperdrive when I was alone. Most days I was Han Solo or Luke, but this day I was Darth

Vader, an invisible lightsaber in one hand, my other forming a C, ready to crush the next jerk to cross my path.

I made my first turn and didn't even notice the cherry red van until the driver shouted out the passenger window.

"Hey there, big guy. Your Mom asked me to do her a favor and pick you up."

It was hard to see much of him because of the angle, but he looked older than Mom's type. "Where is she?"

"Said she had an emergency, asked me to watch you until she got back."

The guy was smiling and looked nice enough, and even if I wanted to read his mind, he was outside my six-foot radius. But still, I just stood there.

He got out of his seat and undid the van's side door. "C'mon on, it's freezing out here. I don't want your mom being pissed at me for letting you catch a cold."

That should have been my clue. Mom never worried about me. But it was a nice thought and he was still smiling, showing all his crooked teeth like he had nothing to hide.

The back of the van was beautiful and the carpet so soft I had to reach down and feel it, the long red fuzziness on frozen fingers. He pointed at the small TV behind the driver's seat and the console below it. "Got a Super Nintendo in there, bunch of games. Hell, if you want we could just play here until your mom gets back." He pointed at the raised bunk to my right. "I just sit there and play. Super Mario's my favorite."

Other kids talked about video games, but we didn't have any, Mom not about to waste money on stupid stuff.

He bent over and pulled out a cartridge, his giant butt just inches from my face. I squirmed away to the side and he went up front and rolled up the window. "Too noisy out there," he said to himself. He held the bottom of the game cartridge to his lips and gently blew along its length. "Nice and clean."

I didn't say a word, just watched as he guided the game into the console, then gave it a hard push. He sat beside me, handed me the gray controller with four purple buttons. All serious, he said, "You gotta promise me something."

I kept my eyes on the TV screen, the letters not meaning anything because I couldn't spell much. "Sure thing."

"Don't break my high score."

I laughed because I knew he was joking, the beeps and bloops from the game making me happy. I kept laughing when he put his arm around my shoulder, hugged me in like Dad never did.

"You seem like a good kid," he said, leaving his hand on me as the tiny man on the screen jumped high in the air and landed on a turtle, knocked him on his shell, then scooped him up. "You deserve this. This is a special treat, right?"

Heck yeah, it was. Not disappointing Mom. Getting to go first on the game. Probably play as long as I wanted because Mom's emergencies could take forever.

The tiny man threw the turtle shell and jumped over it when it rebounded off a block. My controller didn't make him do anything, and I had no idea what to press.

His warm hand wrapped around mine. Almost at a whisper, like he wanted me to really pay attention he said, "Here, better let me show you how to do it."

He extended my pointer finger and used it to push down on the skinny button closest to the purple circles. "To jump, you press this one," he said, taking my finger over to the bottom button. He released my hand and said, "Can you do that?"

I showed him I could.

Tone's voice ripped me from the dream. Him slapping my cheek, calling me a soldier, telling me to open my eyes.

My face was wet, but I couldn't tell if it was my sweat or from Becky dabbing me with the dripping towel. Everything was wet, even my ass, a twisted thought that it might be blood.

Tone's hand was heavy on my forehead. He rocked me back and forth. "Joe, you got to wake up."

I wanted to die, felt like I was bound to, my heart so slow, my stomach aching, everything a blur.

Becky said, "What about one of his pills?" She pulled the bottle from my pocket. "It will kill the pain."

"He can't even swallow," Tone said. "What are those?"

She told him and he asked when I'd last had one.

"Twenty minutes ago, if that. It was just one."

Tone said, "Shit," and told Becky, "Bring the bucket."

I wanted to know what was happening but couldn't even open my eyes.

Someone pried open my mouth and jammed something into the back of my throat. I gagged and tried to move away but it kept pressing until everything came rushing out, splashing back on my cheeks.

The heavy hand patted my back. "You got the bad shit out," Tone said. "You'll feel better soon."

# CHAPTER SEVENTEEN

Fingers stroked my cheek, the light touch of a woman. Soft and sweet like she was talking to Mellow, Becky said, "There you go. You got this."

I forced my eyes open, the lids all crusty. Becky's outline was all I could see in the dark, her face fading in and out with the streetlights' shadows.

She asked, "You okay?"

I was about the farthest thing from that but squeaked out, "Yeah." I closed my eyes, hoping it'd take all the awfulness away, but it only made things worse, Brendan holding a knife to Debbie's throat while she rocked my mother's decapitated head.

"Joe, come on," Becky said, her shock saying she was picking up my every thought.

I opened my eyes and cleared my mind best I could. From behind me where I couldn't see, a man said, "He's up?"

Becky told me, "That's Tone." She read my confusion and said, "The other night outside Kevin's. You know, the Underground. We're in his van."

That was all new to me, and I couldn't have described Tone if my life depended on it. Everything had calmed down, my thinking included, a sluggishness where the pieces weren't quite connecting.

Tone said, "Try some water."

"Think you can sit up a bit?" Becky leaned closer, her cheek swollen and purple. "I can raise your head."

I tried to do it myself, but a stabbing pain spiked the front of my shoulder, put me back down on the futon.

Becky said, "Just relax." She got on her knees beside the futon and slid one arm under my neck, held the water bottle to my lips. "Slow," she warned. "You don't want to puke again."

I'd thought that nasty smell was the van, but it was my breath.

The water helped, revitalized everything it coated. Soon as I felt I could handle the answer, I asked, "What happened?"

Becky said, "The Vicodin. I'm so sorry. I had no idea it could do that."

Tone shushed her. "No one would. Only people with sensitivity to it will react like that." To me, he said, "We'll get you something else for the pain, but no more of that. We'll steer clear of all acetaminophen too."

I kept silent to conserve energy. *What happened with Sara and Danny?*

Becky looked toward the front of the van although she already knew the story.

Tone said, "They got hit this afternoon, maybe three o'clock."

It felt like someone slammed their fist in my stomach. *Hit?*

"Coordinated raid by the Boots. I was posted down the street, saw the whole setup. Two motorhomes pulled up and let out four teams of three. Two took the front, two stormed the back. Very professional."

I assumed Danny and Sara had been killed but braved the question. *They murder them?*

He said, "No shots were fired, either side, as far as I could tell." Knowing where I was going with it, Tone said, "My windows were down. I would've heard the silencer."

Becky said, "The whole house would've been lit up."

Tone said, "About ten minutes after the raid, the Boots walked out Danny and Sara, heads down and handcuffed, but looking unharmed."

*Yeah, for now. They'll execute them. Probably show the whole thing on the news.*

Becky said, "Unless they went willingly."

I asked, *What do you mean?*

"What if Sara called herself in? She did it before to get into Brightside. She could've claimed you forced them along."

*She wouldn't.*

"You know how scared she was, that she kept considering it."

I could barely remember my own name, let alone what thoughts Sara shared around me. *Either way, they're gone. Same with all our things.*

Becky motioned behind her. "We've got way better stuff in those bags than we had at Kevin's."

*Fuck! The morphine.*

Tone said, "We'll find you something to take the edge off."

I was going to need something a lot stronger than that. *How much longer?*

"We're a couple minutes away," Tone said. "Why don't you try sitting up all the way?"

I said I'd try and Becky helped me up, the motion of the van making me queasy.

Becky said, "Just breathe, maybe close your eyes. You're going to be fine, Joe."

Deep breathing helped calm my body, and Tone kept the window down so the cold air would keep me awake. I had just sipped some water when Tone pulled to the curb. There wasn't much to see out the windshield besides a small liquor store across the street.

Tone said, "I'll be right back," and exited the van, walked around the front and up a driveway. He snapped off the chain draped across it and dropped the links to the concrete.

When he got back behind the wheel, Becky said, "That's some heavy-duty security."

"Less is more. You'd be surprised what the smallest deterrent can do." Tone took us into the lot and parked the van so he could put the chain back up.

There were only two spots taken in the parking lot. A beat-up red Buick and a silver Sonata parked beside each other, neck and neck in a race for the exit. Tone took us around the lot, a locked gate blocking us from the back where two SUVs sat. He circled back toward the exit before parking and said, "Always know your way out."

I couldn't tell what the windowless white-brick building was.

Becky pointed out the initials on the sign above the front door. VFW. *Veterans of Foreign Wars.*

When I was a kid, my dad pointed out our local VFW every time we passed it, said there were some great guys in there. It was a special place. A place where his family couldn't follow him.

Tone locked his door behind him and walked around to the side of the van. The door slid open, and Tone stood there, a black submachine gun slung around his shoulder, mostly hidden by his jacket. "Becky, put the guns in that bag and bring it with. Joe, let me give you a hand."

Becky asked, "How about Mellow? Should I leave him?"

Tone nodded as he stepped inside to help me to my feet. "We'll be less than an hour. The key is to keep moving, not stick to one place too long."

My ankle hurt more than I expected but at least the pain took away some of the lingering sickness. When we got onto the concrete, I told Tone I needed a second.

He said, "No problem."

Becky joined us, a black duffel bag in hand. "Ready?"

Tone handed me off to her and said, "Hold on." He disappeared into the van, came right back with a wheelchair. He unfolded it and tossed a cardboard sign onto the futon. "Here, Joe. Take a load off."

I said, "I can make it."

Tone stayed where he was, holding the chair so it wouldn't roll. "I know you can, but I want you resting."

Becky helped lower me into the chair, then fixed it so I could prop up my feet. She asked Tone, "When were you in a wheelchair?"

"Picked it up at the thrift store. Every so often I'll use it for my disguise. No one ever looks at the dude in the wheelchair. Especially if he's got one of these." He pointed at the cardboard sign. Scrawled in messy marker, it read, *Need help. My fuzzy unicorn got bit by a dragon.*

I'd never been inside a VFW hangout, but imagined it'd smell of spilled coffee and day-old donuts.

Tone rolled me up the ramp and waved toward the sign above the door.

I couldn't see the camera. *Where is it?*

He pointed at the black period after the W.

An older guy, squat and short, with an even tighter flat top than Tone, opened the door. He looked like a fireplug in his red flannel, hand on his holstered pistol.

Tone said, "It's all good, Angel," and rolled me in past a desk with a bank of monitors that Angel returned to.

We went through the archway and into the main hall. The overhead lights were too bright for the room, the large square floor tiles, the ceiling panels, and painted brick walls all white.

The only color besides the black metal folding chairs placed along the plastic tables lining both sides of the hall was the goddamn American flag.

*Not in here,* Tone thought as he rolled me toward the dozen-or-so men bunched at the other end by the small stage. *I don't give a fuck what you think outside of here, but just remember all the men that fought for that flag.*

I wasn't in any shape to argue, to try and explain how that symbol of freedom was the biggest hypocrisy. Land of the free unless you have extra abilities.

Tone stopped the chair. *You fucking serious?*

I said I was sorry and counted the tiles, messing up the math but keeping my brain busy so I wouldn't irritate him anymore.

Tone cleared his throat. "Guys, I'd like to introduce you to Joe Nolan, Hank's son, and Becky Glynn. There's over two hundred thousand on each of their heads."

The closest guys were outside of my range, so I couldn't tell if any of them were thinking of turning us in.

Tone said, "They've proven their bravery and have suffered because of it."

The men came forward and introduced themselves, shaking Becky's hand and nodding to me like I looked too delicate to touch.

The names rattled off. Johnny, Jay, Chips, and Sherman. Curtains, Bolo, Dirt, and Stubbs, the only one I knew I'd remember thanks to his wheelchair and missing legs.

"I never knew there'd be so many telepaths in the military."

"Not all these guys are military, and not all of them are telepaths."

I looked around the room wondering who was safe from my thoughts. "So why are they here?"

Dirt said, "Because we all believe you've got to fight for what's fair."

Tone said, "Johnny, you got your medical gear? I need someone to look at his shoulder. He just dealt with a severe reaction to Vicodin. He's good with morphine but lost his supply."

Johnnie walked over, brushed his hair back with both hands. "I'll check him out, but I don't have my gear." He looked around the group. "Anyone else?"

The guys I was turned toward shook their heads. Someone from behind said, "I could spare a couple Dilaudid."

"Thanks, Bill," Tone said. "Johnny, how about you take Joe and Becky over there. We've got some new developments to discuss."

I didn't know why he didn't want us hearing the talk, but I didn't care. All I wanted was to feel better.

Johnny rolled me to the farthest table, backed the chair to the edge so I couldn't roll away. His nose said he was a drinker. His breath said Budweiser. He leaned over my shoulder and raised the damp bandage. "What happened?"

"Couple days ago. Sniper."

"Four," Becky said.

Tone started his speech by saying, "The SSS is quickly becoming the largest police force in the world," but I was paying attention to Johnny, who eased my arm out of the sling and rested it on the table.

Johnny asked if I was cool so I gave him a nod. He unwrapped the bandage and asked, "It's been bleeding this whole time?"

Becky said, "It hadn't been until an hour ago. We fought with Boots."

I hoped the Boot's blood had soaked through my windbreaker, but I guessed it was mine.

Johnny peeled back the final piece of fabric with a wet *schlop*. He covered his thoughts with a song but his wince was involuntary.

I asked, "How bad?"

He did his best to stay positive. "Well, that's not your blood."

"But?"

"This wound hasn't been cleaned."

"We've been running for our lives," Becky said.

"I'm just saying. It's infected. You need more help than I can give."


It'd been about twenty minutes, and I was feeling so much better with the new white T-shirt and clean outer bandage. A couple of the guys came up and introduced themselves. Sherman, a skinny guy with big ears, sat with us. He said he was honored; he'd served with my dad.

Tone stayed on stage with Chip, whose thin glasses and nicely combed hair made him look like an insurance salesman. Everyone else grabbed a seat at the first couple of tables and faced the stage. Becky wheeled me to the second table on the right and sat down beside me.

Chip pulled up a stool several feet away from the wall and set a laptop on it. He messed with it and then went over to the doorway, flipped off the lights.

A bright projection from the laptop lit the wall. I couldn't read anything from my angle and distance but could make out the map.

Tone pointed at the yellow circle and said, "Okay, so here's where we're at. Everything circled blue is Boot activity. Red dots are the base stations we know about."

Dirt, the guy with the gray beard and long hair, who sounded like he was from Georgia, said, "Well, hot damn."

A couple others sighed. The chubby cheeked guy whose name I forgot sitting in front of me thought we were fucked.

Tone said, "Listen up. I know this situation does not look good, but we've been up against worse."

Sanchez said, "Tone, that's half the state."

Tone stared at him. "So we quit? We turn ourselves in?" He looked about the room, connected eyes with everyone. "Is that what we do?"

Sanchez was quick with his, "No sir!"

The rest joined in, even Becky, goose bumps down my arm. All I could think was, *Holy shit. We're all fucking nuts.*

Tone gave a stiff nod, went back to the map. "Yeah, so they're pretty much everywhere."

Dirt asked, "So what do we do? What's our mission?"

Tone said, "There's still been no word from Hank since our last meeting, so the plan stays. Unless we hear different, we strike on Sunday."

Dirt said, "We just sit and wait?"

"Well, there is a side mission that's completely voluntary. Joe and Becky intend on infiltrating a detention center."

Someone laughed. Someone else said, "That's fucking crazy." A couple others close enough to eavesdrop on were thinking the same thing.

Becky stood up so everyone could see her. "They have my parents. I'm going with or without anyone else."

"Again, totally voluntary," Tone said. "Raise your hands if you're in. We'll need help on the ground once we've narrowed down where they're at."

Someone said, "Nearly every city has their own detention center. That's what at least half those red dots are."

Chip asked, "What's the address?"

No one knew what he was talking about.

Chip looked at Becky. "What's your parents' address?"

Becky rattled it off and Chip punched it into his keypad. He tapped the screen, a red marker hovering over a patch of green on the map. "Most likely location." The marker moved across the map, stopped at another patch on the other side of the freeway. "Here's a second."

Becky thanked him, asked him for the parks' names.

Tone held up his hand. "So who wants to pay this park a visit? I'm willing to drive them there."

Dirt stepped forward. "Wouldn't miss it."

Four other hands went up.

"Okay, it's settled. Those that want in can meet us here tomorrow after sunset. We'll aim on leaving at seven."

Becky said, "Thank you."

Angel spoke up from the lobby, where he was watching the TV monitors. "Shit, I think we've got a problem."

Tone asked, "What is it?"

"Two motorhomes just pulled up, each one blocking an exit."

# CHAPTER EIGHTEEN

The overhead speaker buzzed to life. Angel said, "A team of four armed Boots just exited the north motorhome. Second team of four is out the other."

Tone took control, silenced us with his stare. He asked Angel, "What's the exit look like?"

"Still clear. Eight Boots, all out front. I'd hurry though."

Tone told us, "We're secure in here, but not for long. They'll just wait us out."

Dirt gripped the M-16 he had slung across his back. "Then let's boogie."

"We only got two vehicles back there," Tone said. "Fit ten at most."

Angel said, "Don't count me. I'm watching the fort."

Stubbs nodded at me when he rolled past with a smile. "Sorry, Angel, I can't let you be the hero all by yourself." He kept rolling toward the lobby, sounded almost happy. "In fact, I'm going to one-up your allegiance and go have a talk with these inquisitive gentlemen."

No one tried to talk him out of whatever he had planned. Jay saluted Tone and jogged after Stubbs. "I'll cover you."

Stubbs rolled into the hallway and spun his chair so he was facing the front door. "Just get me something white."

Angel announced, "Both teams spreading out, twenty yards from front door."

Stubbs looked right at us and ordered, "No one open the back door until I give the signal."

Everyone nodded. Tone told our group, "The plan stays the same for Sunday. Meet at secondary location."

The speaker was still on and caught Angel speaking to Stubbs at the front door. "You sure about this?"

Everyone but me had a gun out. Sanchez, Chip, and Johnny led the charge for the back of the building. Tone rolled me right behind them, nothing but white walls and floor whizzing by, that and the stress making me sick.

Sherman was close enough that I could hear him thinking he'd protect me, he owed my dad. *You'll be alright, kid.*

Jay, you take this," Stubbs said over the speaker. "Lock the door behind me."

"Yes, sir."

There was a loud creak of the door and Stubbs shouting, "Don't fire! Don't fire! I have information!"

We filled the small room with the emergency exit, the blood red words never more true. We held our breath and waited for gunfire.

Stubbs shouted, "Can I come out? I'm in a wheelchair."

The door clicked closed. Angel said, "Stubbs has eight guns trained on him, but no one's firing. He's being directed to the north motorhome."

Becky thought, *We shouldn't have let him go.*

Angel said, "Most weapons are lowered, two Boots talking with him. Someone in a blue windbreaker just exited the east motorhome.

Becky gripped my good arm, her fingers making dents. *They'll know he's lying.*

Angel said, "The Sentinel is walking over. There are five Boots on Stubbs. Three focused on the front door. Still all clear in the back."

I wished Tone would hurry up and open the door. With all the people surrounding Stubbs, I worried he wouldn't be able to give his signal.

Tone thought, *Don't ever doubt the word of one of my brothers.*

A massive boom rocked the building, my chair rolling into Chip's shoe.

Angel shouted, "Holy shit! Stubbs took out the whole motorhome."

There was no time for sadness, just the back door being kicked open and everyone rushing out.

Tone turned hard out of the doorway and almost tipped me. I gripped the handle hard with my left hand, my right clenched in a useless fist.

The SUVs were roughly ten yards away when Becky stopped running. "You guys go," she said when we passed her. "I'm not leaving Mellow!"

Tone stopped so fast I flew forward, my grip on the chair the only thing keeping my face off the floor. He didn't even notice me on my knees, all his focus on Becky. "Get your ass moving," he ordered. "It's a fucking cat."

Becky stood her ground and stuck out her hand. "The keys."

Tone dug them out of his pocket and tossed them to her.

I used the chair to stand. "Hold still a second."

"What the hell you doing?" Tone said. "Get your ass in that vehicle."

Becky ran back into the building. I started after her and said, "She's my mission."

Dirt broke off from the rest of the men bunched around the SUV's. He threw me a nod and told Tone, "I got 'em, dog. Meet up Sunday."

Angel was at his desk in the lobby, Becky right behind him, gun held like she was going to storm Normandy. He pointed to the top right monitors. Two Boots by the front door, the third standing by the van, holding his head looking at the scattered limbs.

A thousand questions raced through my mind. *Is the door locked? Can they get through? Why aren't we going with Tone? Is this a heart attack?*

Angel said, "I got this," and picked up a walkie talkie. He pressed the button and a giant explosion blasted the two monitors black and knocked me into his desk.

Dirt took position at the front door. "Pop it."

Sherman, who I didn't realize was with us, said, "I'll go left and clear the motorhome."

The door cracked open and black smoke rushed in, sirens growing louder. Dirt crouched down and duckwalked forward, rifle at the ready, disappeared into the smoke.

We held our breath, gripping our guns tight, eyes on the upper left monitor. Three shots were fired and the lone Boot dropped face first.

"Now!" Dirt shouted. "Don't slip."

Becky went first with me right behind, the bitter smoke too thick to see what we were sliding on, or who was still shooting.

We cleared the smoke and Becky sprinted for the van, its lights flashing when she unlocked it with the remote.

My foot caught on something and I spun around screaming, opened fire on the Boot holding my leg. Only he didn't have hands to hold it with, didn't have a head to absorb the bullets ricocheting off the concrete.

Dirt ran up and grabbed my gun. "Finger off the trigger. He's dead."

It took me a second to realize what I was seeing—my entire boot stuck in the Boot's ribcage, bone and blood rubbing on my calf.

Dirt held me still and said, "Come on, we've got to hurry."

The ribcage cracked as I jerked my foot free, rushing sirens blocking out the sound. Dirt pulled me away from the mess, but the scene in front of us was just as awful. Three Boots with holes in their faces, Sherman stretched out on his back sucking his last breaths. The one motorhome was intact, the driver slumped over the wheel. The other was in two, both pieces burning, fire licking the street.

The van's side door was wide open, Becky already inside. We were almost to the door when Tone came running through the smoke. He yelled, "Becky, stay there! Throw the keys upfront!"

Dirt rushed me to the van with an arm around my waist. Tone was in the driver's seat, the van running by the time Dirt set me on the futon and slammed the door behind us.

In all the fire and smoke, it looked like we were driving straight to hell, the taste of sulfur on my tongue, my throat so tight and dry. My heart wouldn't stop racing and I worried it was going to burst.

We thudded off the sidewalk and skidded around the burning metal. Dirt put his arm across my chest so I wouldn't go flying. He kept repeating, "Breathe, Joe."

Becky sat on the other side of him. "Everyone breathe."

It felt like we were going way too slow, that it was just a matter of time before sirens caught up.

Tone assured me we were doing the speed limit. "Dirt, hold his gun for him."

I handed it over, my palm so sweaty it nearly slipped out.

Becky held Mellow tight to her chest. "Where we headed?"

Tone said, "Shelter. At least temporary."

"So how the fuck did they find us?" Dirt asked.

Tone said, "We were either tracked or followed. I didn't see anyone following us."

"Me either," Becky said.

Dirt searched my eyes for an answer before asking his question. "Either of you have any direct contact with the Boots? Any chance they might have placed something on you or the vehicle?"

I couldn't think of anything and shook my head.

Becky said, "We got rid of everything we had from both Kevin's and my parents.'"

I remembered Brendan's radio on my belt, Debbie's phone in the windbreaker pocket. For a split second I considered not saying anything, but everyone had heard the thought.

Tone shouted, "What the fuck? I said dump everything."

"Not to me you didn't."

Tone tore into me, but Becky shouted back even louder. "He was sick! He didn't hear you and it doesn't do any good shouting at him."

The windbreaker was bunched on the floor. Dirt bent over and came back with the phone, pulled the radio off my belt. He asked Tone, "How close are we? Is it safe to chuck it here?"

Tone rolled down the front window. "Do it."

Dirt sent them sailing out the window. Nice and calm, he asked me, "Anything else you might have? Any electronics?"

I shook my head, felt like the biggest failure, more people dead because of me.

The rest of the ride was straight tension but uneventful. We took a large bridge over an empty wash and made the first right we came to. Tone parked alongside the trees that lined the wash's fence.

Tone said, "Dirt, I need you to stay with the vehicle, make sure we weren't followed."

It was a tight fit but Tone joined us in the back, switched places with Dirt. He stopped right in front of me, hunched over so there wasn't but a foot between our faces. "No more fuckups," he told me. "We're running out of chances."

We both nodded because there wasn't any use arguing.

Tone shrugged on his jacket and tucked the submachine gun so it wasn't visible. "Put the windbreaker in the bag. Same with the guns."

Becky brought the biggest bag onto the futon and filled it up.

Tone slid open the door. "Bring whatever you can carry. I don't know if we're coming back."

When I got out, Becky handed me the smallest bag. She carried three, with Mellow balancing on top.

Tone slipped behind the trees. "The opening's this way."

A large hole had been cut in the fence. Tone grabbed one end and peeled it back even more for me. "Through here."

It was hard making out much with just the moonlight, but we were on a path that'd been trampled through the bushes and grass. Tone led the way, gun tucked, making me feel safe.

He said, "Keep your eyes straight ahead and your business to yourself." *Unless it's one of my men, you don't trust anyone. There's plenty of good people down here, but most will turn if a gun is aimed at them. And your asses are worth plenty.*

The trail ended at the top of the wash. Tone took us along the edge until we came to a slope.

"What's here?"

"Shelter," he said in a way that meant he'd had about all he could fucking stand of me.

To our left there was nothing but dirt, mud, and endless debris covering the concrete riverbed. To the right, under the bridge were dozens of tents, just as many shacks, double that for cardboard box homes, only a foot or two separating each dwelling.

Tone took us through the tents, careful not to trip, the sound of vehicles rumbling overhead. More than half the residents were outside, smoking cigarettes, playing cards, keeping an eye on us. Two women with matted hair and dirty clothes passed a bottle between them. At the next tent over, a large bald man with a gray goatee was sitting on a crate and holding a little girl who looked a few years older than Sharon's daughter.

I started thinking some sad shit but Tone shut me down. *How about you look at your feet like I told you.*

We got to the darkest part under the bridge where cardboard boxes, wooden pallets, and pieces of rotting wood were cast together to make several structures. We were four deep when Tone stopped in front of a makeshift shack and set the plywood door to the side. He held back a black curtain and motioned us forward. "Inside."

Becky went first with me right behind, the smell of mold and mildew hitting me hard. It was too dark to see anything, so Becky held still until Tone joined us and flipped on a cheap plastic lamp, the light so low I could barely see the walls.

Tone pointed at the hanging black blanket blocking the corner. "Shitter's in there. To cut down on the bugs, keep your bags zipped and sleep with them on the bed."

Becky set the bags and Mellow on the tiny single mattress taking up half the room. She asked, "We sleep with it open?"

Tone thought of the plywood he'd set beside the opening. "I'll slide the panel in place when I leave. You prop this two-by-four behind it."

I thought that wouldn't stop anyone.

"But it'll slow them down," Tone said. He turned for the exit. "Give you a warning."

Becky asked, "Where are you going to sleep?"

"I'm headed back to the van. Need to do damage control, see what kind of fucking mess we're in now."

Neither of us said a word.

Tone pointed at the small blue ice chest at the foot of the mattress. "Help yourself to anything in there and rest up for tomorrow," he said as he slipped past the blanket.

I pointed to the strip of brown carpet beside the mattress. "I can sleep there just fine."

Becky said, "Don't be foolish. Get on the bed."

"You're sure?"

Becky peeled back the thin blue sheet and helped ease me onto my back, her bruised face looking so fragile.

Sitting made me feel better, but lying down was best, closing my eyes, pretending this shit wasn't real."

"Joe, we've got to get your boots off."

*Why bother?*

"Um, because I'd rather not have that nastiness on our only sheet. I don't know how long we're going to be here."

I tried to open my eyes but couldn't get control yet, the sickness making me an emotional wreck.

*It's okay,* Becky told me. *I got it. You relax.*

I managed to take in a deep breath, hold it for an extra second.

The boot that'd been inside a Boot slipped right off, but Becky struggled with the left because of the tape and swelling.

Becky almost said something about my foot, but changed direction and took off my duty belt, left the gun in the holster close enough to reach at the edge of the bed.

"You think we should take that off?"

"You'll sleep better. And honestly, one extra second isn't going to make a difference." Becky patted my leg and said, "Hold on a second." She picked up Mellow and set him on my lap. "Keep him company while I get changed."

She propped the plywood door in place. "And don't feel bad about me doing all the hard work." She tested the top of the board. "Sturdier than I thought."

Mellow made it easier to breathe, but I felt like shit about not being able to do anything.

Becky knelt and unzipped the black bag, checked both submachine guns and set them beside the holster. "Safety's off. Do not pick up unless you're ready to fire."

I said, "Got it."

Becky took clothes behind the blanket. "And I was joking," she said. "Thank you for having my back."

The mattress which had probably belonged to some kid, was very small. I thought of scooting to the wall but no way I could wiggle over on my own. Plus, I was the one who should be closest to the door. I'd gladly block bullets for Becky.

Whether it was the pill or the sickness, I could barely keep my eyes open. I didn't even hear Becky until she was climbing over me, her gray pajamas pure softness skimming over my forearms, her fruity perfume covering up the sickness and decay.

I felt so much guilt for shoving her into this situation. She stayed hovered over me and said, "Joe. Look at me."

She was less than a foot away, could kill me in a heartbeat. Keeping it quiet, her blue eyes on mine, she thought, *You've risked more for me than most anyone else and you haven't done anything worse than I have. We're trying to live. Thank you for that.*

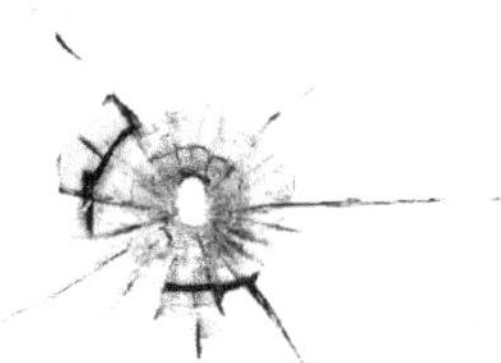

# Night 5

# CHAPTER NINETEEN

Something soft and fuzzy nudged my hand. My eyes were closed, no memory of where I was. A cat meowed. Mellow.

Mellow meant Becky. Becky meant Tone. Tone meant the shack under the bridge.

I breathed in and gagged on the stench of mud and mold, the awfulness of the L.A. air amplified under the bridge. The other smell was scary, a rottenness I swore wasn't coming from me.

There was another smell underneath it all, a hint of sweet mixed into the sour. It brought me back to high school. Janelle's parents asleep in the next bedroom. Her skin so warm, so soft, so smooth.

Mellow was still meowing, but now there was someone's hand on mine. "Joe." Becky shook me. "Time to get up."

It'd seemed like I should've learned by then, but goddamn it hurt rolling onto my side.

"You okay?" she asked. "How's it feel?"

Still groggy, I kept my eyes closed. "Like someone shot me."

"You want a pill? Think it helped last night?"

"Considering I don't remember shit after lying down, I'd say yeah."

"Nothing?"

I opened my eyes, caught enough of Becky's thought to stop me. "Why? Did I do something stupid?"

"No, not at all," she said. It was dark in there with just the fake flickering lantern and slivers of light coming through the cracks, but I could see she had changed. Black T-shirt and blue jeans, a black beanie hiding her hair. "I just wanted to thank you," she said. "It was nice."

I panicked, found it hard to breathe. Yeah, Becky was pretty and had a nice body, but there's no way I ever would've done the thing I swore to myself I'd never do.

Becky touched my arm, left her fingers there to calm me. "Joe, I asked you to hold me. That's all you did."

I breathed a little easier but was still disgusted with myself for having that worry in front of her. To break the uncomfortableness, I focused on whether I was going to heave. "Oh my God. I feel awful."

Becky handed me a pill and a water bottle. "You need to eat. And drink as much of that as you can. When was the last time you even had any?"

I swallowed the pill and gave her my best smile. "Yes, Mom."

She sat beside me on the mattress. "I'm serious."

"So what's on the menu?"

Becky dug into the backpack. "I'd recommend beef jerky or a chia pouch. The Cliff bars are good too."

I wasn't sure I could handle solid food, so I opted for a Blackberry chia, delicious but gross, the squishy seeds stuck in my teeth.

"Guess you're hungry," Becky said. "Want another one?"

I shook my head, used my tongue to windshield wiper my teeth clean. "Better see how I tolerate this one first."

"Smart. And as soon as you're ready, we should get you changed."

"For what?"

"The camp."

My brain was still half asleep. "Camp?"

"Where my parents were taken," she said. "Probably Danny and Sara too."

I pretended like I'd known that all along. "When we going?"

"Soon as you get dressed."

"Was their footage of us from yesterday?"

"I don't think so. Why?"

"Why are we changing?"

Becky shrugged. "How about just because you're bloody and gross?"

"Oh." I looked at my baggy jeans and remembered why I'd wanted to forget what I'd stepped in and splattered all over me. "Makes sense."

She handed me a pile of clothes that'd been stacked beside her submachine gun. "A clean pair of blue jeans in case we use your plan."

I'd forgotten what that plan had been but figured she'd remind me if we needed it. The bathroom was barely big enough for the bucket and crate so I asked, "You mind if I change here?"

"Don't be dumb," she said. "Let me help you."

"If you don't mind."

Becky shook her head. With a little chuckle, she said, "The things you worry about."

I apologized and laid back so she could switch out my jeans.

Becky slipped my right boot on, but set the left one down, took hold of my ankle. "Jesus, Joe. This isn't good."

We were fucked no matter what, my foot the least of our worries, but I kept it friendly. "Matches the rest of me."

Carefully as she could, she eased the boot on and laced up both pairs. She undid the sling and slipped off my shirt. The bandage was stuck to my shoulder. Becky gagged when it peeled off with a wet schlep, the skin an angry red around the wound.

"Looks like I forgot the sunscreen."

"It's not funny, Joe." She put her hand on my chest, her fingers cold. "It's burning up."

"It'll be fine. Just need to get the right meds is all."

Becky didn't call me on the wishful thinking. "I don't have another bandage."

"How about some napkins or something?"

Becky ignored me and dug through the middle bag. "Here," she said, holding out a small pink package and the roll of duct tape.

"What's that?"

"A type of napkin." She tore open the package and pulled out a Maxi Pad. "Now you'll know how it feels to wear one."

I couldn't help but smile as she taped the pad on me. "I feel better already."

Becky helped me sit up and tied my sling, slipped the black sweatshirt over me. "Look, I sliced the inside so it looks like you've got your hand in the pocket."

I felt so goddamn awful but tried to hide it. "So we're really going to do this?"

"I have to." Becky stroked Mellow who was curled up at the bottom of the mattress. "You don't."

"Yeah I do." I waited for Becky to face me. "I go where you go as long as you want."

She looked at me the way she probably looked at her parents. "I'm not your responsibility."

I shrugged my good shoulder. "Decision stands either way."

"Alright then," Becky said. "We need to get going."

"You talk to Tone or Dirt?"

She stood, her beanie grazing the drooping tarp. "They're expecting us soon. At least me."

I clicked my tongue to call Mellow over. He was happy to hobble over, rub his head against my hand. I put him on my lap and absorbed his purr, wished I could hear his thoughts because he was the one guy who didn't hate me. "What about this little dude?"

"No. I'm afraid this is home base for now." She paused, afraid her voice might crack. Trying to sound strong enough for both of us, she said, "If we don't return, he'll find someone else to watch over him."

Becky set aside the door and peeled back the curtain, peeked outside before giving me the green light. The sun had nearly set, a soft glow creeping over the edge of the wash.

I'd never considered the concept of almost dark versus completely dark, but that was because I never had a price tag on my head. I also didn't have a gun to hold, all of them put away in the bag Becky's carrying. So I didn't sound like a sissy, I said, "Should we wait another five minutes? The sun will be down soon."

Becky eased me past her with a hand on my back. "Don't pay anyone any attention and they'll do the same. No one cares about us."

Trusting in Becky is all I had so I followed her past the makeshift houses, passing a tent where a group of people huddled around a trashcan with a fire burning inside. There were a handful of children, but most were adults, everyone somber.

Becky led us left at the next tent and waved to the father and daughter we'd seen the day before. The little girl gave a shy smile and wiggled her fingers to wave back.

*So it's okay to pay attention if they're cute.*

Becky said, "Ha," and walked us out from under the bridge.

It had rained during the day, the ground squelchy. The chia had given me a bit of energy, but it took all I had just to climb the path, sweat pouring down my neck. How sad I'd been reduced to the sorry shape of a nursing home patient.

A bout of lightheadedness hit me. The usual ache in my shoulder now stabbing.

Becky stopped a few yards away. "You okay?" she asked, kind of joking. A little more serious, she said, "Gonna make it?"

I didn't want to know if she'd changed her mind about bringing me, and I wasn't about to send her off so I could die alone in the shack. I blew out a deep breath. "I'll be fine. Just need more water."

She nodded and headed up the slope.

I waited until she looked away before I risked small steps, scared I'd lose my balance.

Becky peeled back the fence at the top. I eased through, careful not to catch my sling on the edges.

The van was right where we had left it, the engine idling. The sound of crunched leaves came from near the rear door. A Boot turned the corner and I jumped back, put my arm out like I could protect Becky.

The Boot put his finger to his lips, raised the brim of the cap to reveal his face. *It's Tone! Relax.*

My hand went to my heart. *Holy shit.*

Becky snickered. *Glad you didn't have my sword.*

Tone said, "I thought I made for a better model. Plus, I don't have half the world looking for me."

"Yet," I said, sounding like Sharon. "Power of positive thinking."

Tone shook his head and opened the sliding door. I was about to step up, but he stopped me with a hand on my chest. His eyes were the same icy cold as Dad's, the type you didn't disobey. "Hold on, soldier."

"What is it?"

Tone studied my eyes, testing to see if I'd crack. "How you doing, Joe?"

"Honestly?"

He nodded. "How you doing with the new meds?"

"Fine, far as I know." The truth was, this felt worse than the flu. If I'd felt like this back in Columbus, I'd stay in bed all day, no way I'd leave the house. But this wasn't Columbus and I was getting a little tired of the way Tone was treating me. "What is this?"

Tone didn't get defensive. "Trying to figure out how much to trust you."

"I'm fine."

"Last question," he said. "What's your mission?"

That was easy. "Whatever she decides."

"Can you handle a gun without accidentally blowing us away?"

I said yes and Tone helped me up and on to the futon. "Then strap up with the Glock Becky's got." He pointed at the holstered gun and extra magazine at the end of the futon. "That one is hers. Got to look official."

Becky pulled out the duty belt and handed it to me before shoving our bags into the back and sliding the door closed. She picked up the black windbreakers at the foot of the futon. "For us?"

Tone said, "They won't fool anybody who's really looking, but if you guys are behind me, I think it'll pass. Especially in the dark."

Dirt was in the passenger seat wearing blue jeans and a black windbreaker. He adjusted the sun visor so he could see me in the small mirror. "You get some rest?"

"Yeah. Those pills knocked me out. You in here all day?"

Dirt's eyes went back to the windshield. "No, we did some damage control to see how hard we got hit. Also got in some recon."

I didn't want to hear what they'd discovered because it'd just be depressing. Our situation was not improving.

Becky wanted to know though. "Anything that can help us?"

Tone climbed into the driver's seat and closed his door. "Yeah, we found out a lot." He was pissed when he said, "We know for sure they were tracking us through the phone or radio. I had the spot scouted and sure enough the Boots rolled up."

I said, "I get it. It's my fault."

Becky put her hand on my thigh. *No, it's not.*

Tone thought, *Shit,* but didn't say anything and pulled away from the curb.

Dirt said, "We've had guys watching the park as well. There's no telling if your parents are in there, but we found the best way in."

Tone said, "But having a way in doesn't mean there's a way out. The place is crawling with Boots." At the corner, Tone made a right and headed toward the freeway. "This mission does not have a high-percentage success probability."

"Doesn't matter," Becky said. "Joe and I are going."

Both men nodded. I squeezed her hand to let her know I'd be beside her.

Dirt turned in his seat to face us. "I sent up a drone to see the layout. Looks like whatever is going on is happening in the middle of the park, the entire thing tarped off, a big patch of blue."

I asked, "That's where they're keeping everyone?"

Tone said, "Most likely. Either that or they've got them crammed in the small rec center and bathrooms. Those are the only two structures on site besides the tiny shed and baseball dugouts."

Dirt ran his hand down his beard. "I brought the drone down low to get a peek but it got fried." He shook his head and faced the front. "Not sure whether it was shot or disabled some other way. Everything went black on my end."

Tone said, "Yeah, they definitely don't want anyone snooping."

"How far is it?"

"Five more minutes at most. It's just south of Whittier Blvd and north of the 5 Freeway."

The names meant nothing to me, the city a geographic jumble I'd never exit. I stopped looking out the front window and sat back, worried the van must have been reported. I hadn't considered we could be pulled over any minute.

I didn't realize Dirt was eavesdropping, but he found me in the rearview and said, "We're good. We've got eyes and ears in their network. Not as much as we'd like, but enough to know we're clean."

There wasn't any talking the rest of the way, everyone off in their own world. Tone turned onto a residential street and parked in front of a small brown house halfway up the block.

"Where is it?" I asked.

Tone cut the ignition. "Straight ahead. We're on foot the rest of the way."


The door slid open, and Tone and Dirt got out, both with their Boot regulation submachine guns at the ready.

Tone said, "There's no getting caught. That's a slow death."

Dirt said, "A coward's death."

I tucked the magazines into the windbreaker pocket that Becky helped me into. The gun felt heavier than I'd remembered.

"But." Tone held up a finger and paused to make sure I was listening. "No one other than Dirt makes a move until I give the order."

I didn't know if it was the fresh air, the pill, or adrenaline from knowing death was one mistake away, but I felt much better. The sun had set, the streetlamps low. Just an ordinary street in an ordinary neighborhood.

The three of them started down the sidewalk, but I noticed two little boys pointing at us from the house we'd parked in front of.

Becky came back for me. "Come on. They think we're Boots. No reason for them not to."

At the end of the block, two motorhomes were pointed in a V, their headlights bright, just enough space between them to drive a car.

Tone waved us forward. "And remember to speak out loud so we don't look suspicious."

Dirt said, "Yep, just four dickheads returning to base."

Most of the houses on either side of us had their blinds closed, the front yards all empty. "What are we walking into?" I asked. "Is there a checkpoint? What kind of security?"

Dirt said, "They've got cheap fence all the way around covered in blue tarp." He pointed toward the right. "The entrance is one street over. There are several large motorhomes parked alongside the fence on that side. They've got two guards at that gate at all times and another six pour out anytime people approach with a suspected telepath."

Tone pointed ahead. "Up here's the side entrance where they bring in their cars, usually with prisoners in the back.

Two guards up here but it seems mostly like facial checks, not real security."

I walked slower, could see that the motorhomes were positioned to block traffic from both directions, leaving only the one way through the entrance. "Are we just going to walk in?"

"That's the plan," Tone said.

*Holy shit. We're dead.*

Becky said, "No we're not. Believe, Joe. Only way it's going to work."

Tone said, "Remember, kid, we'll know what they're thinking. If we're compromised, we'll improvise."

I took the gun in my weak hand to wipe my sweaty palm. "Alright."

Tone said, "Dirt, stick to my left. If we get past them, I want you hanging by the exit."

We were about twenty yards away from the motorhomes when both driver side doors opened. It was hard to see much with the headlights messing up my vision, but I could make out a Boot exiting each vehicle and walking to the front.

"Wrong gate, fellas," the guy on our side of the street said in an Asian accent I couldn't place. "This is for vehicles only."

Tone kept walking and thought, *Follow my lead.* "It's all good." He thumbed over his shoulder and said, "Vehicle's back there."

The other guy, a white kid who looked a year out of high school, said, "Sorry, but we've got orders. Foot traffic is through the front."

Tone motioned at us. "Come on. I got new recruits and they're both late. I don't want them getting fired."

Both Boots waited at the front of their trucks, neither with a hand on their weapon. We weren't a threat, just a nuisance.

I was about a dozen feet back, too far to hear their thoughts.

Becky thought, *That didn't make sense to either of them.*

Dirt headed for the guy on the left, put his hand in his pocket. "Hold on, I got paperwork in here."

The Boot on the right, who looked a little like Dr. Osaka, said, "Nelson, don't bother." Speaking to us, he said, "We don't have time for this, guys. Just take it to the front."

Tone switched his gun into his left hand, reached into his back pocket. "Trust me, you're gonna want to see this."

# CHAPTER TWENTY

Chang and Nelson stayed where they were in front of their motorhomes. Becky and I stopped a good ten feet back from them. Tone and Dirt closed the distance to an arm's length.

From that far away, I couldn't hear any thoughts other than Becky's frantic, *We're cool, we're cool, we're cool.*

Chang's hand now rested on the butt of his holstered pistol, his gaze jumping from Tone to the rest of us.

Nelson didn't seem to care what Chang had told him because he was holding out his hand waiting for the paper Dirt promised.

Dirt said, "Here it is," but it had already come, a flash of his blade before it plunged into the side of Nelson's neck, the blood spraying Dirt's windbreaker.

Tone was a split-second slower and Chang a little faster, jumping back as Tone's knife sliced the air just inches from his face.

Chang tugged on his gun, but the holster kept it stuck to his hip. He stumbled back and banged into the motorhome's grill.

Tone lunged forward, stabbed at Chang's chest, but Chang swiveled his torso like he was in the *Matrix*, turned his back on us to dodge the knife.

Chang popped the holster, raised his gun, the red dot on Tone's forehead.

Tone covered his face and dropped to a ball because he saw what Chang couldn't.

From behind, Dirt gripped a handful of Chang's hair and yanked, his knife filleting the Boot's neck into the widest smile I'd ever seen.

Chang's gun clanked off the concrete without firing. Tone retrieved it and got to his feet.

Becky said, "Oh shit," and ran at Nelson, who was crawling to his gun, a trail of blood behind him.

With one hand holding his neck, Nelson picked up the submachine gun.

Becky kicked his hand, the gun flying from his grip and skipping under the motorhome. She got both hands under Nelson's arm and tossed him over. He landed on his back with a loud oomph. She dropped a knee on his gut causing an even louder one.

Nelson tried pushing Becky's knee off his belly, but she wasn't going anywhere and pinned down both his hands.

*Why?* Nelson couldn't speak, couldn't understand what was going on. *Why?*

Becky kept him pinned, the blood pouring from his neck. Her face was set in determination, but her mind screamed, *What am I doing?*

Nelson was fading quick, his only thought to stop the blood flow. *Let go. Please.*

Becky kept her weight on him but released his right hand, ready to snatch it if it was a ploy.

Nelson was out of tricks and had just enough strength to bring his hand to his neck before he went limp.

This whole time, my aim alternated between the motorhomes, sure someone would barge out and open fire on us any second.

There was only silence from the vehicles, the slam of a door down the street, kids playing in a backyard. Dirt and Tone had taken what they needed from Chang, and each had a hold of two limbs. Tone thought, *On three,* and counted them off, tossing Chang beneath the motorhome.

Dirt threw Chang's windbreaker over the one he was wearing, popped on this hat, put in an earpiece.

Becky thought my name. *Help me get his jacket.*

She was holding Nelson by his collar, so he was nearly sitting up, his head dangling back.

The windbreaker slipped off. I handed it to Becky. I wasn't cut out for this. *You wear it. You're the better actor.*

A pair of headlights from behind us lit up the scene as Tone and Dirt got ready to make Nelson disappear. Tone said, "Joe. Handle it."

I was closest, my gun drawn. The lights were blinding and coming right at me, maybe twenty feet away. I raised my weapon, finger on the trigger.

The vehicle screeched to a halt. I couldn't see because of the headlights, so I stepped to the driver's side, kept my gun trained on it.

It was an old Ford four-door, a Hispanic couple up front, two teenage boys in the back. They all had their hands in the air. The mustached man behind the wheel, shook his head back and forth. *Oh, Dios mío.*

I drew from the Spanish tapes I'd studied and asked, "Qué haces?"

He pointed at the house to his right. "Vivimos aquí."

From the backseat, one of the boys thought, *That guy's dead.*

The other boy said, "Look at all that blood."

None of them suspected anything, but all were rightfully scared. I figured the kids could translate if the parents didn't understand because I'd screw it up in Spanish. "We just got attacked, and there may very well be another one. Go somewhere safe. At least for an hour, all night if you can."

The wife said, "Oh, God bless you."

The man held his hand in a half-salute. "Yes, sir. Thank you." He turned into their driveway, backed out, then drove away.

Dirt and Tone tossed Nelson under the motorhome. To me, Tone thought, *So you just let them go? No worries they might recognize you?*

*It doesn't matter.* I walked past him and joined Becky, who was standing in the shadows where the back of Chang's motorhome met the edge of the park. The family didn't care about me, but even if they did, I knew, *I can't get any more wanted than I already am.*

Both baseball fields were lit, but they were in the far corners, their light ending a good forty yards away, nothing but field between us and the giant tarped area that stretched from one second base to the other.

Dirt came up close enough to share his thoughts, looked just like a real Boot if it weren't for his beard. *Alright guys, good job. The rec center and bathrooms are to the left. Stay away from the main entrance to your right.*

Tone thought, *We'll keep this exit secure as long as we can without unnecessarily risking our lives.* He looked right at Becky. *That means fucking hurry up and do what you came here to do.*

The night was still early and the neighborhood awake, but operations had ceased or at least slowed down inside the camp. On the back end of the park, there were a few people milling outside the row of RVs that blocked the view from the street to our right.

If it hadn't been for the lights on them, I wouldn't have spotted three small buildings off to the left. A silhouette walked between the buildings and disappeared in the darkness. There was no telling who else was roaming about, ready to stumble upon us.

Becky tugged my sleeve and headed forward. *Come on. Let's do this.*

The ground was squishy, a muddy mess from all the Boot activity. I worried about the noise we were making, but Becky assured me, *We're fine. We're Boots. We work here.*

*You talk to anyone who stops us.* I wasn't proud telling her this, but I wanted us to get out alive and it wouldn't be smart to withhold information. *I can't do it.*

*Deal.*

Halfway to the tarp, I could finally see under it. There were three large fenced off areas, pigpens full of prisoners. The largest was to our right, packed full of people, many huddled together and covered with packing blankets, loners spread out amongst them.

The middle pen was about the same size as the first but had fewer than half the people. Number 3, the small pen to the left, held the fewest, just a dozen or so.

*This is the back side of the cages,* Becky thought. *Look, the guards are on the far side.*

She was right, but we still had no plan. *What the hell are we going to do?*

Becky kept moving forward toward the middle pen where the porta potty touched the fence. *We find my parents.*

I stood beside her, my heart thumping so fast.

*Joe, I need you to calm down. Can you do that?*

I took a deep breath and blew it out, peeked around the potty. The two guards at the gate on the other side hadn't moved. Even if they were to turn around, I doubted they'd see us with the light so low.

*Anyone there?* Becky focused her mind. *Anyone hear me?*

I couldn't hear a response, but Becky flashed me four fingers, then two more a second later.

*I need your help,* she thought. *Peter and Paula Glynn. Fifty-something couple. My dad has brown hair, clean-shaven, businessman. My mom is thin and tall with dark hair. Would've come in yesterday or the night before.*

Becky nodded like she was listening, but I got nothing. There was a shuffling on my side of the potty, and an older man thought, *You've got to help us.*

A woman I hadn't known was there joined in. *You aren't Boots?*

A teenage girl crawled closer to the cage. *You getting us out of here?*

Becky answered, *We're sure as hell gonna try.*

There was silence but Becky was concentrating on something. She asked, *Where are you?*

I was just a few feet to her side and didn't get why she was asking. *Right here.*

*Not you, Joe. Quiet.*

The porta potty door opened and closed. A woman thought, *Can you hear me?*

We both answered yes. Becky thought, *My parents. Have you seen them?*

The lady thought, *I haven't heard either name and I've taken it on myself to document every person I cross paths with. It helps keep us human.*

Becky asked, *You hear everyone's name?*

*Everyone that comes into this cage. The ones that are telepaths at least.*

I thought, *Not everyone's a telepath?*

*Hardly. Maybe one out of every three or four.*

Becky asked, *So what's the difference in cages? Could they be in one of the others?*

*Possibly. Over to your right is intake. No telling how long that stay can be. From there you visit the rec center and if you're lucky you get sent in here or to the left.*

I asked, *What does it take to get moved?*

*From what I've gathered, they stick you in here if they think you're valuable, either for ransom or personal reasons. The third is for telepaths destined to be Sentinels.*

I asked, *How about Sara or Danny?*

The lady was already moving, the door opened and closed. I started saying something to Becky, but she held up her finger, wincing at whatever she was taking in.

I asked, *What is it?*

She shoved her finger at me. *Chill.*

It's hard to fucking chill sitting in the shadows surrounded by Boots and Sentinels, prisoners trapped in cages, but I did my best to calm my mind.

After a few seconds, Becky thought, *Stirling.*

I repeated the name, marveled how she thought it with such anger.

*Reyes.*

*Reyes?*

*Donner.*

I asked, *Who are they?*

Becky thought, *Our top three most wanted.*

A gunshot froze us in place. Another shot was fired.

My first thought was that Tone or Dirt had opened fire, but these shots came from our left, muffled from being indoors.

*It's one of those three buildings,* Becky thought as she led me along the back of the small pen, everyone wrapped in a blanket, no one paying us any mind. *My guess is the rec center.*

Becky paused at the corner of the pen, forty yards of darkness between us and the buildings. A Boot exited the bathroom to the right. He turned back to the door and locked it, wiping his palms on his pants as he headed toward the rec center.

I asked Becky, *You think that's the shooter?*

The Boot entered the rec center, the door closing behind him. Becky slipped her gun into the holster and slid the sword from the sheath on her back. She left the safety of our corner, holding the sword along her leg. With more hate than I'd ever heard from her, she thought, *I bet that's Stirling.*

I kept my gun in hand because I wasn't a quick draw.

Becky thought, *I suggest putting it away. Too many Boots with Dirt and Tone way back there. Any shooting and we're done.*

It felt like a dumb move, but I holstered my gun and pulled out my cheap plastic stun gun.

Becky walked with a purpose, her intention set. I couldn't believe she was only sixteen and that I was the one who had forced her into this mess.

*Joe, shut up. Seriously,* she thought. *These are not good guys.*

I didn't mean to think it as it went against the rationalization I constantly told myself to deal with the guilt, but my mind went to the newbie and his wife, their little boy. *Not all of them.*

Less than ten feet from the door, Becky thought, *What they do in that bathroom, you don't want to see. I'm getting my parents out of here.*

*I'll cover you best I can.* There was no one to our left, just a flatbed truck parked behind the bathroom and loaded with black trash bags filled with lumpy material.

Becky stopped at the door. I took a last look around. A Boot sat in his car on the baseball mound in the far corner, its headlights on the backstop and bleachers. I told her, *It's all clear out here, but we're walking in blind.*

*So be prepared to react.* Becky put her shoulder against the door, sword at the ready. I didn't know if she was talking to me or herself when she thought, *Strike first. Strike fast.*

Becky slipped inside without a sound, and I followed her. After the darkness outside, the fluorescent lights seemed so bright. There was a hint of sulfur in the air.

I'd expected Becky to pause before turning the corner, but she walked into the main room like she belonged. The room's floor and walls were white tile, just like the VFW, a flashback to the slaughterhouse.

The Boot who'd been in the bathroom was at the table along the back wall fixing a cup of coffee. Looking right at him was another Boot, a forty-something, heavyset blond resting his boots on top of the receptionist's desk. Sounding a little too happy, he hitched a thumb at the closed door behind him. "Got a cleanup on aisle seven."

Becky headed for the Boot getting coffee. I stuck my stun gun in my windbreaker pocket, felt I should say something to give her some time. Quickest thing I could think of was, "Goddamn, it's getting cold."

Neither man paid me any mind. The coffee Boot turned to the desk guy. "What happened?"

"Donner didn't care for her response and—" the blond said, cutting himself off when he noticed Becky, who was arm's length away from his partner. He got his feet off the desk, his voice suddenly all official and kind of creepy when he told her, "You're new."

Coffee guy held up his mug to Becky. "Care for some?" Before she could say anything, he said, "Whoa, what happened to your face?"

The blond Boot thought, *Oh shit*, because he saw the sword. He scrambled out of his chair and shouted, "Stirling!" But Becky was already moving, kicking out Stirling's leg and pushing him over, driving her sword into his chest when he hit the ground.

The blond Boot fumbled with his holster. "What the fuck?"

Stirling was still fighting, both hands on the sword, but Becky wasn't budging. I ran around the desk, the stun gun out and clicking. The blond looked my way as he took aim at Becky, but I got to him first, buried the stun gun into his neck, kept driving forward as he spasmed to the floor.

I held that trigger as hard as I could, his body spasming, his feet smacking the tile.

Becky was on her feet, facing the side room where someone was turning the knob.

A man's gruff voice said, "What the hell's going on out there?" The door opened and a stocky Boot with a graying crewcut stepped out. He turned tail at the sight of the body and Becky's dripping sword. He slammed the door behind him.

Becky threw the door open and tackled him, a sharp cry of pain that wasn't hers.

I still had the stun gun going but my guy had ceased movement. I hurried into the office and found Becky mounted on the Boot, her sword an inch above his mouth, blood spreading out from his torso.

*Becky, you don't want to do that.*

She didn't acknowledge me. "What's your name?"

His face scrunched up in pain. "Captain Franklin Donner."

Becky thrust the sword through his mouth. He tried rising up, and I could see the blade sunk into the carpet, Becky holding it down with all she had. His legs flailed, but only for a second before flopping back down. There was no escape.

# CHAPTER TWENTY-ONE

Captain Donner's eyes were closed, the sword pinning him to the carpet. His heart still beat, one thought repeating. *Help will come. Help will come.*

Becky walked behind the captain's desk. "No, it won't," she said. "Not for you."

My heart thumped, a throb rising in my ears. Blood poured out the back of Donner's neck, turning the carpet into a soggy mess. My vision wavered and all that red became black. Sensing that I was about to pass out, I backed down on a folding chair.

Becky and Donner were thinking, but their thoughts were muffled, the thrumming all I could hear, images from the last week flying in front of me. Rachel without a face. Wayne with a hole in his forehead. Boots burning in the helicopter, heads barely hanging on from a shotgun blast, splattered on the ground from a 200-foot fall. Boots murdered in their cars, blown to bits, choked, stabbed, stunned. So much fucking death.

That is what we had become.

Becky said, "Joe, you gotta breathe."

I tried, blew out what little air I brought in. I sat up straight and opened my eyes, felt a little better.

Becky was on the captain's laptop, flying through the different windows. Behind her, the whiteboard was divided into three sections with colored magnets spread about, the majority taking up the first two sections.

I couldn't read the names on the magnets, the writing too small. "Are those the prisoners?"

Becky didn't hear me, all her attention on the spreadsheet, searching a list of names for a Peter and Paula.

Captain Donner's thoughts were weak and far apart, but so goddamn sad. *Laura. Oh, Laura.*

Becky looked up, not in the mood for my sensitivity. She walked around the desk and hovered over the captain, twisted the sword as she pulled it free. She wiped the sword clean on his pants and hocked a loogie on his cheek. "Fuck him," she said. "Fuck all of them."

The pressure in my skull swooped back, but I pushed it away with my breath. "Your parents?"

"Nothing yet."

I pointed to the nametags. "Are they up there?"

She glanced at the board. "Don't know. I'm going to gather all I can, but you got to pull it together and watch the front door. If anyone's alerted, we're not getting out of here."

Not ready to give up, I got to my feet. Stirling lay where he'd been, his blood mixing with the spilled coffee. Not wanting to get messier than I already was, I went over to the blond guy who hadn't moved either, no thoughts, no heartbeat.

I took his radio and clipped it onto my belt. There were some papers on his desk, but they didn't mean a thing to me when I looked over them. The top drawer was full of office supplies, nothing useful. Middle drawer was more of the same. The bottom drawer empty.

An angry grunt came from Donner's room as a plastic trashcan came flying out, magnets scattering across the floor.

I assumed it had to be her parents but asked, "What is it?"

The soft clank of keys and bootsteps approached the front door. *Oh shit.* I didn't know if Becky could hear me with a wall in the way, but I thought, *We got company.*

The door opened and a young Boot with a buzzcut walked in, his windbreaker so tight everyone could see he spent plenty of time in the gym.

The entryway blocked his view of the bodies, but that would all change in two steps. I hurried around the desk and held up my hand. "What are you doing in here?"

My question stopped him, made him mumble his answer. "I need to ask Captain about something," he said, leaving out he was going to ask for time off.

"Well, he's busy and doesn't have time for anyone's bullshit."

He stood a little taller, puffed his chest. "It's not bullshit."

I couldn't have been more than five years older, but I asked him, "What's your name, son?"

He deflated. "Waterman."

"Well, Waterman, head to the side entrance and switch places with Nelson. Captain wants to see him immediately."

"The side entrance?"

I couldn't remember the term Tone had used and didn't know if that was the correct one anyhow. "How fucking long you been here? Look for the two huge motorhomes on the south side."

He looked more confused than defiant. "But I'm posted at the front. I told them I'd be back in five."

"Not anymore. I'll get someone else over there."

He wasn't a fan of being treated like a child, but he'd faced bigger dicks in the Army. "Yes, sir," he said, keeping, *you fucking asshole,* to himself.

I got on the radio and said, "Nelson, I've got Waterman headed your way. Switch with him and report to the command center."

It took a second for Dirt to reply. "Copy that."

Waterman left without a word, his mind picturing what he'd do to me in a street fight.


The door closed behind Waterman. I wondered if I should lock it.

"I wouldn't," Becky said from just a few feet away, getting a kick out of my jump.

I hadn't heard her sneak out, but there she was, pressed against the wall, sword in hand, close enough to strike if Waterman had taken another step.

"Hope that was a smart move," she said.

"They can handle him better than I could."

Becky sheathed her sword. "Well, it is what it is."

"What now?"

"Take Stirling's keys." She grabbed the blond's wrists and dragged him to Donner's office, his mouth peeling back on the floor.

I was back to being a soldier and unclipped the keys from his belt, didn't care what I was stepping in.

Becky repeated her process with Stirling, tossing him on top of the blond. "Go to the men's room and film everything."

"What's in there?"

She slipped off her backpack and handed me a phone. "Use this to record."

"What's in there?"

Becky didn't answer, busy putting the laptop into the backpack. She brought out a gray package and remote control, set them on the desk.

I asked, "You have his password?"

"Oh shit."

"Tone probably has someone that can hack it."

Becky had her sword back out and lined up her chop. *Look away.*

I was happy to, but there was no stopping that sound. One thwack, then another.

Becky wrapped the finger in a napkin and set it in the backpack. "All done."

"What are you gonna do?"

"Get ready. There's been a change of plans."

"Should I meet you back here?"

"No. Once you've filmed in there, you get on the radio. I'd do it but they don't have any females working."

"What do I say?"

Becky repeated the message Tone had given her. "All available units report to the command center. Those at a station remain there until relief comes."

I repeated the whole thing so it would sink in.

"When you radio it in, I'll meet you at the cages. You take the one on the left, and I'll go right. Tell those guards that they're relieved for the meeting." She grabbed all her stuff and locked Donner's door behind us.

The swirl of coffee and blood brought back stepping in the Boot outside the VFW. "So what exactly are we doing?"

"Following orders. Getting everyone out."

*That's what we tried in Brightside.*

"Yeah, well that's what we're doing again." Becky glanced about the room. "And when you radio it, be sure to add for someone to bring a mop, the last interrogation got messy."


The rec room door clunked closed behind me. I waited for my eyes to adjust to the darkness, imagined I was walking in front of a firing squad. No shots were fired, no Boots in sight. With my gun holstered and stun gun in my windbreaker pocket, I made my way to the men's bathroom, key in hand.

The bathroom looked no different from any other you'd see in a park, but it felt so wrong, like it was cloaked by an evil cloud. I knew that was bullshit, just my mind messing with me because of what Becky had said, but I couldn't shake the feeling, the eerie light slanting out the window slits only making it worse.

I paused at the door, listened closely, couldn't hear a thing, real or thought.

The key slid in, the lock clunked open. A sharp sob came from inside, but it didn't sound like a man.

The door creaked and the sobbing grew louder, a woman's panicked thoughts on the edge of my range. *No. God, no. Not again!*

I didn't want to get any closer, but I had my orders.

Another step and the edge of a mattress came into view, wedged between the stalls and the wall, no sheet covering it. The counter beside the sink had a stack of folded towels. Beneath it, a pile of waded up dirty ones.

The smell hit me hard. Piss and shit, blood and semen. It took me back to being fourteen, Mandy teaching me to be a man.

I brought out my gun before turning the corner, reholstered it when I saw the naked woman curled on the mattress, her bloody wrist handcuffed to the base of the farthest stall.

"I'm not one of them," I said, my voice cracking. "I won't hurt you."

The woman, who looked about my age, cradled her head with both arms, bruises spotting her legs and butt, her thoughts on a loop. *No! No! No!*

I grabbed a bunch of towels from the counter, laid them over the woman, my tears falling.

*Don't believe him, Corina,* she thought to herself. *It's a trick.*

Calm as I could, I whispered, "No, it's not. Corina, I'm here to help."

She peeked out from behind her arms, her face battered. *You can hear me?*

I nodded. *Can you her me?*

Her face showed she couldn't. "I don't know if you're talking. I'm not a telepath."

"Jesus Christ." Time was short, no telling who might stop by for a privileged bathroom break. "We're getting out of here, but I have to film this. Let's cover up your face, but we need the world to see what the fuck is going on."

She took a towel and laid it over her face, then set it to the side. *No*, she thought. *Show them everything. Let them see what kind of monsters they are.*

I turned on the video, starting with the counter and wadded up towels. Speaking low, but loud enough for the recorder, I said, "I am in a bathroom at Salazar Park in Los Angeles, where the SSS have a detention center. This is what these officers, the men who have undisputed authority, are doing to protect everyone."

I focused on the handful of hair on the mattress by her feet. When the camera got to Corina's face, she flinched but kept strong while I finished.

I put the phone in my pocket and got out Stirling's key, used the smallest one to remove Corina's cuff, the skin so puffy and red where it'd been rubbed raw.

Corina crawled into the stall and came out in a minute with black yoga pants and a UCLA sweatshirt.

"I need to move forward with our plan. If you want to leave with us, you need to get to the two motorhomes parked in a V at the south entrance."

"Do I follow you?" she asked, not wanting to leave my side.

I shook my head. "Not yet. Too dangerous. We're breaking everyone out."

"How?"

Instead of telling her I didn't know, I handed her my gun, showed her how to take off the safety. "Only use this if you have to. It's ready to go."

Corina wondered how many bullets she had, if there were enough for each of the men that had violated her.

I held up a finger to show I needed silence. "This'll just take a minute," I said as I got out my radio. "All available units report to the command center. Those at a station remain there until relief comes. And someone bring a mop. The last interrogation got messy."

# CHAPTER TWENTY-TWO

There was no way to know how many Boots questioned my transmission, but enough copied to give me the courage to leave Corina behind washing off blood.

The bathroom door closed behind me and I set my course for the front of Cage 1, the field lights making it easier to see. I was nearly where the cage met the infield when three Boots turned the corner. The shortest one said, "Wrong way."

I kept walking. "I'm relief."

None of them cared and they continued to the rec center.

I rounded the corner and looked through the fence. Several silhouettes on the other side of the cages all headed for the emergency meeting.

The Boot guarding Cage 1 didn't look old enough to drink. He asked me, "Any idea what's going on?"

"No." I rubbed my forehead to cover my face a bit. "Donner seemed like he was in a good mood. Think it might be about a bonus."

The guy slapped my bad shoulder. "Fuck yeah. Be back in a bit."

I ignored the pain and put my back to the gate, listened for thoughts of the telepaths behind me. A man kept thinking, *Fuck,* while a woman prayed, *God, my savior, my light, watch over your children.*

If I could hear them, they could probably hear me. Not ready to explain I had no idea what I was doing, I ran through multiples of five, got to 3,125 before a Boot approached from the right.

The stun gun didn't give me much hope, the plastic feeling like it'd shatter under my grip. The next closest Boot was in his car facing the bleachers. If this guy confronted me, I had no choice but attack.

The footsteps came close enough I could hear Dirt's thoughts. *It's all good, Joe. We took out Waterman. Thought you could use some backup.*

*You see Becky?*

He motioned behind him with his submachine gun. *She's at Cage Three. I got Two.*

*Your guards already gone?*

*Yep. Nothing left to do but get everyone the fuck out of here.*

*Where they going to go?*

*Open your gate on our signal. Send them to the south entrance.*

*What's the signal?*

*You'll know.* Dirt turned and walked back to his post.

I checked my gate to see what kind of lock they had on it, figured I should find the key.

*There isn't one,* a woman thought. *One gun does the trick.*

She was right, nothing but a latch I had to lift. There were only two women in my range, but I wasn't sure which one I was talking to. *You know who I am?*

*No, but I'm praying you're Underground.*

*As quietly as you can, spread the word that we're getting out.*

*The lady wrapped in the brown blanket looked up, a flash of hope in her eyes. When?*

Metal clicked on Cage 2, everything amplified in the wide open. Prisoners crept out both gates and headed toward Becky, who was barely visible, guiding people around the corner.

My heart thumped, my eyes darting between both cars on the infield. All it would take was a look in their rearview.

From one of the other cages, a woman screamed, "No! No!"

I said, "Oh fuck," and threw open the gate, told the prisoners to go my way instead of Becky's. The second I said it, the door to the rec center opened, two Boots stepping out to see what was going on.

The woman who sounded a whole lot like Sara yelled, "You can't—"

A giant explosion tore through the night, the rec center exploding in a big ball of flame, the Boots obliterated.

"Go! Go! Go!" I shouted as prisoners hurried through the gate, but just as many stayed balled up on the ground.

Gunfire popped off by the main entrance, prisoners hitting the dirt, no way to tell if they'd been hit by bullets or were taking cover. One burst then another erupted from our side, Becky and Dirt returning fire.

Both Boot vehicles drove off the pitcher mounds. I thought the closest one was headed for the rubble of the rec center, but he was coming right for us, the car just a few feet from the fence we were running beside.

I yelled, "Scatter!"

There was no time for anyone to react, the car mowing down an older couple twenty yards behind us, everyone screaming.

Loud as I could, I shouted, "Against the fence! Everyone!"

I grabbed the teenage boy beside me and jumped into the fence, praying we wouldn't bounce back. The fence held for a second and we started to rebound, but then bodies plowed into us, enough weight to knock the entire length of the fence onto the grass, the car's tires tearing right by.

I screamed in pain, all that weight driving me into the ground, but I could barely hear myself with the gunshots, prisoners screaming as their bodies bounced off the car's hood and disappeared under the wheels.

The man on my back rolled off me as the car flew past the corner of the cage and smashed into a man the size of Wendell crawling on all fours. The driver's side wheel left the ground as it rolled over him, and the driver couldn't regain control, the car spinning in a circle, coming to a stop on the grass.

My stun gun was worthless from so far away, no chance I could make it to the car before the driver got out and mowed us all down.

Some of the prisoners fled back into their cage and huddled with those that'd stayed behind, but the rest took off running. The car's interior light went on as the driver stepped out, blasts of gunfire as he picked off the closest escapees, bodies thumping to the ground.

I got up and told the kid I'd grabbed, "Stay down." These people were dying because of me. I ran for the car, didn't care about the bullets.

There was another blinding blast, but it came from right behind the driver, put him face down on the hood of the car. It was Corina, the gun hanging loose in her hand.

Dirt came running around the corner. "Load that car up and get the fuck out of here!"

A bald guy with a matted black beard threw the Boot off the hood and got behind the wheel. Four others jumped in and they sped past us as we ran for the exit.

Dirt was beside me, close enough to hear my worries. *I think she made it out the front. Tone's there.*

I wondered who was watching the south entrance and figured I'd find out soon enough.

Bursts of bright gunfire came from the cluster of cars to the right. One, two, three people collapsed, smacking the ground in front of us.

Dirt pulled something out of his windbreaker and chucked it at the cars, dropping to his knees and yelling, "Get down!"

I was too slow to react and the explosion knocked me on my ass.

Dirt jumped to his feet and ran for Chang's motorhome, stopping in the shadow that we'd been hiding in only fifteen minutes before. "Everyone, down this street," he yelled. "Run! Hide!"

I stayed beside Dirt, knew it was the safest place to be.

He grabbed an able-looking man who'd been helping a young boy. Dirt handed him keys and a phone. "The white van down the street. Take it and as many people that'll fit."

The guy didn't know what to say, so Dirt pushed him in the right direction.

I couldn't understand. *Why'd you do that?*

Dirt took one look back in the park. *Get in the motorhome.*

*What?*

He peeled back from the corner and ran for the door. *They're coming!*


The first sign that Dirt had this planned was the motorhome's cab light not turning on like it had when Chang exited the vehicle.

The second was him guiding me down the narrow corridor despite only the faintest light streaming through the curtained window. Dirt stopped us before the doorway to the bathroom and wedged me between the wall and the dark plastic bags stacked chest-high along the right side of the RV.

*Sit tight*, Dirt instructed. Men yelled outside. *Keep your thoughts clear as you can. Remember, they got Sentinels.*

There was no way he'd be able to fit into the space with me. I worried he was going to leave. *You going in the bedroom?*

*Nah, first place they'll look.* Dirt toed my boots so I brought my knees to my chest then he laid one of those thick plastic bags over my legs. *I'll be right behind the cab.*

*I don't have a gun.*

Dirt reached under his windbreaker and pulled a pistol from the shoulder holster. *15 plus 1. Use them wisely.*

I felt better with the gun, but sirens were screaming toward us. *How long we gonna hide?*

He headed for the front. *Long as it takes.*

The air felt too thin like my first day in Brightside, the elevation kicking my ass. But this was just my mind dealing with claustrophobia and the fear I wouldn't be able to get out if I tried.

The sirens grew louder as my eyes adjusted, able to see the bags were stacked four high.

Tires squealed to a stop by the front of the motorhome. The sirens ceased but strobing red lights flashed through our window. A car door slammed shut then another. Sounded like a couple more cars rolled up, the doors opening and closing.

Men talked outside, but too muffled to hear. A savage intensity of hate hit me hard, someone thinking, *Gonna kill these motherfuckers.*

A gravelly voice barked, "Blake, you're with me. Merkin, go with Saenz."

Everyone said, "Yes, sir," with one of them calling him Sergeant.

I'd hoped they were going to go straight past us, but the motorhome door opened. The sergeant said, "Fucking light's busted."

Someone outside said, "Same with this one."

There was the slightest shift when the sergeant climbed aboard. The back of the motorhome was illuminated with the click of a button, a high-powered flashlight showing everything.

Quiet as I could, I brought the bag over my head, made it so just my right eye peeked out.

The sergeant said, "If anyone's in this vehicle, announce yourself now. This is an order."

I hoped Dirt's hiding place was better than mine, but I expected a gunfight any second.

Another set of footsteps entered. The sergeant said, "Blake, clear the back."

"Yes, sir."

Everything went black but only long enough for the sergeant to adjust his light around Blake, who was headed my way, one slow step after another.

Sounding irritated, the sergeant said, "Go. You're covered."

Blake walked faster and right into my range, his thoughts flying. *Be empty. Be empty.*

Staying hidden behind the black bags, I leveled the gun where I figured his chest would be. I wouldn't shoot unless Blake saw me. If that happened, Dirt would have to take out the sergeant, and then it'd be the two of us versus the two in Nelson's motorhome, plus who knows how many Boots hanging around outside.

Blake shuffled forward and stopped right in front of me, the barrel of his submachine gun sticking into the bathroom. Unlike the others we'd seen, he was all SWATed out with a bulletproof vest and helmet. I'd have to hit his neck, a tough shot from my position.

*Okay, okay,* Blake told himself as he swiveled to clear the left side of the bathroom, pausing when he turned back my way, the flashlight reflecting off his narrowed eye.

He started talking and I nearly fired, the trigger halfway there when I realized he'd said, "Bathroom clear."

From the other motorhome, one of the men shouted, "All clear, Sergeant."

Blake entered the back room and banged around on the cupboards and closets. He came back through thinking, *Thank God.* "All clear, Sarge."

Someone outside shouted for the sergeant. "Fuck, we got one of ours out here."

Another Boot said, "Shit, under that one, too."

The flashlight clicked off and the sergeant left our motorhome, Blake right behind him.

"Goddamn it! Get them out from there," the sergeant said. "News crews are coming. Let's show them what they did."


My stomach clenched so hard it woke me. It tightened again, a loud gurgle going with it. I breathed in deep and gagged on the smell of shit and piss.

I checked my pants, relieved to find my crotch dry. The smell had been there all along; I just hadn't noticed it.

I slipped the phone from my pocket, kept it under the bag to check the time. 10:18. I'd been sitting over three hours in the same position, my shoulder screaming at me to find a pill or something to take away the pain.

The first hour had been the worst, Boots and news crews walking past us, in and out of the park's entrance, so many thoughts jolting me out of a semi-conscious state.

The light from the phone shined off the zipper of the bag by my hip. I eased open the zipper and reached inside, no question I touched flesh, the round of someone's shoulder.

I felt stupid not guessing what the smell had been, a stack of forty bodies on a slow decay. But what I really felt right then was that I was going to shit my pants in a matter of seconds, my stomach furious.

As far as I knew, Dirt and I were alone in the motorhome. There was going to be the noise and smell of my bowels letting loose, so I figured it was worth the risk to use the toilet, the desire to die with clean underwear stronger than my fear of death itself.

I slid the phone back into my pocket and holstered the pistol. Getting up was going to hurt, but I was determined. Everything went pins and needles, except for the lance of fire driving through my shoulder.

My eyes had adjusted, and I could see the length of the corridor, the cab looking empty. As quietly as I could, I set down my empty body bag and eased into the bathroom, struggled to get my jeans down in time, a flood of nastiness pouring out of me, the splash even louder.

Someone outside said, "You hear something?"

"Nah."

I'd come to terms with there being no toilet paper, but then I noticed the roll on the back of the toilet. Three quick wipes and I had my pants up, my gun out. The instinct was to flush but I just closed the lid, prayed it didn't smell any worse than the rest of the place.

I was returning to my spot when the cab door opened and someone dropped into the driver's seat. I sat down on the toilet, swiveled my legs so they couldn't be seen down the corridor, readied my gun.

Another door opened and closed. A new voice, full of anger, said, "Whatcha waiting for, Jones?"

The engine started and Jones said, "HQ, this is R6 headed to DS14. Repeat, R6 to DS14."

HQ copied Jones over the radio, said he was all clear.

The motorhome eased forward and down the street. Jones sounded kind of scared when he said, "I can't believe this shit is happening."

"Why?"

"Did you go back there? You see how many guys we lost?"

"Nothing like Fallujah. This ain't shit."

"Yeah, Hoop, but this is our soil." Sounding disgusted, he said, "Our own people are attacking us."

The Boots kept up their conversation but I leaned against the bathroom wall and tuned them out so I could concentrate on breathing and feeling better. There were a bunch of turns, but I didn't keep track of those either, no way I'd ever retrace our steps.

We'd been driving about ten minutes when I risked a peek. The empty street was in an industrial area, buildings lit for their graveyard crews.

The motorhome's turn indicator clicked and we slowed to a stop at a solid metal gate with razor wire on top. A window up front rolled down. "R6 with drop off."

An intercom buzzed and a voice said, "Copy that." He paused before he asked, "Is it true what happened?"

Jones said, "Afraid so."

"Any chance they'd try something on a place like this?"

Hoop said, "You better act like it. Twenty-four hours a day. Shit happens when your guard's down."

The gate guard said, "Yes sir," and the gate rolled open.

# CHAPTER TWENTY-THREE

The gate slammed closed behind us as we drove to the right, bins upon bins of newspaper, plastic bottles, and aluminum cans in rows along the fence. The warehouse's overhead lights were on with two floodlights aimed at the mountain of cardboard covering the concrete in front of it.

We circled the cardboard and headed for the backside of the building, pulled to a stop beside a loading dock. Jones lowered his window and raised his voice so he could be heard over the roar of machinery. "Am I good?"

"Back up two feet," someone said not far from me on the driver's side of the vehicle. "Come on, just a little more."

I couldn't remember whether there'd been a door in the back of the motorhome, but I had to be ready for someone to come in that way. This time I wouldn't hesitate to shoot.

Both Boots exited the vehicle and started talking to the recycling guy. I was sure this was it. They were going to be coming in here sooner or later and we'd be trapped. And we had no way of knowing how many Boots surrounded us.

I peeked into the corridor, saw someone coming.

Dirt thought my name so loud I put down my gun. *You're right, Joe.* He helped me up and thought, *It's our turn.*

My knees buckled and I would've collapsed if he hadn't grabbed me. *I'm sorry. I'm not doing so good.*

Dirt checked over his shoulder. *Well, buck up, soldier. These next five minutes will be the most important five minutes of your life.*

I took in as much air as I could and blew it out, stood on my own. *Fuck it. Let's do it.*

Dirt crept down the corridor, gun aimed at the cab. *Here we go.*

Jones was talking with someone to our left, but I couldn't hear what it was about. Dirt crouched along the right side of the corridor so he could see out the driver's window. I did the same on the left, nothing out the passenger window besides bins, a fence, and buildings on the other side of it.

With the window down, it was easy to hear Hoop's irritation when he said, "Where's the forklift driver?"

The recycling guy sounded stuffy, like he was fighting a cold. "Working the baler."

"So who's working the forklift?"

"No one. I got Jose on the Bobcat filling containers."

"We're not moving all these ourselves."

Jones must've been leaning against the motorhome because I picked up his thoughts, how going back in with the bodies was the last thing he wanted.

"Well, I don't know what you expect me to do," the guy said as he sucked back snot. "There was an accident with one of the workers and another one ran off a few hours ago."

Hoop said, "This is East L.A. Go pick up some fucking wetbacks."

"Easier said than done, muchacho."

Jones said, "Why don't we just bring in workers from the centers? Got no shortage of bodies."

"Look at that baler. You got the first idea on how to work one of those fucking things?"

Hoop said, "No, but I can figure out how to drive a forklift."

"Knock yourself out. Keys are in it."

Dirt thought, *Hold tight. We move when he drives back.*

No one was coming my way so I focused on the front window. The warehouse had a rear wall of corrugated steel, its massive roof at least forty feet high. The far end of the dock had stacks of cardboard and plastic bales. A man with a green bandana over his mouth, safety glasses, and a thick pair of headphones sat behind the controls of the giant machine.

The recycling center Boot asked, "That guy always such a dick?"

"Pretty much."

*I've got these three*, Dirt thought. *You be on the lookout for the intercom guy and any other Boots.*

*Copy.*

Dirt crept into the cab, fired three shots through the open window. He pushed open the door and jumped onto the loading dock before Jones and the other Boot collapsed to the floor.

I crouched beside him, my head on a swivel. The forklift was headed toward us, Hoop not seeming to notice anything had happened, the roar of the baler covering the gunfire.

Dirt popped up and fired three more times. One ricocheted off the forklift but the other two hit Hoop in the head, knocking him back in his seat, the forklift blades impaling a bale of cardboard.

There wasn't anyone around us besides the baler operator, who hadn't noticed anything. There was a light on in the office on the other side of the warehouse. Keeping my gun by my leg, I walked along the conveyor belt stacked with body bags. Sandbags surrounded the main body of the baler, but I didn't pay them any mind until I stepped over them into a blackish pool of muddy blood that went halfway up my shins.

Movement by the office made me look up. A Boot stood outside the doorway, his hand on the walkie talkie clipped to his windbreaker.

The Boot was twenty yards away, not a good distance for my pistol, but I had no choice. Although it looked like he was just curious where the others were, I wasn't taking chances. He saw my gun being raised and tried darting back into the office, but I was already firing.

The Boot clutched his right hamstring and scrambled for the front of the dock.

I reached the edge of the dock the same time he did but a good fifteen yards away. He flung himself onto the pile of cardboard and slid toward the blue building beside the front gate. I fired three rounds, but they all missed.

Not able to rely on Dirt saving the day, I jumped onto the cardboard, the jolt to my shoulder making me scream.

I climbed over the cardboard and found the Boot limping to the building's front door, only a few yards to go. I fired and he collapsed, his hand going to his hip.

The Boot grabbed his radio and dragged himself behind the short wall. "DS14 is under attack! Agents down! DS14 under attack!"

*Fuck.* I hurried over, careful turning the corner in case he had his gun out.

The Boot was pressed against the door, both bloody hands clutching his radio, no gun in his holster. He was thinking about his mother, how he wanted her to hold him. Through tears, he said, "Please don't."

His chubby cheeks and watery blue eyes burned into my memory. I felt awful, no anger and only remorse. I said, "I'm sorry."

The hole was an oozing black crater an inch above the Boot's left eye. It stared right through me.

The clanking and banging of the baler ceased, the night suddenly silent, just me and the innocent young man I'd killed.

Dirt yelled my name, but I couldn't look away.

"Joe! I need you!" Dirt was on the loading dock next to the motorhome. The baler operator and another worker, both in dark blue coveralls and filthy yellow safety vests, sat off to his side. "Now!"

I didn't look at the kid again, confident I'd never forget his face. The cardboard in this section was only a foot high but so soggy. I trudged through the pinkish-red sludge, my gun out in case anyone was hiding.

"Use the ladder." Dirt pointed at the end of the loading dock, his submachine gun ready but not aimed at anyone.

I holstered my pistol because I only had the one hand. Dirt helped at the end by pulling me up by my windbreaker.

He stepped close, only inches between us, his steel gray eyes penetrating mine. "Look, son, these fuckers are the enemy, every one of them. If you don't kill them, they won't hesitate to kill you."

"But—"

"No, buts." Dirt shook his head real slow so I knew he was serious. "You did what you had to. And you did a good job."

I nodded, not sure if I believed that at all.

The pep talk was over. Dirt motioned at the workers sitting on the crates. "See what these guys know." He waved at the operation. "Then get all this on film. We don't got long."

Dirt ran for the front building before I could ask why he wanted me to do the questioning. I stopped a few feet from the men. "What are your names?"

The little guy with the short brown hair said, "Jose."

The baler operator pulled his ponytail out from under his uniform. "Esteban." He tugged his ponytail, positive this wouldn't end well. "Habla espanol?"

I made a so-so motion and said, "Si. Te hacen trabajar aqui?"

They both nodded. Esteban said, "Vienen hace tres noches, dijo que mi jefe es un pinche telepata."

Jose said, "Hacen lo que quieren. matan a quien quieren."

Esteban said, "No es mejor que el federales."

I got enough of what they were saying to know they wouldn't be a problem. I brought out my phone and started filming. I didn't know who, if anyone, would ever see it, but I pretended like the whole world would be watching. I reigned in my emotions and buried the pain, acted like a real reporter.

"This is Esteban." I zoomed in on his face, caught a tear slipping out. "The Boots forced him to work this machine the last three days at this recycling center in East L.A."

I turned in a circle to show the location. "Since they came in and seized the property, the Boots have been disposing of suspected Thought Thieves that they killed with no trial. In that motorhome alone there are over forty bodies from Detention Center 14 at Salazar Park."

Instead of wasting time with the motorhome, I told Jose, "Muéstrame los contenedores."

Jose got up and walked me past Hoop flopped back in his forklift, but I kept the camera on the conveyor belt with all the body bags.

Jose took me around the back of the baler. "Cuidado, es resbaladizo."

I filmed the ground, slick with watered down blood and gore, a pool of it around the clogged drain where they'd been hosing it. "Let's see what they do with the bodies after they go through that machine."

Jose pointed out the small bulldozer. He said, "Ahí," and pointed at the container pulled up to the dock, a chunky red trail between them.

The smell of rotting meat grew worse with each step, the light from my phone, just enough to see the bales of squished bodies and bags. The walls of the container seemed to be closing in on me, my vision going blurry.

I don't know if he saw me swaying or could read my mind, but Jose said, "Salir de allí." He stood at the edge of the container and waved for me to follow.

The air wasn't much better on the dock, that smell permanently part of me. I shook off as much as I could and resumed filming, turning the camera to the conveyor belt. I asked Jose and Esteban to unzip the bags so I could see faces.

I began halfway down the line, zoomed in on a teenage boy, probably still in high school, his hair slicked back with gel. "This is someone's son."

Next was a chunky-faced middle-aged woman, her jowls stretched down, her mouth open. "Here is someone's mother."

I had no way of knowing if what I said was true, but I hoped people got my point. "This is someone's brother."

"Someone's friend."

"Someone's lover."

"Someone's sister."

"Someone's dad."

There were only four more bags before the belt dropped them into the mouth of the baler. I froze on the next face, forgot how to breathe, just stood there, everything stopping because I was staring at Danny. Into those brilliant brown eyes with the flecks of gold. A strained grimace instead of the smile that'd never shine again.

Goddamn it. Not Danny. He didn't deserve that.

His cheek was cold, the first time I'd ever held it. The nicest guy I knew until he met me, became a killer, died in agony.

A hand grabbed my shoulder and I jumped, nearly dropped the phone.

Dirt said, "Joe, put that away. We gotta go."

I hadn't noticed the sirens before, but they sounded close. I didn't care. I was zeroed in on Danny, wishing he could hear just how fucking sorry I was.

"He knows." Dirt took my phone and slipped it into his pocket. Red lights flashed down the street and he pointed at the back fence. "Let's split."

The chain-link fence with razor wire along the top separated the recycling center from the railroad tracks. Dirt had out a pair of wire cutters and started snipping from the bottom when a giant boom came from the front of the property.

Another huge crash followed it, metal on metal. I climbed on a crate and looked that way, watched as the Boot's RV smashed into the gate, knocking it free.

I shouted to Dirt, "They're in."

He yelled at me to hurry. He'd clipped a line up to the halfway mark and then over a couple feet, peeling it back by the corner. "Go!"

I bent over and squeezed through the opening, my windbreaker snagging on the fence, the metal tearing into my arm.

Dirt ripped my windbreaker off and tossed it aside. He wriggled through the fence as the Boots stormed into the center, one car after another rolling over the downed gate, their headlights flooding the warehouse.

The train tracks were about twenty yards away from us, another twenty past it to the back of the buildings on the opposite side. Dirt pointed out an opening between two of the buildings to our right and started jogging.

I followed, figured they'd never see us in the dark, but then a small RV with a flashing siren on top flew around the back of the warehouse. It only had one headlight because it'd been the rammer. I froze when the headlight flashed over us and prayed the driver hadn't seen us, but the RV cut its turn short and whipped back, flying at the fence.

Dirt was a few feet in front of me. All I could keep thinking was, *Holy shit!*

I kept pumping my good arm, going as fast as I could, looked back at the crash. The fence tore in half, one of the poles smashing in the RV's passenger side, the windshield all cracks. *They're fucking nuts!*

Dirt thought, *Next left. Car will be on the right.*

I didn't know what car but he was out of my range, ducking against the wall behind a discarded couch, taking aim at the RV.

The RV was only two lengths behind me and jumping the tracks. It was going to run me down, probably splatter me against the wall.

A short blast of automatic gunfire ripped through the cab, the driver jerking the wheel hard, the RV smashing into the brick building and sliding to a stop just a few feet behind me.

There was movement in the cab, the passenger with a bloody forehead raising his gun, thinking he had an easy shot at me.

I was the faster draw and put a bullet through his head.

From the other side of the vehicle, Dirt yelled, "Run!"

I did what he said and took off for the corner.

A Boot stepped out of the motorhome's backdoor and brought his weapon up to mow me down. His brains blew out his forehead, no clue Dirt had been behind him.

A Boot cruiser drove over the downed fence and turned our way. I ran through the alley, heard Dirt right behind me. He passed me where the alley dumped into a quiet industrial street. He ran for the dark sedan parked on the right side.

I thought it might be a Boot car and shouted, "Wait!"

Dirt threw open the backdoor and jumped inside. It looked like two Boots in the front seat, but no one was shooting. There was someone in the back with Dirt who was yelling for me to hurry.

I kept my gun out when I got in the car, breathed so much better when I saw it was Tone behind the wheel, Becky beside him.

# Night 6

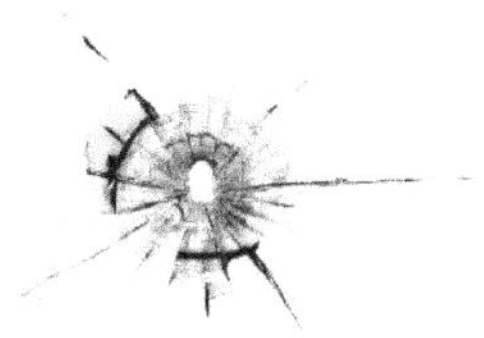

# CHAPTER TWENTY-FOUR

Everything was black except a faint light coming under the door. I couldn't tell if this was part of the real nightmare we'd been going through or the awful one I'd been stuck in all night. There were voices, but tiny and muffled so I couldn't even make out the language. The smell was death and disinfectant, my skin slick with sweat.

The sweat became heavier, thicker, dripped from my fingers with a loud plop, plop, plop. The light flicked on and I was in a large white room, a puddle of blood spreading on the floor ten feet away, directly underneath my mother's decapitated head.

Mother stared at me with dead eyes, but her mouth moved. "My little superhero."

I told myself it was a dream, to wake up. Everything went black but the darkness only held a second.

We were in the backseat of the helicopter, Becky snuggled beside me. Two Boots sat directly across from us. The one facing me was the newbie, clean shaven with mushy gray stuff coming out the smashed side of his head.

The newbie pressed his palm against the bulge, pushing back some of the brain matter but spluttering out just as much. His voice came out all wrong, real slowly like Danny's. "Heard you met my family."

Chang was across from Becky, his head bowed like he was sleeping. Dirt leaned out of the passenger seat and pulled Chang's head back by the hair. Chang's throat peeled open, a clean slice across his throat. The broken puppet lip-synced to Becky's soft voice. "I'm worried."

The pilot turned in his seat, his skin charred blacker than his windbreaker, half his forehead crumbling to ash when it banged against Dirt's shoulder. Acting like nothing was wrong, the pilot sounded just like Tone when he asked. "Is he hot?"

Chang's throat pulled all the way open, the sides of his neck ripping slowly. "Hah! Hot! I get it!"

Everything went black and silent, entirely too cold. Except my feet, rubbing back and forth on a soft red carpet. My shoes and socks were off, my feet so small.

"Told you it'd feel good," the man said. "Hold on. I'm going to do mine."

I looked back at the small television screen, ducked under the giant bullet, banged the top of my head on the block, chased after the mushroom. Jumping on dragons with a beep and a bop.

Spit sprayed my arm when the man whose name I didn't even know said, "Oh, yeah, that feels good."

His feet were twice the size of mine, his toes bunched up and pulling at the carpet, the knuckles red and swollen.

I concentrated on the game, realized it was all timing, the coins there for my taking.

"You know what else I like to do?"

I said, "Un-huh," my focus on the screen, trying to figure when to jump.

"Playing in shorts or even my underwear. The sheets feel so good on your legs."

I had on my usual brown corduroys. "Maybe I can wear shorts next time."

"I don't know if this will happen again." He sounded all disappointed like Mother, when he said, "That's fine. You don't have to if you don't want to."

Dad didn't care if I sat around in my underwear if we weren't in public. Plus, I hated wearing pants and how the patches rubbed my knees raw. "You don't mind?"

"Not, not at all." He put his hands over mine and pressed a skinny button, held the controller for me. "There, it's paused. Wouldn't want to mess up a high score, right?"

I said, "You know it," and yanked off my pants, took back the controller.

"You know what?" Before I could guess, he said, "That looks too good not to join."

His long, hairy leg brushed against mine. The van smelled like my parents' pile of dirty white laundry.

I threw a turtle shell and knocked down like a dozen, but then one in a football helmet knocked the life out of me.

"What's wrong?" His breath blew on my cheek. "You keep on dying."

My voice shook like an old lady's. "I don't want to play anymore."

Everything went black and a woman called my name from far away. Someone shook my leg. The woman said my name again, but she was fading, the cold air on my thighs, which were covered with goose bumps.

The man put his hand on my thigh. "Watch. I'll make those go away."

I only heard others' thoughts when I wasn't distracted, and I was too scared to read his. It was nice having someone care for me, touch me without hurting, but it no longer felt right and I wanted to run.

"What's the matter?" he asked. "You still cold?"

I said yes and reached over to get my pants.

He grabbed the back of my shirt and spun me around, put my chest to the mattress, my face inches from the gray sheet metal siding.

The stupid happy music kept playing and it was hard to breathe, but I said, "What are you doing?"

He covered me with his body, all his weight pinning me down. His voice lowered a few levels, dark and raspy. "Warming you up."

I tried to scream no but could barely breathe. "Get off."

One hand snaked around my throat, the other ripped down my underwear.

"Joe! Wake up!" Something slapped my cheek. "You're screaming."

I wasn't screaming anymore, my stomach stuffed in my throat, worried my insides had been rearranged.

Becky said my name, sounding very serious. "Open your eyes."

It felt like molasses was weighing them down, everything black around her outline.

Becky's voice got like Father's when she said, "Wake up. We need you."

I didn't know who *we* were or what good I'd do, but I'd already decided I was with Becky to the end. I blinked and wiped away the gunk. "Holy shit. I feel awful."

"They gave you a shot for the pain a few hours ago."

She must've felt me digging at her thoughts because she said, "You're pretty sick."

My words came out slow. "What'd they give me?"

"Not sure. We gotta trust them though. Because really, what do we know? Plus, they're all we got."

I couldn't argue with that.

I was on a couch in a small storage room, metal shelves to my side, disinfectant and shaving cream nearly covering the yeasty smell from my wound.

She handed me a water bottle. "Drink a bit and give it a minute. Let's see if we can get you to your feet."

The water helped with my throat, not my burning skin. "What happened last night? How'd you get away?"

"Luck and strategy. These guys aren't a joke."

"Yeah, I'd be dead ten times over if it weren't for Dirt."

Becky held the side of her head and grimaced. To herself, she thought, *I'm strong. I'm unbreakable. I won't be stopped.*

I asked, "You okay?"

She nodded and took the bottle from me, offered her hand. "So what do you think? You look a little better."

I swung my legs off the couch, not so sure I'd be able to stand. "Let's do it."

Becky guided me by my good arm and opened the door, the fluorescent lights blinding. I told her I could use a second.

*As long as you need.*

My legs almost buckled, my belly threatening to purge. I blinked open my eyes to help with my balance.

We were in a barber shop, big black and white tiles, four barber chairs along the wall to my left, three on my right. The other two walls were giant windows with the blinds drawn, Tone and Dirt over by the door in the far corner. Bill, who'd given me the Dilaudid, was in the far chair on the right. He tipped his mug to me, said, "Welcome back."

Chip was in the far one on the other side wiping down a machine gun. Johnny, who had changed my bandage and said I needed more help than he could give, sipped from his Budweiser in the chair next to Chip. There was a television above each window, both stations on the same channel, a raging bonfire behind a blue and gold banner that read Torch all Thought Thieves.

Becky walked me toward Bill. "Let's get you seated."

I started for the first chair, but she said, "Not that one."

I didn't get it, so she nodded at the counter, the row of photos lining it, groups of Marines posing in the desert. *Angel*, Becky thought. *This was his place. His chair.*

My limited memory of Angel wasn't enough to be able to recognize him in the photo until Bill pointed him out. I hadn't pegged the man as a barber.

Bill said, "That was his thing. Angel would just ask customers about their day and then listen. Said that way at least he wasn't eavesdropping."

Dirt said, "Plus, these are some old ass photos." He pointed to the photo of Angel and three other Marines, dressed out in Blues. "You see him?"

I thought he meant Angel, but he was talking about my dad, guy on the right. "Looks different without glasses," I said. "And I'd never seen him in uniform."

Bill said, "He's a good man."

Tone agreed. "Wouldn't be here if it weren't for him."

It was hard to believe he meant in a good way, so I turned to the last photo of Angel sitting atop a tank, three Marines on either side of him. One might've been Bill but just as likely some random white guy.

I looked up, my reflection in the wall-length mirror making me sick. My sunken eyes were the only thing I recognized, my face pale and gaunt.

Johnny chugged more beer and motioned at my shoulder. "Glad to see you're keeping it clean."

The sling was a mess of muddy grass stains on the bottom, bloody yellow discharge seeping through the top.

I climbed into the chair beside Bill, felt so much better off my feet, able to rest my head.

On the bench that ran along the left window were several black windbreakers, blue jeans, and SWAT gear. In front of the other window a pair of card tables were pushed together, weapons stockpiled on top. One of them looked like a grenade launcher.

I heard Bill's smile when he said, "Mary, my M320. She's my baby."

The news was playing on the TV, the sound muted. Becky followed my gaze. "Just more of the same. More proof that we're heartless murderers and a threat to the country."

"What about our video? I gave it to Dirt."

Bill said, "The problem is getting it seen. The second it goes up they'll shut it right down."

Tone walked over to the weapons, inspected a machine gun. "We got some good leads thanks to the laptop. If we can secure the right access, we'll be able to blast the videos."

"Not that anyone's going to give a shit," Chip said. "Everyone wants us dead."

"Sharing these videos will be the biggest blow we can deal," Dirt said.

I pointed at the new screen where Boots in the park were being covered with blankets. "Looks like we dealt them a serious blow."

Tone glanced up and shook his head. "Twenty-two Boots dead but double that in prisoners."

"And they'll recruit that in an hour," Becky said with disgust, not defeat. "News keeps telling everyone to be brave and strong, help the Boots crush and eradicate us."

Like he was playing a grade-school teacher, Bill said, "And don't forget that terrorists are hiring Thought Thieves to help their evil plans."

The laptop was on and open, resting on the bench beside Tone, Donner's severed finger beside it. My queasiness returned and it became hard to breathe.

Becky handed me a water bottle and told me to sip. "I'll be right back." She walked into the bathroom and came back with a fuzzy white cat snuggled against her chest.

"Mellow? He's okay?"

Becky said, "Tone got him this morning." She set Mellow on my lap. "He missed you."

I never knew I was a cat guy, but his purring helped me calm down. I looked to Tone. "So how do we get access for the video?"

He set down the machine gun and held no hatred looking at me, almost sounded respectful when he said, "You've sacrificed enough, Joe. We need to get you to a doctor."

"I'm not going anywhere without Becky."

"And I'm not stopping until I make them pay for my parents."

I turned to her. "What'd you find out?"

Becky didn't say anything for a second. Calm, like she was telling me the weather, she said, "They were on your video. The conveyor belt."

*Oh, no.* I hadn't recognized her parents, but all I knew about them was from a glance at a ten-year-old family photo. I wanted to hold her, to make it better, but I just said, "I'm so sorry, Becky."

She nodded and turned to Tone, a deep groove that ran above her ear like a bloody lane between corn rows. "So what's the plan?"

He said, "We need to nab someone in charge of their social media accounts. I've nailed it down to three men, but only one is local."

Dirt said, "And the entire operation is on high alert after last night."

Bill pointed to the gear on the bench. "But they won't see us coming."

Tone said, "Our best chance is to get him leaving work. Dirt and I will go with Bill."

I asked, "What about us?"

"You'll stay with Chip. Johnny will find you a doctor."

Johnny sighed. *Fat fucking chance.*

Becky said, "No."

Tone said, "No, what?"

"We go in shooting and we stand too great of a chance of him getting away or killed."

Dirt said, "Well, it ain't like we can just go in and ask him to come with us."

"No, that's exactly what I'm going to do," Becky said.

The girl I'd first thought of as frail and fragile stood tall in front of the vets, waited for them to finish their objections. Like it was already decided, she said, "I'll go in alone and bring him out."

Tone shook his head. "If you haven't noticed, you got a little lucky last night. Another half-inch and you're dead."

"But I'm not."

Dirt said, "What are you suggesting?"

"That this guy is susceptible, just like any other man."

"Are you talking about sexually?" Like he couldn't believe it, Tone asked, "You want to seduce him?"

I was just as shocked. "You're sixteen."

"Seventeen tomorrow."

Tone shook his head. "That's ridiculous."

She looked right at him. "Really? He's not going to imagine what it'd feel like squeezing my ass?"

Tone turned away but we all saw him blush. He picked up a vest, pretended to examine it. "You're not going."

Becky looked at Johnny. "What about my mouth? You don't think he might wish he had my lips wrapped around his dick?"

I said Becky's name so she would stop it, the tension running so high, no one breathing.

"They're not my words." Becky turned Bill's cheeks red with one glance, then shook her head like she'd had enough. "This Boot will think something and I'll capitalize on it."

Dirt asked, "What if he's gay or just not into you?"

She shrugged. "We'll deal with it then."

Tone turned around. "Or recognizes you?"

Becky stood tall, met his gaze. "Like I said."

"I don't like it," Tone said.

"I didn't ask you to," Becky said. "In fact, I bet I like it less than any of you, but I also know it's our best chance."

I said, "So where do we find this guy? What do we know?"

Dirt said, "Fredrick Anders, retired U.S. Army, now a director of the SSS."

"He's scheduled to be picked up from work at eight. Private plane to D.C. leaves at 10."

Becky said, "Then we better hurry."

Bill was behind the wheel, Dirt in the passenger seat, a shotgun standing up between them. We'd been crawling through traffic for forty minutes and just turned onto Pacific Coast Highway, the ocean a dark void on our right.

I sat behind Bill, the three of us dressed the same: blue jeans, black windbreakers, and hats. Becky had on a hat too, but hers was pink and flowery, drooped enough to cover the bullet groove.

Becky was dressed as a civilian in a pair of beige pants and a blue blouse, the top three buttons undone to show cleavage. Her mind was a mad scramble running through all the possible outcomes.

I squeezed her hand. "You're going to do great."

"How much farther?" she asked, her nervousness peeking through. "We even going to make it?"

"It's only a few more minutes," Bill said. "Their building is right on this street."

Dirt looked up from the laptop. "We're on the wrong side of this battle. They get all the fancy cars and prime real estate, meanwhile all we got is a barbershop."

Becky tested her radio, tucked her earpiece under her hat.

Tone, who was riding in another car with Johnny and Chip, said, "Copy, loud and clear."

Becky blew out a breath, ran through her mantra. *Unstoppable. Unstoppable.*

The car was quiet, the wheels rolling on the road, waves crashing on the shore. Dirt slapped his knee and said, "I knew I'd seen this slimy fuckhole before. He's the one they praised for turning in his own wife."

Bill asked, "Anders? When was this?"

"Few years ago. Start of all this shit." Dirt read from the article. "Director Anders is being praised for his exemplary patriotism, putting his country before himself and his family, something he did his twenty years serving in the Army. 'What higher honor is there?' Anders asked. 'My wife is an enemy of the state and has to be held accountable.'"

Bill said. "I remember that dude. Said he was a true American hero."

Dirt said, "Yep, although by the looks of his wife, I'd say he did it for himself as much as for his country. Bet he got stuck with her in Boot Camp.

I asked, "What happened to his wife?"

"Never made it to Brightside," Dirt said. "Found her guilty of treason and duly executed."

Becky asked, "Did he remarry?"

Dirt typed away, took about ten seconds. "Not from anything I'm seeing."

Becky asked to see his photo again. Dirt held up the laptop and expanded the picture, a serious-looking forty-something with a strong jaw and crew cut, eyes so narrowed I couldn't tell the color.

Bill said, "Three more blocks."

Becky was shaking. I whispered to her, "You okay?"

"I have to be."

Bill said, "No, we can scrap it and take them out on the road. They only have the one vehicle assigned to him."

Becky looked out her window, pretended to be interested in a passing building. "No, I'm just being a baby."

I said, "You're sure?"

"Hundred percent."

I had to get her to focus on me. "Okay, Becky. What are you going to do if he's on to you?"

"Shoot him in the face? Kick him the balls?" She forced a smile. "Haven't decided yet."

Bill put on his blinker and pulled to the curb. "They are two blocks up, that four-story building on the corner."

Becky asked, "How much time do I have?"

Dirt said, "They're scheduled to depart in seventeen minutes."

"Okay." Becky climbed out of the car, shut the door, clutched her purse like it was invisible and everyone could see her gun.

It looked like she was about to lose it so I told Bill to give me a minute. "I'll be right back."

Becky stepped to the edge of the sidewalk, afraid someone might see us. "What are you doing?"

"What is it, Becky? What are you afraid of?"

"Where do I start?"

"You've got this."

She didn't want to say it, but finally asked, "How do I look?" She uncrossed her arms and let the purse hang by her side. "I need you to be honest."

My first thought was that she looked like a girl about to go to her first date, but I said, "You look great. You're going to do fine and I'll be right there if anything goes sour."

"But what do you really believe? Is it sexy enough? Too slutty?" *Just look at me. You don't have to say it.*

I didn't care that we were probably minutes from death. Here was a young woman unsure of herself, needing to hear the words she'd never been given.

I stared into her ocean blue eyes, couldn't have been more sincere when I told her, "You're beautiful, inside and out."

She met my gaze. "You're not just saying that?"

I leaned in, my cracked lips on her bright red ones, the lightest kiss so I didn't mess anything up. "You're perfect."

# CHAPTER TWENTY-FIVE

No one said a word when I got back in the car, all eyes on Becky walking down the street with a slight limp.

Bill thumbed a happy beat on the wheel, waited until she crossed the street. "Joe, aren't you the one who said she was sixteen?"

We all knew he was joking, but I didn't want to hear it. What just happened with Becky wasn't supposed to. Even when I try to do the right thing, something gets screwed up.

"Got it," Bill said as he pulled into the first lane.

I checked my gun, put it back in the holster but left the strap undone.

Bill found my eyes in the rearview. "Remember, that shit's the last resort. No gunfire unless absolutely necessary."

I said I understood. We passed by Becky just as she stepped onto the last block. She was doing a better job with her purse, but still clutching it tight like she was about to get robbed. A black limo with tinted windows sat at the far corner. Bill parked directly behind it.

Dirt got on the radio. "We got two on the front door. Can't tell if the driver is in the limo."

Tone said, "Assume he is, if not others."

I tried not to sound nervous when I pointed out, "They're looking at us."

Dirt said, "Not anymore," because Becky had just stepped up to them, looking relaxed, purse loose at her side. "We're up, youngster."

I got out of the car and heard Becky's husky voice when she asked if Officer Donovan was working.

The pudgy white guy with the round, droopy face said, "No, he got off at six."

The big Hispanic to his left admired Becky's ass, wondered what she wanted with that loser.

Becky turned to him, her hand brushing his windbreaker. "What a jerk," she said. "He promised to show me the breakroom."

"Excuse me, honey," Dirt said to Becky when he shuffled past her and through the door.

Becky got a huge smile for me. *Play along.* Like it should be a secret, she said, "I know you."

I pretended to be embarrassed, figured it'd explain my flushed skin. "Deanna, right?"

She said, "You never called me."

The big guy asked me, "You know her?"

I took hold of the handle. "Sort of." My smile felt creepy. "Time well spent."

Becky touched his arm. "So what do you say? Want to escort me to the bathroom?" She turned so her ass rubbed against him, her voice playful. "You can pat me down."

The white guy kept smiling, but was thinking, *Fucking Garcia. Lucky bastard.*

Before the door closed behind me, I said, "You two have fun."

The building was quiet, no one walking around the first floor. Dirt was in front of the receptionist's podium with its lush green planter circling behind it. At his feet lay a body in blue jeans and black boots. Dirt shrugged his shoulders. "Couldn't fool him."

"I think they're coming in."

Dirt pointed at the women's bathroom to my left. *Get in there!*

I hurried into the first stall, straddled my legs on the door like I was giving birth, counted to twenty-two before the bathroom door opened.

Becky's footsteps were soft on the tiles. "Oh, what's wrong? You don't want to come in?" She lowered her voice. "I was serious about the pat down."

His response was muffled and they were too far away to hear their thoughts. I breathed a little deeper, tried to calm my body.

More spirited than I'd ever heard her, Becky said, "You worried what Kendrick might say? Don't be. He'd be just as guilty as you."

I didn't know who Kendrick was, but seeing how this guy bought it, I assumed Dirt had slipped Becky the name of the dead receptionist. Loud enough to hear his hope, Garcia said, "Really?"

Soft footsteps came closer, heavy boots clomping right behind. Becky stopped by the sink directly across from my stall. *I got this. Stay out until I say so.*

Garcia stepped between Becky and the stall, the hem of his blue jeans barely a foot away, the black of his windbreaker all I could see out the crack.

No one said a word and I worried how loud I was breathing, whether I could keep my legs up, my stomach cramping. If he turned around, I'd be fucked.

As carefully as I could, I slid my hand onto my holster, raised the flap.

With only a hint of irritation, Becky said, "Hey, not so fast. Your friend will watch the front."

"Pyle? You do him too?"

"No." Her voice got deeper. "Why? Would you like it better if I did?"

Garcia blurted out, "No."

"You just need to relax a minute," she said, soothing, caring, her mind repeating her mantra as she ran her hand across his chest and down his stomach. "You guys have a high-stress job trying to save our country. You need time to unwind."

"I know," Garcia said, playing it cool but thinking, *Holy shit, this is happening. I shouldn't do this.*

"Give me your hands," Becky said. "Good, now hold onto the sink."

That voice was intoxicating, almost made me holster my pistol.

He asked, "What are you doing?"

Becky walked behind him, whispered, "Good. Now step forward just a bit."

He obeyed.

Each word took a second like Becky was savoring them. "Now, let everything relax."

Garcia grunted. *Holy fuck.*

Becky went down on one knee, then the other, her hands gripping the front of his thighs.

He tried to turn to face her, but Becky held him tight.

"Hold still. My rules." To prove she was the boss, Becky said, "Undo your belt. Your zipper."

Sweat dripped from my chin, onto my collar, the gun slippery in my grip. Garcia mumbled okay, and Becky pulled down his jeans so they were bunched around his ankles.

"Your underwear, too."

He bent over and I felt so sick for Becky, couldn't stop from thinking this was all my fault, that I should just get out and put a bullet in the fucker's head.

Becky silently screamed at me so loud I nearly dropped the gun. *Joe! Stop thinking!*

I thought an apology as Garcia's blue boxers bunched on top of his jeans, a tiny shit stain right in the middle.

Becky shot forward, her shoulder slamming into Garcia's low back, her arms jerking his legs out from under him. Garcia's loud oomph was cut short by a thudding crack, a chunk of the sink shattering on the tile. A page straight out of Wendell's playbook.

My feet hit the ground, everything pins and needles, made it so I could hardly think. I pulled open the stall door and took aim, lowered the gun because there was no need for it.

Becky rolled off Garcia, blocked my view. "Don't look."

The remaining half of the sink was sprayed red. I used the stall to help me stand, looked anyway because I was the one who made all this shit happen.

Garcia's face was turned to the right, his eye wide open in the spreading pool of blood.

Becky picked up her hat and put it back on, washed her hands, threw water on her face,

"Becky, I'm so sorry."

She looked at Garcia, all the blood. "There's no cleaning this up."

"We'll put the trashcan in the doorway, make it look like it's being serviced."

"Good idea." She dried her hands with a paper towel and threw it in the can. "Let's finish this."


Dirt sat on the stool behind the receptionist's podium, nodded at us as we hurried to the elevator. *Good luck.*

Becky thought, *Can't let anyone in there.*

*Or in here,* he thought, motioning at the planter. *Should be okay though. Ghost town in here.*

I pressed the up button for the only elevator, spotted Kendrick's hand sticking out from behind the bushes in the planter.

We were too far from Dirt for me to hear what he had thought, but Becky's response was clear. *No. I'll bring him down.*

I asked, "Sure about this?"

Becky glanced at the directory beside the button, only a dozen names on it, Anders the sole person on the fourth floor. "It's our best bet."

The elevator was small, not like the one we had at Brightside Travel. Becky pressed the button for the fourth floor and said, "As long as he's like ninety-nine percent of the population and doesn't take the stairs."

The floors crept by, my grip on my gun.

Becky said, "We need him alive."

I let go of it, wiped the sweat on my jeans. The door opened onto an empty hallway with a thick white carpet, the smell of lavender all around.

Becky pointed to the left. "He's the first on the right. Go past it for the stairs."

The elevator door closed behind me, a staticky voice crackling in my ear. "Copy?"

I walked to the left, the carpet so cushiony I couldn't hear my steps. Becky didn't respond to the transmission, so I whispered, "No. Repeat."

Dirt said, "The driver and backup are silenced. Allow the target to come down on his own. We have their car."

An ornate gold nameplate on the solid oak door stated the office belonged to Director Anders. Light shined under the door.

I hurried past and radioed," I don't think Becky can hear us."

Tone said, "Then go get her."

I turned back to the elevator, froze when Anders' door opened. He stepped out of the office, strode toward the elevator, a black briefcase to match his suit, cell phone to his ear.

Anders was much bigger than I pictured, more of an athlete than I imagined he'd be at forty. He pressed the button, kept talking, facing the elevator.

The door opened and Becky exited, pretended not to be paying attention and bumped into Anders. "Oh, I am so sorry," she said, holding up her hands.

Still talking on the phone, Anders jerked his head to the side, irritated she was blocking the way.

Becky said, "Sorry," but moved so slow the door closed.

Anders kept talking and shook his head, jammed the call button.

Afraid he'd hear me talk, loud as I could I thought, *Becky! He's not biting! Tone said to let him go.*

Becky broke off from almost interrupting him again and turned my way. Anders spun around and looked right at me, his penetrating gaze destroying any hope my disguise might work.

I couldn't hear either of their thoughts, but saw what was going to happen, Anders winding up with his briefcase. *Becky! Duck!*

Becky dropped to her knees, but Anders adjusted his swing, the corner of the briefcase slamming into her side, knocking her over, her hat coming off.

Fighting him one-handed was a losing option so I went for my gun.

Anders ran past Becky before I could get it out of the holster. She tackled his ankles and he fell face first, the briefcase sliding my way.

Becky kept hold of Anders' legs, drove into his hamstrings to keep him pinned.

Anders looked over his shoulder and swung his fist hard, blam right on Becky's nose, the crunch so loud it had to be broken.

Becky lunged forward, arms around his neck, both feet hooking the inside of his thighs. She squeezed.

I pulled out my baton because Anders had blocked Becky's choke with his chin, his hand pulling on her wrist.

Anders thought, *Nice try, bitch,* and threw himself back toward the wall. Becky rebounded with a thunk, the right side of her face smashed into his skull.

Her letting go wasn't what scared me. It's how fast it happened, from full squeeze to nothing.

Anders shook off the headbutt and rolled to his knees. He turned his head to the snap of the baton extending.

Becky was knocked out, her face a bloody mess. I swung that baton as hard as I could on Anders' collar bone, none of us prepared for his scream.

"Holy shit," Dirt said over the radio. "What the fuck's going on?"

Anders fell to the carpet, his left hand holding his shoulder. "You motherfucker."

I hit him again, this time in the face, the skin on his cheek split in two.

*Joe.* Becky rolled to her knees, her nose resting to the right, raining blood. *Don't!*

I lowered the baton, my arm shaking, my whole body shaking. I wanted to hit him again. I looked right at him when I swore, "One mistake and I bash your fucking brains in, you fucking piece of shit traitor."

He smiled through the blood.

Becky tilted her head and pinched her nose shut, snapped it back in place. "Not the first time." She matched Anders' smile. He never saw the kick coming, her shoe slamming into his nuts from behind, so hard it almost dropped me.

Anders rolled back and forth in a ball, juggling pain and nausea, holding it all in.

Becky picked up the cellphone, saw the call was still going. *Breathing. Listening,* she passed on to me. She told the caller, "I'm sorry but Director Anders had an accident. He'll call you back as soon as he's able."

Still balled up, Anders thought, *Yeah, bad accident where someone called me a motherfucker and wanted to bash my brain in.*

Becky slid the phone into her back pocket. "It was facedown, they didn't hear shit."

I wasn't sure who she was lying for, but it was probably all of us. At the least the caller would most likely hesitate contacting the authorities.

I said, "So what now?"

She looked at Anders. *We can't leave with him.*

I couldn't think straight and had no ideas. "So?"

Becky got on the radio. "Change of plans. We're doing it here."

No one questioned it, just copied. Trust. Teamwork. They knew she wasn't someone to mess with.

She kicked Anders in the ass. "Get back in your office. You fuck up once and he'll do what he said." Becky waited for him to look at her. "And I won't stop him."


Anders' right arm was useless so I controlled his hand, held it up to the palm reader, his lips biting back the scream.

The door clicked and I pushed it open, told Anders, "Move it."

I'm not sure if it was intended for us to hear, but Anders thought, *You'll all pay.*

Becky shoved him inside. "That's all we've been doing. Now it's your turn."

The office was immaculate, bright white shag carpet and black leather everywhere. A giant marble desk sat near the expansive window that overlooked the dark ocean. The door to the right was open, a king-size bed with black sheets and a glass shower in the corner.

I didn't feel good and had to sit on the couch, watched Becky guide Anders to his desk, sit him where a guest would go. She moved around to his side of the desk and dropped the briefcase in front of him. "Open it."

It looked like he was playing along but I got up with my baton, still a little woozy. Anders was navigating the 5-digit combination with his left hand, but I walked over and rested the baton across his swollen clavicle, just enough pressure to make him squirm.

The lock clicked open. Anders pushed the briefcase to her, blood running down his cheek and staining his shirt. "I don't know what you plan on accomplishing. I don't control anything going on. I'm not responsible for any operations."

Becky took out the laptop and set it in front of him on the desk. "No shit," she said. "Log in."

Anders realized what we wanted with him and shook his head.

I pushed down on his collar, drove him into the chair.

"Okay! Okay!"

I said, "No more warnings."

Anders typed in his password and turned the computer to Becky.

Becky stuck something in the USB port and radioed, "We're in. Do your thing."

Chip said, "On it."

I asked Becky, "How long do you think this'll take?"

She looked out the window, didn't see any flashing sirens. "Won't be long."

A knock came from the front door. "Director Anders," a man said. "You in there, sir?"

Becky warned him, *Don't answer!*

He knocked again. "Director Anders? There's blood out here."

Becky pointed to the door. *I got Anders.*

I headed that way, no idea what I was supposed to do. The red light blinked as the door clicked and a young Boot opened it, froze when he saw me. "Oh, I'm sorry. I heard a scream. Anyone in here hurt?"

I won the award for most ridiculous lie of the year when I said, "We're fine."

He looked at my baton, his mind flying, trying to place me, figure why a woman was in Anders' chair, blood spotting the carpet, all of our faces a mess.

"It's ours." Chip's voice crackled over the radio. "We control their feeds."

Casually as I could, I slipped the baton into my back pocket. "Anders is meeting with his niece. She got a little hysterical."

He thought, *Dude's lying.* Trying to be sneaky, the Boot rested his hand on his holster, "I understand."

I whipped out my gun, aimed it at his chest. "Wish you didn't."

He went for his gun, left me no choice but to fire, the bullet punching through his stomach, doubling him over.

Becky said, "Shit," and hurried over to Anders. "Get up."

Anders said, "Why, so you can shoot me too?"

Becky grabbed hold of his broken clavicle and jerked him out of the chair, pushed him to the sliding door of the balcony.

The door slid open. Anders would've laughed if it weren't for the pain. Through gritted teeth, he said, "You guys are fucking amateurs. What are you going to do, put out one video and shut us down? What good do you think it'll do?"

I could hear he was scared, covering it up with anger. All I got from Becky was her mantra. *I'm strong.*

I headed for them so I could help, but Becky thought, *I got this. You get the briefcase.*

Anders turned to face her, his low back pressed against the railing. "Your attacks only make us stronger, will make the world hate you that much fucking more."

Becky looked him in the eyes. "Did you know people are being raped and tortured, all without any conviction?"

"I have nothing to do with operations."

"Well, let's make that permanent." Becky dropped down and popped back up with his legs, tossed him over the edge. "Scum bag."

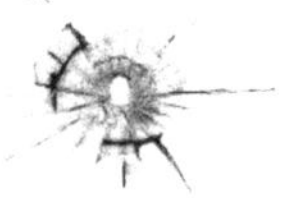

# Night 7

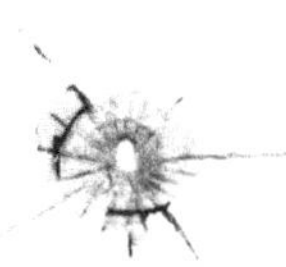

# CHAPTER TWENTY-SIX

I've been standing here with my back to the blanket for far too long, my foot an angry throb, my body burning one minute, shivering the next. But I'm not ready to find out why Becky's crying. She's probably been able to overhear my every thought from the mattress where she's safely out of my lesser range. All I know is that whatever she's thinking about is destroying her.

The bottom of the blanket brushes against my ankle. I put my back to the plywood, chalk it up to another hallucination. The blanket pushes in again, Mellow's little head right behind it.

I click my tongue three times like Dorothy's shoes. "It's okay, boy. Come on in."

Mellow slips under the blanket and sits, his eyes on me, probably wondering why I didn't have the decency to use a litterbox.

I bend down and offer my hand. "Yeah, yeah, you're the boss."

Mellow rubs his head against me, purrs so hard I feel it up my arm.

The purr gets louder, reverbing in my brain faster and faster, my vision going black. I push Mellow out of the way because I'm going down.

"It's okay," Becky whispers, her hand cold on my forehead. "Don't move, Joe. I got you."

The blanket that'd been hanging is bunched up beneath me, my legs sprawled out, my good foot resting against the overturned shit bucket. Becky's behind me, holding me close, her body supporting mine. "Shuhhhh." She's not crying anymore but her voice shakes. "It's okay. Relax."

Her fear is coming through loud and clear, but it's all aimed at me. I almost ask what happened, but my shoulder's throbbing intensely. I must've landed on it when I passed out.

From here I can see the loose piece of plywood we have for a door, the four-by-four beam wedged behind it as a lock. A paper plate full of cat food sits beside it. "Is Mellow okay?"

The cat comes on cue, rubs against my thigh, slides his body up my hip.

*Oh fuck.* I forgot I was naked, Mellow just inches away from my tiny little dick, all shriveled up like my soul. I grab for the blanket, but my ass is pinning it down, and I'm too weak to pull it out. I try to cover up with my hand, but Becky hugs me even tighter, makes it so I can't reach.

*Joe. None of that means anything.* She rests her forehead against my neck. The tears return, run down my back. *I thought you were dead.*

The needle's resting on the carton next to my phone, the flashlight still going. *You thought I killed myself?*

Becky shakes her head, wipes her tears with her arm. "I heard you thinking about it, but I know what you decided. You plan to complete your mission."

"But?"

*What everyone's been saying*, she thinks, too afraid to hear herself speak. *You're not doing good, Joe. We've got to get you help.*

I set my hand down and Mellow curls up on top of my palm. "I'm fine."

She sighs. "Yeah. I can totally tell."

It's true I'm doing a little better, but it's still a shade of awfulness. I take a deep breath and hold it in, notice Becky's heart beating against my back, my heart slowing to match it. I close my eyes, appreciate the moment, her arms around me, her skin against mine.

My heart spikes because, holy shit, she's naked. It used to be that a stiff breeze could give me a boner, so I look about the room for something to focus on, finding nothing. As a distraction, I ask, "Why were you crying?" knowing she has a thousand legitimate reasons.

*The videos.*

I'm looking at the plywood but seeing flashes of the park, Corina, the bales of pulverized people. "They didn't go up?"

She sniffles. "No, they did. Chip tagged everyone he could, used all the right hashtags, asked people to share if they love America and all it stands for."

"Boots take them right back down?"

"They're down now, but even when they were up no one gave a shit."

"But we showed all the bodies. Half those people weren't even telepaths."

"Doesn't matter," she says, so defeated. "The rape, the torture, the confiscations, the killings. None of it."

All I can do is sit here, Mellow weighing down my hand.

She says, "They've condemned the Citizens against the Unethical Treatment of Telepaths and are scooping up anyone who has shown support."

"Jesus."

"We should've known this would happen." The blare of a big rig's horn makes her pause. "Ten minutes ago they announced all cleared citizens will receive a bonus check along with unlimited streaming movies for the month. A little bonus for their loyalty."

"With what money? We've got the biggest deficit in history."

"Probably with the money the Boots have been acquiring. Houses, vehicles, businesses, pretty much anything they want. You've seen it. All they need is a supposed accusation."

"I'm sorry, Becky."

"But we're never shutting down the machine," she says. "The machine isn't the Boots. It isn't the government. It's the country. It's fucking everyone."

The thought is so depressing I can't consider it. "There are still good people."

"Yeah, all the ones who want us dead."

"So what now? Find a safe house?"

"I doubt there are any left." Becky says, "The whole system's been compromised."

"We can try Mexico."

She doesn't say no, just tells me, "Come on. Let's get you on the bed."

I say okay, and she helps me on to my knees so I can crawl onto the mattress, eyes down so I don't see her.

Becky's on her feet, draping the blanket over me. *It's okay. Just rest.*

As I thank her, I notice a purple bruise the size of a grapefruit below her right breast. I jerk my head away and say, "Sorry."

She sits on the edge of the mattress, the side of her leg just a foot from my face. "I'm not a little kid," she says, but not defensive like the first time I mentioned her age.

A chill rips through me, my skin cold and clammy without her against me.

Becky scoots closer, puts her hand on my chest, the blanket between us. "And you're not responsible for anything that's happened to me."

I look up, her nose swollen, both eyes black and blue, her right cheek ballooned. "Yes, I am. All this is my fault."

"No." Her eyes don't waver, the light flickering off the watery blue. "You didn't do this to me. I wanted to leave Brightside. I made that decision."

Another spasm shakes me, Becky's hand holding me still. She takes a breath and blows it out, waits for me to look at her. "All you've done is watch out for me and care for me and treat me with kindness," she says. "You've shown me more love than anyone ever has other than my parents."

"I've been nothing but a piece of shit all my life."

Becky wipes the tears I didn't know I was crying. "Well, good thing I'm only judging you by the week I've known you."

"Thank you," I say sounding pretty choked up. *Thank you for everything.*

Becky says, "Of course." She turns to her phone vibrating on the mattress.

"What is it?"

"Tone. Says they're ready to go." Becky types a response. "I told him we need a half hour."

The last thing in the world I want to do is leave this spot, but I play strong and say, "I can get ready now."

Becky sets the phone down and says, "Not yet." She pulls back the blanket and slides underneath it, her skin warm, her breasts soft against my side. Her thigh slides over mine as she melts into me.

A flood of emotions hits hard, my brain in a panic. "What are you doing?"

Her hand goes back to my chest and she shushes me. "Joe, I've never been touched."

Half a lifetime ago was my first time, with Mandi my broken teacher. "I'm not the—"

"I need someone to hold me," she says, praying I won't reject her.

I don't want to say the words that feel so right yet so wrong, but I owe her an answer. I say, "I can try."

Before Brightside I manipulated my way into women's hearts and bedrooms, knew it was wrong every time. But this feels so different, my brain shouting stop but my heart pounding beat for beat with Becky's.

My erection is a surprise, the only part of me that's working. I say, "I'm sorry," and try to pull away but she holds me there, her leg wrapped around mine, her arm across my chest.

Becky brings herself on top of me, lowers down until we're touching, wipes the tears from my eyes. *Shush. I don't want you to feel sorry for me, Joe. I want you to hold me. I want you to feel loved.*

# CHAPTER TWENTY-SEVEN

Becky's clad in black, looking badass, submachine gun strapped to her chest. She disables the shack's security system with a sweep of her boot, knocking loose the four-by-four wedged against the door. Time to go.

I'm sitting on the mattress in matching black sweatshirt and pants, figured since we're the bad guys we might as well start dressing like them.

Becky sets the wood to the side. *I think it might have something to do with not being seen.*

With someone else maybe I'd get irritated at the sarcasm, angry they were in my head, but with Becky I only smile. I've given her access to everything, be it good, bad, or nothing. "There is that too."

She slips on her black beanie and shrugs on her orange sweatshirt, looks like a shriveled-up pumpkin.

"A pumpkin?" She shakes her head but keeps the grin and playful voice. "Nice to know how you really see me."

My gun's holstered on my hip, safety off because we left that zone a long time ago. Becky's my mission. Keeping her safe until I can't.

"You ready?" she asks like we're headed to a sock hop.

This is the least ready I've felt for anything, but I say, "Let's do it."

She giggles. "Oh shit, you are old. Sock hop?"

"I don't really call it that."

Becky throws her backpack over her shoulder, says, "Well, if you do a good job, I'll ask Tone to take us to the diner for a root beer float."

Laughing hurts but gives me hope. "How do you stay so positive and happy?"

"Happy is not the right word," Becky says. "Just appreciating what we have. Living in the present." She bends down and snaps her fingers. "Come here, boy."

I forgot about Mellow curled up at the far end of the mattress. He lifts his head and hobbles over, rubs against Becky's cheek when she picks him up.

"Are we leaving him here until we return?"

Becky holds Mellow with one hand, pulls me up with the other. With only a few inches between us, she sets her eyes on mine, no hope, just certainty. "You know we're not coming back."

I pretend she's just talking about this shack and say, "I know."

She rises onto her toes and places the lightest kiss on my lips. "Let's do this."

Becky slides the plywood to the side, brushes the blanket out of the way. She steps into the night and pauses, takes everything in. *All clear.*

I exit the shack, don't bother putting the door back, follow Becky between the tents. She stops beside the trashcan fire, the flames lighting the battered face of an angel. I think she's giving me a chance to catch my breath and tell her, "I'm okay."

Becky doesn't respond, her attention focused on the tent to our right.

I can't see what she's looking at, so my hand drops to my holster. I step beside her, see she's looking at the bald guy with the graying goatee sitting on a crate outside his tent. He's braiding the hair of the little girl in the yellow shirt.

Becky walks over to them, stops a few feet away. "Do you mind if I interrupt?"

The man's eyes match his mustache. "Not at all," he says, much gentler than I'd expected.

Becky kneels in front of the girl, who's braiding her doll's hair. "What's your name, sweetheart?"

The girl looks up but doesn't say a word.

"Hi, Isabella. I'm Becky, and this is my friend, Joe."

The girl smiles, but I'm too far away to hear her thoughts.

Becky says, "I was hoping you could do me a favor."

Isabella studies Becky with deep blue eyes.

"I need someone smart, strong, and loving to watch after this guy," she says, holding Mellow up to rub on her face. "You seem like you would be perfect. Do you like cats?"

The girl nods her head, looks back at her father.

Before he can say no, Becky hands him a roll of bills. "This will help with food and whatever, maybe get you somewhere safer."

He flips through the bills, his eyes wide. "There's nowhere safer," he says and hands it back.

Becky shakes her head. "That's for you guys. There's also a shack back there that's a little sturdier, has a mattress."

I say, "The bathroom needs cleaning."

Isabella looks at her father with puppy-dog eyes, begging for the kitty-cat.

The man says, "If you want to keep him, you need to tell her yourself."

Isabella spins around, the half-finished braid flying, her smile so big, eyes shining.

Becky says, "You're wel—"

"Out loud," he says, stern but calm.

There's a moment's hesitation, then she locks eyes on Becky.

Becky says, "Who cares what anyone thinks? I'd like to hear you."

The girl stammers before starting over. "Th-th-thank you, Be-Be-ecky."

"You're absolutely welcome. I know you'll take great care of Mellow." Becky kisses his head and hands him over. "Got him?"

Isabella nods, holding him tight like he might run away. "Mellow?"

"Short for marshmallow. It's a dumb name."

"No. I like it." Isabella rubs her cheek against Mellow. "He's so s-s-soft."

Becky says, "In case you don't speak cat, Mellow says I did a good job picking you."

Isabella smiles then gets a little sad.

"What's wrong, honey?" Becky points at her bruised face. "Is it all this? I'm okay. It doesn't hurt."

The man puts his hand on his daughter's shoulder and says, "Isabella's a smart girl. She figured out who you guys are."

Becky nods, clears her throat. "It's all good, sweetie. I honestly couldn't be happier at this moment. Thank you for that."

Isabella bursts into tears, the two of them hugging Mellow between them, a life-size s'mores.

Becky's cry turns into laughter. She tells Isabella, "He just called us graham crackers."

That gets Isabella laughing and a humongous grin from her father, who's absorbing the shit out of this moment because you never know how long you've got.

Becky's explaining some cat care tips, but I get a bad feeling and search for a sniper. Fuck, for all I know we're in someone's crosshairs.

Mellow gets one last pat on the head before Becky gets to her feet. "It's okay, Joe. Relax."

I hadn't realized I was swaying back and forth, but I can't stop, my vision doubling.

Becky rushes over. "No, no, no." She takes hold of my arm but I can't see her, everything black, my hearing getting fuzzy. "Sit, sit. I got you."

I obey, ass to the ground, the jolt shocking me awake. "Oh fuck."

"Breathe. You're okay." My angel tells me, "Breathe."

Becky leads me up the hill by my hand. She said I wasn't out long, but I feel better, hope that was just the rest my body needed. A fresh little recharge, face first in the dirt. If only my mother could see me now.

If only my mother could see.

Her eyes so big, so green, so empty. What was the last thing she saw? Hopefully it was fast. Maybe she didn't see it coming.

"Stop it. Enjoy what we have," Becky says. "Come on, we don't want to be late for the sock hop."

I say, "Sure," but the blood doesn't stop dripping from my mother's severed head.

"Okay. What about, hmmm?" Becky taps her chin, pretends she's reading my mind. "How about we survive this thing and we go on a real date."

"Where no one shoots at us?"

"And real food."

"And a bottle of Jack," I say, the ridiculousness of our relationship smacking me hard. I break down in tears, so fucking ashamed for crying, for not being a man.

Becky holds me. *We don't have much more to get through. One more round. We can do it.*

*I'm not a fighter like you.*

*Then that's some bullshit about me still at number five. I'm pretty sure I beat your body count.*

"I gladly concede my spot. You know, so you can win and all."

She pecks me on the cheek like I were Mellow.

"Holy hell, you're a needy one," she says, leaning in and planting a soft kiss on my lips.

"That's what I've heard." I take her hand and let her lead the way, concentrate on my breathing so I don't faint.

Becky squeezes through the fence and holds it open for me. I can't get up without her help. Some goddamn hero.

She helps me up, hums the G.I. Joe theme song, probably got it off Danny.

"That's not funny," I say.

Becky leads me through the bushes. "Wasn't meant to be. They murdered your friend. They murdered your mother. They murdered my family." She turns around. "Screw being a hero. I'm exacting vengeance."

There's no van parked on the street. I ask, "Where they at?"

Becky heads right on the sidewalk and nods toward the blue motorhome parked around the corner. The window above the cab is curtained, a small part where the sliding middle window is open an inch. I can't make out the driver, the Boots baseball cap hiding his face. He tips his cap, Dirt's rock-solid expression same as always.

We go to the backdoor, and Becky helps me inside, leans me against the stove because the table is full. All I can see of the guy sitting across from Tone is the back of his head. Johnny stands beside them, and Chip's on his belly in the bunk, laptop in front of him, sniper rifle to the side.

Chip looks up from the computer. Meaning me, he asks, "He okay?"

Becky thinks, *He's fine,* but she's tapped into Tone, the motorhome so somber, the air heavy.

"What is it? Becky asks. "How bad?"

Tone said, "Very. They took out Underground headquarters." He ducks his head, averting her eyes. *Televised their executions.*

Chip says, "Same exact hashtags we used."

Neither of us knows what to say. "I'm sorry about your friends," Becky tells him.

I figure Becky means in general, but both she and Tone are thinking about Shine, Bill, Curtains, Bolo, Tobbie, and

Jay. "Team two," Tone says. "Just hit them, Gomez the only one who escaped."

"Can we do it on our own?"

The man sitting with his back to us says, "Only one way to find out."

I lean over to make sure it's actually him, that I'm not hallucinating. "Dad?"

Tone gets up and squeezes into the front passenger seat. Johnny moves out of the way so Becky can help me around.

My father winces when he stands. His blue polo is clean, but the front of his jeans are marked by a fresh blood stain. He wraps me in his arms, buries his face against my good shoulder. *I'm so sorry, Joe. So fucking sorry.* He takes a deep breath and breaks off the hug, his tears scaring me. *But so goddamn proud.*

I ask, "Are you okay?"

He smiles. "I'll live."

I don't have the courage to say the same thing, to lie to his face.

Dad points for me to sit. *I didn't say for how long.*

From the front, Dirt says, "Well, how about another hour or so? We're about forty-five minutes out, fifty-five tops."

Dad's sitting across from me, Becky's shoulder rubbing mine, barely enough room for us at the small table.

She's afraid she doesn't belong and tells me, *I can stand.*

I pat her leg and tell my Dad, "Becky's the only reason I'm here. She's my mission."

Dad looks ten years older than he did last week, his dusty brown eyes brimming with death and disappointment as he considers his mission. I can't believe it's only been a week since I've seen him. He nods. "I completely understand."

I'm glad he's too preoccupied to dig deeper into Becky, to question my decision. "Thanks."

Dad asks, "So how you holding up?"

It hurts to laugh but the other option is crying. "Fucking barely."

He thinks of what Tone and the others have said about me, that I probably don't have long. The look of worry and concern is so foreign on his face. Dad's never worried, usually just mad.

I say, "What about you?"

He shakes his head. "All the years spent planning for this type of situation, yet I never once considered this possibility, that they'd turn the entire world against us, make us the scapegoat so they can control the country."

My entire life was spent avoiding him and Mom, so afraid to hear their thoughts, how much of a disappointment I was. I embraced anger, contempt, and all the shit that made a man but ran from anything that resembled weakness. But that life is over, this moment all we got. My sob scares me. "I can't stop seeing her."

Dad reaches across the table and grabs hold of my hand. "I know," he says gently. No yelling, no soldiering up. "Believe it or not, but I loved that woman more than anything."

I never believed that but took him at his word.

"And she loved you."

That is harder to accept, Becky squeezing my thigh under my table to let me know she's there, that I am lovable, that my father is speaking the truth.

I can't thank either of them, my voice gone. I give Dad a small smile, realize he's just another man who's been through hell.

He thinks, *And given up everything.*

"Makes you think, huh?" I say but not like I'm being a dick. "Like maybe we fucked up pretty bad. Like maybe all of this was the biggest mistake ever."

"What could we have done differently?"

"Run. Hide. Not jump into the middle of it."

Dad shakes his head. "No. All this," he says, spreading his arms wide, a grimace as pain rips through his stomach. "All of it was inevitable. They had this planned for such a long time."

"But did it have to be us?"

"Joe, it had to be someone." Dad takes off his glasses and cleans them on his shirt. "I'd rather fight for what I believe. Fight for what I love."

Becky squeezes my leg. "We understand. Least I do."

I lean against the wall, the glass window cool on my forehead. The wheels on our bus go round and round. Round and round.


Becky says, "Wake up." She shakes my shoulder.

"You okay, Joe?" Dad asks.

I keep my eyes closed, a furnace raging in my chest. I feel fucking awful, hope it'll get better in the next thirty minutes.

Dad says, "Twelve minutes."

Dirt says, "Eleven."

I hadn't thought I was out that long, but barely have the strength to lift my head off the window. I feel like such a failure when I admit, "I don't know if I can make it."

From up on the bunk, Chip says, "We've got something that'll help, give you some clarity and energy."

"What?"

"It's a temporary fix," Dad says, nodding at the small black bag beside him.

Chip says, "A little cocktail I put together. I call it the Berserker."

Becky asks, "Do we want to know what's in it?"

"Let's just say only one of the seven substances wouldn't get me arrested, and that's the water I mixed it in."

I say, "Cocaine?"

"And then some."

I expect Dad to be looking at me, surprised that I'd experimented, but he's focused on the yellow pad in front of him.

Chip says, "I made enough for everyone. A little clarity before battle."

Becky trembles, squeezes my thigh. *Should I?*

I turn to her, my beautiful angel all banged up. *Your body. Your choice.*

*I've never done drugs.*

*Well, I wouldn't worry about a piss test.*

*It's not that.*

Dad says, "I'm doing a half dose, fortifying my body and mind, keep me focused on completing the mission."

Johnny's sitting on the stove, tossing a grenade back and forth. "I'll have what Joe's having."

Chip climbs down from the bunk and grabs the black bag. He sticks his head in the front, "Assuming no for you two."

Dirt says, "Correct."

Tone says, "No, count me in."

I tell Becky, *There's no pressure. No judging. Do what you want.*

She blows out the breath she'd been holding. *I'm with you.*

Chip sets the bag back on the table, Johnny scooting beside him.

Dirt says, "Eight minutes out."

Dad says, "Then let's get this rodeo started."

I jump when Chip drops a black tube on the table. "Shit, I thought it was a snake."

He says, "I suggest using it if you've got bad veins."

Dad picks it up and wraps it around his bicep, makes a fist.

I've hated needles since I passed out giving blood in second grade. I turn the yellow pad so I can see what looks like a huge rectangle around a bunch of squares and arrows, lines going this way and that. "What is it?"

Dad waits until Chip pulls out the needle. "Oooh boy," he says, rubbing the cotton swab up and down his arm. He points at the pad. "That's our mission."

I blink away some of the cloudiness, flick my ear to keep me awake. "Looks like a giant house."

Dad unties the tube and hands it to Johnny. "A mansion in Bel Air. We got a party to crash."

# CHAPTER TWENTY-EIGHT

"Breathe." The whisper's weird coming from me. Becky's curled on my lap, hands hiding her face. I'm propped against the backdoor, praying it doesn't pop open and dump us both headfirst on the street. "Breathe."

She shakes. *Shouldn't have done this.*

I hold her tight and say, "It's gonna be okay," because I'm a fucking liar and she did the exact thing for me two hours ago.

*Holy shit, holy shit,* is all she keeps thinking, rocking back and forth.

I stay calm, my mind the sharpest it's been since this mess started, my heart beating like a horse sprinting down the track. *It's okay.* I place a light kiss on the back of her beanie, breathe in the perfume mingling with all of our sweat, fear, and sickness. *It's just the drugs. You got to chill.*

Our roles have completely reversed, the first time Becky isn't on top of the situation. *I can't. I can't. I can't,* the saddest mantra I've heard from her.

I think, *Maybe you can't.* When Becky started tripping, thinking of jumping out the door, I worried we all got a bad dose. But not anymore. The cocktail's working wonders for me, my pain nearly gone, the nausea a minor inconvenience. It's my turn to be the strong one. I believe it when I think, *But together we can.*

Becky grabs my hand, presses it to her slippery check. *I don't want to die. Not on my birthday. Not any day.*

*Then don't.*

*Joe, we're out of chances. This is it.*

I've had plenty of time accepting my impending doom, but only my own, the movie in my head always ending with Becky making it, living a wonderful life, experiencing everything she dreamed of. That dream feels way more like a fairy tale now, but I stay positive and parrot advice Sharon had passed on. *We're alive right now. And right now is all that matters.*

From the front, Dirt says, "Pulling over in one minute."

Chip pops his head out from the bunk. "I'm in their system and looped the feed. No telling how long we have before they figure it out."

I wipe Becky's tears. *Right now, I'm giving comfort to a beautiful soul who has done ten times that for me. Right now is special.*

Johnny walks over to Dad, who's lying on the table, his legs dangling off the edge. "How you doing, Hank?" he asks, offering his hand. "How's it feel?"

"Ooooh boy," Dad says, his face scrunched up when Johnny helps him sit hunched over, elbows on his knees. "Barely felt a thing."

Johnny laughs and hands Dad a tiny scrap of shiny metal. "And they said I wasn't smart enough for med school."

Dad looks at the metal and says, "How cute. I should have kept Joe's and made us matching necklaces." He tosses what I'm guessing is a bullet onto the floor and uses his hands on his knees to straighten up. "Goddamn, that cocktail ain't no joke, Chip."

Keeping his head facing the front window, Chip says, "Only the best for you guys."

Dad looks about the RV, spots us. "Johnny, you watch after them."

Johnny helps Dad to his feet. "You know it."

Becky's been too busy listening, her panic subsiding. While she's in the right frame of mind, I tell her, *You got this, Becky. You ready?*

She wraps her arms around mine and makes me squeeze tighter. *I don't want this to end.*

*I don't either.* Whether she means the hug, the closeness, or our lives, it doesn't matter, I'm right there with her. But Dad is saying his goodbyes and heading our way. I tell her, *Come on, we got this. On our feet.*

Becky lets my arms go and sits up a little, sucks back snot. *I'm sorry.*

*No apologies. Let's do this. Pretend we're kids playing cops and robbers.*

*It's not a game.*

*Kind of is. And we've been pretty damned good at it so far.*

The motorhome slows and pulls to the curb. I pat Becky's back and think, *And who wants to get old and sick anyway? All the stress of not knowing what's going to happen, when you're going to die. If it's gonna be a heart attack, stroke, car accident or cancer.*

Dad stands a few feet away from us, his polo spotted with fresh blood a few inches above his waist. He points at me and says, "Your arm."

I hadn't realized it, but I'm rubbing Becky's back with my left hand, my arm out of the sling. I test it up and down, side to side, nearly no pain. *Becky, we've got a chance to make a difference.*

Becky stands and helps me to my feet.

I glance over at Dad and think loud so they can both hear. *A wise man told me nerves are there for a reason, to prepare our body for performance.* I take off the sling and throw it on the stove, hold her close. *Breathe deep and get ready for the final match.*

Becky hugs me tight and says, "Thank you," her voice calm like her mind.

"Hate to break this up," Dad says, "but I've got some work to do."

I let go of Becky and face my father, the man I hated for all the wrong reasons, never understanding who he was or why he acted.

Dad shakes his head. "No time for that, son."

Even if my brain wasn't messed up, I'd be able to count our hugs on both fingers, no one in our family ever showing affection. I wrap my arms around him and try not to cry. "I'm sorry…"

"Be sorry for nothing." Dad steps back and takes off his glasses, tosses them into the corner, the lenses cracking. He waits for me to lock eyes. "This isn't goodbye," he says. "I'll see you inside."

Dirt takes a right at the stop sign, everything clear in all directions, not a car on the street, the privileged all parking within the gates of their estates.

Becky's doing better, standing by my side, both of us holding onto the bunk. It seems like we should be used to this by now, but, holy shit, this is it. This is the part of the game where you go against the big boss and we're out of extra lives.

Becky nudges me in the side. *Relax. We got this.*

It's nice having the old Becky back, exactly what I need to keep me focused. But my heart, it's fucking racing. A goddamn motorboat with no brakes.

She chuckles. "Brakes?"

Chip's crouching on the bunk a few feet away. He smiles and says, "It's just the crystal meth, caffeine, and a few other ingredients."

Becky says, "I need this for my next match."

No one says a word but we're all thinking that this is the next match. Our last match.

"Time to rock and roll, boys and girls," Dirt says, the turn indicator ticking. He takes us right at the stop sign and says, "Approaching the rear of the property."

Chip gives us a small wave and lifts the hatch directly above him. He stands on the bunk, his upper half sticking out the roof. He radios, "Slow. Southwest corner is best option."

Dirt says, "Everyone hold on."

Becky and I are already clutching the bottom of the bunk, but I let go with my right hand so I can hold her closer, my last chance to make her feel safe.

Chip says, "Cut the lights."

Beyond Brightside

The street goes dark, and we thump onto the sidewalk, coast to a stop, the ivy-covered fence just inches from our passenger window.

Chip says, "Here we go," and there goes one boot then the other out the hatch.

From behind us, Tone says, "Women first."

Becky climbs onto the bunk, sword sheathed on her back. Without hesitation she raises herself onto the roof.

Tone and Johnny help me up even though I could do it on my own. Tone claps my leg. "Save your energy, soldier."

The mattress is soft enough to sink into but difficult to crawl on. It is tempting to lie on the cool sheets and go out peacefully, but I made a promise.

Chip says, "Hold up," and lowers onto the bunk, scoots next to his rifle. "Good luck, Joe."

The night is darker than I expected, the breeze energizing. Becky's crouched near the edge of the motorhome's roof, looking past the manicured yard of green grass and hedges at the huge mansion a good fifty yards away.

*Seventy-five*, she thinks in total mission mode.

I don't see a front door, just rows of brightly lit windows, eight on each of the first two floors, another four on the third.

*Guard to the left by the pool. Another on the third-floor balcony.*

Everything's blurry half that far, but I trust her. I'm almost to Becky when my foot gets caught and I fall forward. Becky sticks her arm out and pulls me onto her, saves me from the rows of razor wire spiraled atop the fence beside the motorhome.

My heart's jackhammering, my mind matching it. *It's okay. It's okay.*

Becky and I get on our knees by the edge of the RV. Johnny joins us with Tone right behind him. Tone whispers into the radio. "We're set."

My dad and Chip both copy.

Dirt says, "You're a go."

Tone picks up the rope that I'd tripped on and tests the knot with a hard tug. He says, "Watch how I do it. Whatever you do, do not touch that fence."

I've already imagined what those blades would've done to my face and don't need the reminder.

He creeps to the edge of the vehicle and jumps, swings back toward the fence, letting go for a soft landing on the grass.

Tone tosses the rope to Becky. Johnny tells her, "Go."

Becky leaps without hesitation, Laura Croft swinging through the jungle, dismounting in a three-point stance, head scanning left and right.

Johnny reels in the rope and offers it, looks a little wobbly.

I'm nervous about my shoulder and tell him, "You first."

"Got it," he says with a smile. He jumps farther than either of them but swings back faster. He thinks, *Oh shit,* and lets go, but his momentum runs him face first into the fence, a loud crash and zap, crackling as the smell of burning flesh wafts past me.

Tone says, "Fuck," and wraps the rope over Johnny's twitching body, rips him off the fence.

A flashlight's moving over by the five-car garage to our right. It turns our way, both Tone and Becky scattering into the shadows.

There's radio silence and a twelve-foot drop, now or never. My feet spring off the roof as Tone radios, "Guard coming."

I land on both feet, a loud rip coming from my left ankle. There's a sharp sting, but I pray it was just the tape tearing.

The radio clicks on. "Stay down," Tone whispers.

I bury my face in the wet grass, hope all my black blends in. Johnny's still crackling a few feet away, burnt hair and skin making me gag.

The flashlight comes closer, the beam bobbing over the hedges. I figure I have a few seconds and grab Johnny's grenade off his belt, clutch it in my left hand tight to my chest.

The beam flies over my shoulder, hits the fence.

The grenade pin feels like it'll pop right out, but there's no time to switch hands, and I don't know how far I can throw with my bad one. Last resort I'll blow myself to hell, not give these bastards the satisfaction of bringing me in.

The voice shouts, "Hey!" and I'm sharing the spotlight with Johnny. "What the—"

A thunk cuts him off, the thud of his body traveling through the ground.

The flashlight clicks off, but I can't see anything. Footsteps approach. Becky thinks, *It's okay. Let's move.*

I get up. *Johnny's dead.*

She looks over at the Boot, his head hanging on by a thick slice of ham. *So is this guy. Come on.*

The Berserker has heightened all my senses, but they're still shit. I have no idea where we're supposed to go.

*Tone's to our left,* Becky thinks, her sword dripping by her side. *Stay low. Boot on the balcony and another round the corner.*

I follow her hunched over like it's *Mission Impossible,* slipping the grenade in my cargo pocket and pulling out my gun. Ten times the fun of paintball with none of the worries about cleaning up after.

Becky says, *Stick to the plan.*


The pool's an abandoned paradise in the shadows to our left, a piano playing inside the house straight ahead. Becky pulls me down to a knee, points at the bobbing beam of light approaching from the side of the cabanas.

There are about twenty yards between us and the corner, the clank of a chain giving me goosebumps.

Becky thinks, *Just stay still.* Our back is to the bush. *He won't see us.*

*Fuck. His dog might.*

The rottweiler is on a leash, the Boot with the flashlight focusing straight ahead. The path they're on runs about ten feet from us, no chance the dog won't pick up our smell.

The dog stops and cocks its big boxy head.

Becky pulls me around the bush as the bark rips through the night. She puts me behind her and readies her sword. *Stay down.*

"Fender," the Boot calls, but not very loud, like the dog does this all the time.

Fender tears around the corner, five feet between us. He leaps at Becky, mouth open, ready to crush.

Becky thrusts the sword, piercing his chest, one hundred pounds thudding down on the ground.

*Holy shit,* Becky thinks, steadying herself as she slides out the sword. *Oh my fucking God.*

Fender's front paws twitching. "Come on, boy," the Boot says, lighting up the grass an arm's length away. "What is it?"

One step, two steps, three and he turns the corner. Becky jumps at him, her katana missing his neck but slicing deep across his chest, the flashlight falling. The Boot stands there petrified, remembers his gun too late because Becky's taking another swing. This one connects with his neck, sends him to the ground.

I grab Fender's paws and pull him deeper into the shadows, help Becky do the same with the Boot.

We're both breathing heavily, surprised we didn't shit our pants. Becky looks sick but shakes it off, peeks around the edge of the bush.

My eyes are fully adjusted to the dark, the Boot's face still shocked. One of the guys on the conveyor looked just like that, both eyes big, mouth open. Someone's brother, I'd called him. Just like this guy. Someone's brother.

Becky's furious and turns on me. *Stop it!* She shakes her head to show she's not playing around. *They're the enemy.*

"Harris," someone says right behind me, making me leap.

Becky pulls me back down so I'm below the bushes. *His radio. Grab it.*

I'm picking it up and it says, "Harris?" *What do I do?*

The Boot on the other end says, "Sounded like Fender."

Becky says, *Answer him.*

I've got no idea what Harris sounds like, so I keep it deep and muffled. "Just a squirrel."

The other Boot copies. I go to turn the radio turn off but he's still talking. "Meet me at the front door. C.O.N."

I say, "Copy," and power it off, toss it beside Harris.

Becky thinks, *We need to get in there fast.*

I kneel beside her and take in the scene: a house six times the size of the one Mom died in. *We've got this.* The Boot on the balcony is the only one I see, and he's facing the far wall. *No one's looking.*

*Stay right behind me.* Becky runs straight for the thick row of bushes that backs up to the building. There's a small opening toward the middle. Becky squeezes through it and crouches below the windows. The sharp tip of a branch breaks on my forehead, an inch lower and I'd be blind.

Becky points to our left where a small set of stairs is lit about twenty yards away. *Tone's clearing the backdoor.*

The door swings open and a Boot appears, gets on his radio. "Rufford, come in," he says, a faster voice than the last guy. "What's your twenty? Why aren't you at your post?"

I ask Becky, *Where's Tone?*

*Supposed to be controlling that door.* Becky creeps toward the Boot, prepared to sprint and stab him the second he turns our way.

The Boot's radio says, "Largent, you seen Harris?"

Largent, stays on the porch, maybe ten feet from Becky, no idea how quick she is with that blade. He says, "Last I saw he was rounding the front. Maybe ten minutes ago."

Becky slips a little closer. *I can get him if I have to. That happens and you're straight through that door.*

Largent reaches for his belt and pulls out his flashlight, shines it back and forth across the yard.

Becky's losing it, frozen to the wall. *What do I do?*

*Fuck, I guess get him.*

*Hold up,* Tone thinks, scaring the shit out of us. *I'm right behind you.*

I look along the building in the opposite direction but can't see him.

Largent puts away his flashlight and turns to the door, disappears inside.

*Alright,* Tone thinks. *We're missing out on the party.*

The window to my right slides open, lets out the music, a classical piece I probably once knew. Makes me think of a commercial with cats tiptoeing, but I'll blame that on the Berserker.

*Für Elise,* Tone tells me. *Now hurry up and get in here.*

# CHAPTER TWENTY-NINE

We're in a gigantic living room, fanciest one I've ever been in. Dark oak bookshelves built into two walls, a huge TV taking up the third. The only door is closed, the piano cold and crisp, cutting through the murmur of voices. Tone switches off the lights and slips into the corner behind the green armchair.

I'm still by the window, can see the backyard with the living room dark. Way off to the left, there's someone heading this direction, scanning back and forth with a flashlight. *Shit. He keeps going and he'll see Harris.*

*Let him be*, Becky says. *Stay focused.*

I can't listen to her because this guy's going to sound the alarm, fuck all our plans. He's still about thirty yards out but all I've got is this Glock.

Becky lays her hand on my cheek, turns me so we're facing, only inches apart. *We can't do anything about it now.* There's a fire raging in her eyes, a battle for control. Fear and love. Hate and honor. *All we can do is finish this.*

She's not expecting the kiss, but doesn't pull away, a light touch that might be goodbye.

There's movement to my right, so I push Becky out of the way and drop to my knee, raise my gun. My finger's on the trigger starting to squeeze when Becky grabs hold of the gun and says, "No!"

I wait to get shot, but there's only the blue and green waves pulsating on the TV's screen saver. *Shit, I'm sorry.*

Becky tells me, *Forget it,* and walks to the door. *Gotta make sure no one heard me.*

Tone thinks, *We're good. No one down this hall.*

I don't know what kind of range Tone has but I'll take his word for it. I'm useless past six feet, Becky about five times that. I ask her, *You picking anything up?*

Becky blows out a breath and presses herself against the door, lets in a line of light as she cracks it open.

I check behind us, breathe a little easier when the Boot with the flashlight walks out of sight, past the spot where we ditched Harris.

Becky thinks, *Damn. Your father wasn't kidding about it being a party.*

Tone tells her, *Eyes and ears.*

Becky nods. *At the end of this hallway there are several people standing around, drinks in hand. Three middle-aged men, fancy suits. Five women in dresses. One Boot.*

Tone asks, *Can you tell where the main party's taking place?*

*Well, there's nothing going on between us and them, and there isn't much house left to our left.*

*So the right,* Tone thinks. *Should've known with the piano they're probably in the ballroom.*

Becky wants to move, to do something. *So how long do we stay here?*

*Until his dad says so.*

*Well, I don't think....* Becky straightens up, takes a step back from the door.

I ask, *What's wrong?*

*Someone's coming.* She grabs my hand and runs to the couch.

I think we're taking cover behind it but she throws herself on the couch, lands on her back, pulls me on top of her, our guns clanking between us.

*What are you doing?*

She plants her lips on mine. *Kiss me!*

I expect to be shot in my back but do as she says. This won't be such a terrible way to go, Becky beneath me, her heart and my heart a duet of drumbeats. Her mouth warm, tongue darting. She tells me, *This is it.*

It's been ten seconds, maybe twenty. *No one's coming.*

Becky keeps me close, our lips locked. *Two of them. They're texting.*

I break off the kiss and suck in some air, don't want to pass out if I get up too fast.

Becky brings me back down, her hand on the back of my head.

The door opens and a teenage boy says, "What the fuck? You turn this off?"

I think he's talking to us, but a squeaky voice says, "Wasn't me."

The room lights flick on and Becky stops kissing. She looks over my shoulder and says, "We're sorry. Didn't think anyone was in here."

"Well, this is our room." The entitled little shit stuffs his phone in his front pocket and thumbs to the door. "The party's out there."

*Let me up.* Keeping it nice and friendly, Becky says, "Just a sec and we'll get out of your hair."

I roll off Becky and get to my feet. The boys look related, probably in high school, uncomfortable in white button-downs and black ties. Squeaky's probably a couple years younger, all his attention on the TV, which just flicked on, a game controller in his hand. His arrogant-looking brother shakes his blond shoulder-length hair, his chubby cheeks jiggling with it. He's checking out Becky, wonders if I was the one who beat her up.

She says, "Sorry to interrupt, boys. Back to the boring party."

Squeaky chuckles from the couch. "Have fun."

Blondie's looking at my forehead. "Why you bleeding?"

I didn't know I was but before I can say a word, he asks, "Who are you?"

Tone slides out from behind the chair and closes the door, submachine gun aimed at them. "Enough talk. Get your ass on that couch."

Blondie doesn't even blink when he sees the gun. "You know who we are? What the hell are you doing?"

Tone steps forward, eyes crazed, shoves his gun in the kid's face, the barrel smashing into his cheek. "Telling you to sit the fuck down," he says so calm that it chills my blood. "Another word and I splatter your head all over the place."

Blondie plops on the couch next to his brother, furious at himself for trembling. He doesn't say a word, but thinks, *Grandpa's going to kill you.*

I say, "Who's Grandpa?"

Squeaky doesn't know why I'm asking and says, "General—"

Blondie smacks his arm. "Shut the fuck up, Matthew."

"Here we go," Dad says, making me jump.

I spin around, expect to see him climbing through the window, but no one's there.

Becky thinks, *Radio*, just as Chip and Tone copy Dad's transmission.

Tone stands striking distance from the brothers, motions at the big screen behind him. "How do we watch the security cameras on here?"

Matthew points to the remote. Tone hands it over and Matthew switches it to channel 3.

A red alert flashes on the bottom of the screen with the words, *Person Approaching*. Dad limping up the driveway.

I ask, "What's he doing?"

"Following the plan," Tone says.

Dad pushes a button on the box by the gate and a buzzer rings. There's the click of someone picking up. "Hello," the no-nonsense voice says. "How may I help you?"

"My name is Hank Nolan, the number two most wanted man in America."

Becky puts her hand on my shoulder because I'm freaking out inside.

The voice says, "Stay right there."

"On one condition," Dad says. "I would like five minutes of the General's time. I will give a full confession of my crimes, all my knowledge of the Underground, but I will only give it directly to the general."

"Do not move or you will be shot."

Dad leans against the gate. "I'm not going anywhere. I'll take you to public enemies, one and five." He looks directly at the camera and says, "My boy is reckless and needs to be stopped."

The piano is no longer playing, people chattering down the hall. Matthew is on his knees, shirt off, cheek smashed against the floorboard, a gun buried in the back of his skull. His face crunches up as Tone applies pressure.

Tone turns to the one named Kirk, who's cringing on the couch, hugging himself. "Don't make me do it, fat fuck. Gonna get your brother splattered over a shirt?"

Kirk's the same age as Becky, but new to this game. "Fine. You can have it," he says, his voice trembling.

Tone turns the gun on him, keeps his voice low. "So take it off."

Kirk's taking too long and Tone's gonna fire. I cover my face so I don't get splattered, but Tone's expression gets Kirk moving. He pops the buttons free, hands over the shirt, covers his saggy breasts.

Becky's at the door looking like a waitress in Matthew's white button-down. She says, Hurry up."

The upper right quadrant of the TV screen shows the front gate, where five Boots surround my father.

Kirk's shirt is tight on the shoulders, but I get it buttoned, tucked in my pants. I grab my gun and hold it underneath a *Time* magazine, hope it'll look like I'm cleaning.

*Or reading on the job*, Becky thinks. *Also convincing.* She grabs a newspaper from the end table and pulls out the sword sheathed inside her pants.

*Hold up.* Tone grabs my discarded sweatshirt off the floor and wipes the blood off my forehead. *Anyone asks, say you're boyfriend-girlfriend, got into a little scuffle.*

That sounds like an excellent way to get arrested, but I understand there won't be any talking. On the bottom screen, three Boots march my father down the driveway.

Becky nods at the scared shitless and shirtless brothers curled up on the couch. *You got them?*

Tone says, "I'd rather be out there."

"Only way," she says.

He doesn't want to hear it and shakes his head. "Go then."

Becky steps into the bright hallway like she belongs, walking with a purpose, the folded newspaper in her right hand. The white marble sparkles, gaudy pieces of art spaced along both walls. She keeps to the left of the hallway so I don't accidentally put a bullet in her back.

*Smart girl.* There's no one standing around anymore, but someone in black pants is sitting in one of the high-backed chairs up ahead.

Becky thinks, *That's the rear of the foyer and main staircase.* She continues through the intersecting hallway, which is empty except for a fancy couple headed away from us.

We're only ten feet away from black pants, but I can't make out a face. It's definitely a guy by the size of his hand holding the armrest. A very tan hand.

Becky tells me, *Act natural.*

The guy leans forward and looks right at me, a shiny, silver Sentinel collar wrapped around his neck.

*Carlos,* Becky thinks because my brain's so slow I forgot my old boss.

Carlos doesn't recognize Becky but is all over me, his brain battling what to do as he stands.

Becky hears his decision and thinks, *Cover me.*

I don't know what I'm covering, but I step where she was as she leaps at Carlos, knocks him down in the chair.

Thank God no one's watching, a crowd of heads all facing the giant front doors, phones recording from every angle, their talking so loud they don't notice the thump.

*What are you doing?* Carlos screams in silence.

I move toward the middle of the hallway, make the mistake of looking back, Becky's foot smashing Carlos's balls into the chair, her sword midswing.

There's a waiter's black tray with two empty glasses on the console table. I get hold of it, knock it off when there's the loud clank of metal on metal, my shattering glass and a clattering tray a split second after.

I don't know what's happening behind me, my eyes on the crowd, a few of the women looking back. I hold up my free hand and wave them back to what they were doing. "Sorry," I say, surprising myself how calm I sound. "Had an accident."

They all look away, join the excitement as my father approaches.

From behind, it looks like Becky's comforting Carlos, cradling his head against her stomach. Another step and I hear her crying, see she has one hand holding his head there, the other holding her sword, the hilt buried between Carlos's chin and the metal collar.

Becky can't speak, just cries. *He said his daughter. They have his daughter.*

The front door opens to the clapping crowd.

*I don't want to do this*, she thinks. *I just want it to end.*

I put my hand on hers and pull out the sword, unleash a flood of blood, the bottom half of her shirt soaking red.

The sword's jagged, broken in half by the collar. Becky lays it on Carlos's lap and says, "Sorry."

The clapping dies down, a man telling everyone to be quiet.

I make out the top of my father's hair, the man in a black suit questioning him, nearly half a head taller. The man gets in Dad's face and barks, "You Hank Nolan?"

"Yes, I am. I need to speak to General—"

"Where are your son and the girl?"

"I said—"

The slap echoes across the room before I register the man's movement. He says, "Where are they?"

Dad groans.

I wait for him to give me up again, Brightside all over.

"Up the hill," he says. "The blue motorhome."

"You heard him," a powerful voice booms from the side room to the right. "Go get those pieces of shit."

# CHAPTER THIRTY

The ballroom is huge, nearly the size of the VFW hall, with a ceiling twice as high. A shiny wood floor and ornate curtained windows instead of white tile and brick. Nestled against the wall of windows are fancy tables with wine glasses and cheese platters, two dozen empty chairs, the guests in their thousand-dollar outfits standing in a half-circle around the stage that takes up the front of the room.

Becky and I are at the rear of the crowd. I'm keeping right in front of her so I can hear her thoughts and no one sees her blood-stained shirt.

The stage is two feet high, just tall enough for me to see the top of the piano in the corner. The wall is a magnificent marble fireplace with an enormous painting hanging above it. Lights above and below shining on the gold-framed mountainside scene, the sun breaking over the trees. Like I'm back in Brightside looking out my window. The one Rachel splattered with her brains.

*Joe! Focus.*

I say sorry and look for Dad. He's down on the stage where I can't see him. That's where he's been since he got dragged in by the two Boots standing on either side of General Voltier, his forehead carved with the kind of deep-set wrinkles you get from seeing some serious shit.

The general dons a creepy smile, waits for the crowd to quiet. "Thank you all for coming to our special day of celebration. What luck to have unexpected guests make it so much sweeter." The general faces the TV. "Turn to the front gate," the general says like he's speaking to Alexa.

The flat-screen filling the side wall pops on, switches to a view of the street, our blue motorhome just visible at the top of the small hill.

The general holds out his arms like he's some magnificent magician. "Let us watch what happens to enemies of the state."

I ask Becky, *What now?*

*We wait for the sign.*

Four Boots walk in a line toward the motorhome, submachine guns ready. Holy shit, the tension's high, the room silent except for their minds screaming for my blood.

*Joe, put it back,* Becky thinks.

I look down, see the grenade in my left hand, slip it back in my pocket.

The general says, "It's okay, sweetheart. You can come up."

I can't see who he's talking to until a pudgy preteen with long blond hair steps on stage and hugs him.

The Boots on screen plod forward, split the distance between the motorhome and the front gate.

The general wraps his arm around the girl's shoulders and keeps her close. "It's okay, Natalie. He can't hurt you."

The chubby cheeks and blue eyes say Matthew and Kirk are her brothers.

I'm watching the general, but everyone else is glued to the screen, so many minds with one message. *Kill that motherfucker.*

There's a loud pop from outside, a communal gasp in here. Another pop and a second Boot flops to the street. Pop, pop, the other two collapse, no one saying a word.

The general barks, "Get them!"

The motorhome's headlights blink on as more Boots run on the screen, sticking to the trees and shadows.

The Boot to the general's right shouts, "Secure the gate!"

No one besides Becky recognizes Dirt walking onto the bottom of the screen, and none of the Boots see him aiming his M27 at their backs. Dirt puts three pops in each target, drops them all.

The women are screaming, the men shouting. Two Boots I hadn't seen have their guns pointed at the windows toward the front gate that's halfway closed.

The motorhome blasts forward, its lights growing bigger. One of Dirt's victims is crawling to the sidewalk, almost there when the motorhome flattens his head, the general hiding the girl's face against his chest.

"Lockdown! Lockdown!" an official sounding voice shouts over the speaker.

Unseen locks slam into place, steel shutters descend, people screaming and pushing, the motorhome filling most of the screen, the gate nearly closed.

A Boot yells, "Protect the principal."

The gate looks solid, but the motorhome is huge. It changes direction at the last second and slams into the power pole to the right, the entire motorhome exploding, rocking us to the ground, blowing in the windows, the power gone.

A flickering light is coming from the flames outside. A woman nearby cries for help. "Someone," she says. "My husband's hurt."

No one cares, everyone crawling over each other through broken glass, trying to get away.

I don't know where Dad is, but he thinks to Becky so loud it echoes in her head. *Get him!*

I'm on my feet, gun in hand, Becky beside me. I tell her, *You get the general. I'll grab the girl.*

My heart's pounding, finger on the trigger, can't see a fucking thing with all the bodies bouncing off each other, shining their phone flashlights in everyone's wide-eyed face, screaming out names. An overwhelming cry of *Help!*

I don't know where Natalie went, so I scramble to the stage where I last saw her.

From the foyer, someone shouts, "The door! The door's locked!

I pass a Boot who thinks, *These assholes wouldn't make it a day in the field.* Loud enough for all to hear, he says, "We're safe inside."

I kick the bottom of the stage a second before a flashlight flicks on, that same Boot behind it. He points it at the foyer door and says, "Everyone he—"

There's a loud blam and an "Ooomph!" The flashlight clatters on the floor, his body right behind it.

"Down!" It's another Boot, but sitting down, his back to the wall. "Everyone down! Get below the windows!"

I stay on my feet, hope that Dirt won't open fire. The flashlight's beam is angled my way and lights Natalie, who's balled up a few feet away by the leg of the piano.

I hurry to her side and get on my knees, her thoughts a chainsaw cutting through the shrieks. My head's high enough to be taken off, but I'm trusting Dirt, focusing on my mission. I lay my hand on Natalie's shoulder, my arm shaking from the sobs wracking her body. "Everything's okay, sweetie," I say loudly because whispering won't work. "I'll take you to your brothers."

She looks up but it's too dark to see her features. "Are they okay?" she asks, the voice of a child.

"Yeah, my friend's keeping watch over them."

Someone picks up the flashlight, and our side of the room is back in darkness as he heads for the foyer. I put my hand on Natalie's back and say, "Hold on."

The guy with the flashlight makes it one, two, three steps before the explosion knocks him off his feet.

His partner crouching between the windows shouts, "Sniper pinning us down in the ballroom!"

Natalie squeals, "They're gonna shoot us!"

I shush her and say, "Stay low and keep hold of my hand. Can you do that?"

She thinks she can and squeezes so hard it hurts.

The door leading to the foyer is packed full of people, and the door on this side of the room is where they took the general.

The hallway is dark, a few inches of night giving us just enough light to see about three feet in front of us. I keep it slow while I get my bearings and listen for Becky. I ask Natalie, "You doing okay?"

She starts sobbing again, stops moving. "No!"

"Come on, Natalie, we've—"

The ballroom door bangs off the wall, the Boot who'd been hiding below the window is running full speed, shotgun in hand, no time to slow down.

There's going to be a collision, so I snatch Natalie and draw her close, use my back to shield her.

The Boot jukes to the side because he just wants away from the bullets, but his shoulder catches mine, all three of us falling. I land on Natalie, the Boot not so lucky, his head thunking on the baseboard.

I can see in the dark, his head's right there, the shotgun out of his reach. Natalie's facing the other way, and I've got my Glock aimed, my finger on the trigger, but I can't pull it. This guy's a coward, pretending he's knocked out, thinking about how he should've listened to his wife.

The emergency lights flicker on and the steel shutters descend, click into place.

I help Natalie to her feet and ask, "Do you know where they took your grandpa? That room would be the safest for you."

She seems like a sweet kid, nothing like her brothers. "There's only one room we're never allowed in," she says. "Upstairs at the back."

I feel terrible tricking her, but say, "Good job, Natalie."

The Boot keeps still, his mind tries to place my voice. I kick his shotgun farther down the hall and head for the stairway at the end. We're heading up when Natalie says, "What about Matthew and Kirk?"

I say, "Hold on." I press my mike and radio, "Bring the boys upstairs soon as it's clear. Safe room is at the back."

Natalie squeezes my hand. "I'm scared," she says, sounding like a mouse.

I whisper, "Everything will be okay," and start up the next flight of stairs.

We're nearly to the top when Becky thinks, *Stop!* but it's too late. She's standing in front of me on the landing, looking away, both blood-stained hands in the air. There's a dead Boot by her feet, her knife buried in his neck.

*Your pocket,* Becky thinks. *Do it!*

I let go of Natalie's hand and pull out the grenade, step to the side so I can see where to toss it. The woman on the other side of the landing has a silver Sentinel collar around her neck, her gun aimed at Becky's head.

Sara.

We need to hurry but any quick movement and Sara's shooting. I'm hiding behind Becky, hiding Natalie behind me. Sara blocks the door ten feet away at the end of the hall, black pants and blue blouse, the outfit of the enemy. There's another closed door to Becky's left, an open one on the right. I've got no idea what Sara's aim is like or if she's ever shot a gun, but if she empties it she'll probably hit all three of us.

Becky says, "She can hear you."

"And I can shoot," Sara says, her solid stance backing her up. "Don't move, Joe. And put that away."

Natalie wonders why Sara's pointing a gun at us if she knows my name.

I speak softly, don't want to upset Sara, whose rosy red cheeks pale in comparison to her much brighter lipstick. "I can't do one and not the other," I say as I take a small step to Becky's right, slip the grenade back in my pocket.

Sara switches the gun from Becky to me, fading bruises on both her cheeks. "Stop!"

I keep Natalie behind Becky and tell Sara, "Look, she's only a child. Let's get her out of the way."

Sara can't see who it is, but doesn't say no.

I bring down Becky's hand and guide it to Natalie's. "Becky will take care of you."

Natalie says, "Okay," but is trying to figure out who we are. Thinking of the Sentinels, she says, "I thought they work for us?"

Sara says, "I do."

"Then—"

I face Sara, blocking Becky and Natalie with my body, step over the Boot with the knife in his neck. I take one side step then another and say, "You don't need these two."

Sara sees what I'm about to do and says, "Stop!"

I push Natalie and Becky through the open doorway, realize I'm close enough to read Sara's thoughts. I tell her, "You're not hurting them."

Sara's got the trigger pulled halfway, her eyes narrowed, burning into the spot on my forehead she's about to blast.

This isn't the way I thought I'd go, but it's all good. Death is death, it's all the same. Not wanting Sara to feel guilty, I think, *It's okay.*

Her face is all anger, eyes like spears. "I fucking hate you."

"I did everything I could to—"

"No!" Sara screams so loud everyone in the mansion can probably hear it. "You ruined everything!"

My blood's thrumming through my veins, my heart drumming on my chest, but I stay calm. More curious than mad, I ask, "Why are you doing this?"

"Why do you think?"

"Because you hate me."

She says, "Not everything's about you."

"You're right. It's about you. You helping the enemy."

From the safety of the side room, Becky thinks, *Joe, we got to hurry.*

Sara keeps the gun aimed at my head, her arms steady. "Tell your girlfriend I've got all day."

Neither one of us says a word.

Sara's face falls, any chance of forgiveness gone. "Oh my God. I should've known. You're a fucking predator."

Becky says, "No, he's not!"

Sara shakes her head. *I never meant a thing to you.* "You're just a user!"

I can't argue with her. "We need to get through that door."

Sara's still stuck on our kiss, how I thought it silenced everything, collapsed my universe.

That was Day 99. Only eight nights ago, but might as well be forever.

Her gun lowers a little but her finger's on the trigger, ready to blast me center mass. "I hate you."

"Yes, Sara, I'm a huge piece of shit. I dragged you and Danny into this mess and I'll always be sorry for that. Shoot me if you want but let them finish their mission. Don't help these people."

Tears run down her cheeks, much of her anger now aimed at herself. "If I don't cooperate, they'll kill Danny."

"You don't know?"

"Know what?" she says, voice cracking.

Becky reminds me we got to move. *Backup's got to be coming.*

"They killed Danny."

"I don't believe you."

"I don't know when but it was before we got to the park. They were going to pulverize him with all the other bodies at the recycling center."

Sara shakes her head, the silver collar around her neck unmoving. "You're lying," she says, so softly it's more like a question.

Tone warns he's behind me to my left so I don't block his shot. He asks Sara, "Want to see the video?"

She aims at Tone who's crouched at the top of the stairs, his M-16 trained on her. "I can't leave," Sara says. "Next it'll be my parents. Someone else I love."

Becky steps out from the room, gun down by her side. "I'm sorry, Sara, but they're probably already dead. They murdered mine."

I say, "And they're never going to stop unless we make them."

The radio buzzes, then goes to heavy breathing. "Not looking good out here, fellas," Dirt says. "Got reinforcements flying in."

Tone says, "You two figure this shit out later. We need the general."

I ask him, "Where are the boys?"

"Downstairs."

Sara asks, "His grandsons?"

Tone nods.

Her eyes go big. "Oh my God, you killed them!"

Natalie screams, "No!"

I say, "What the fuck, Tone?"

Tone keeps his gun trained on Sara, his hate on me. "Fall in line, soldier, and do your goddamn duty. How many more lives you going to let this bitch ruin?"

There's a loud blast and Tone's thrown forward, dead before he hits the carpet, the back of his head a big mess of blood, brains, and buckshot.

The Boot who had crashed into us down below is pumping the shotgun, running up the last stairs, aiming at my chest.

I fumble for my gun, can't get it out the holster.

A shot's fired, but not from his gun, the bullet whizzing past my ear and punching through the Boot's forehead, his body thumping down the stairs.

Sara lowers her gun and sobs. "I'm sorry."

I get my gun out in case anyone else is coming. "You just saved me."

"It's my fault Danny's dead," she says, the most despondent I've ever heard her.

I step toward her, see all the makeup was to hide her bruises. "The Boots killed him."

Becky tells me, *She turned them in, just like I told you.*

Sara says, "I'm sorry. I thought it was the only way."

"None of that matters. Help us get…"

"What is it?"

"Your collar. There's a row of red lights around it."

Sara drops the gun, both hands flying to the collar. It's not budging.

I take hold of it, a dull buzz aching my bones. There's no button to press, no way to get it off her. I don't know what's going to happen, but I stay calm, tell her, *Look at me, Sara. It's going to be over.*

*Joe.* Her eyes are so blue, so beautiful, drowning in grief. *Joe, I'm scared.*

There's a sharp click and Sara winces, shrieks as rivers of blood pour out from under the collar and run down like lava. She goes limp and crashes to the carpet.

I kneel beside her, ignore all the blood, tell her it's going to be okay.

"Joe, stop." Becky pulls my hand off Sara and says, "Remember your mission."

# CHAPTER THIRTY-ONE

The wood door Sara was guarding is locked, and we don't have time to look for keys. I hurry over to the Boot Sara plugged and scoop up his shotgun, peek down the staircase but don't see anyone.

Becky and Natalie have their backs to the wall. I tell them, "Cover your ears and eyes."

The shotgun blows a hole in the door that's big enough to reach through. I unlock it and ease it open, waiting for return fire.

The bedroom is gigantic, several times the size of the one I had in Brightside. To my right is a closet with a sliding mirrored door, a bathroom beside it. The middle of the room is taken up by a massive four-corner bed, and taking up the left side is a sunken hot tub that looks like it could hold a dozen people.

Becky brings Natalie in, and they follow me as I clear the bathroom, check under the bed, even make sure there's no one hiding in the hot tub. *It's a dead end.*

Gunfire explodes, wheels squeal, metal crashes, all barely muffled by the shuttered windows. There aren't any other doors in here. *We're trapped.*

The radio buzzes. "Heading inside," Dirt says. "Can't hold them long."

Becky's looking to me for the answer, a beautiful angel covered in blood and bruises, a chorus of gunshots blazing below.

Natalie's been hunched over since she heard about her brothers, hasn't said a word. She jerks back when I touch her arm and tell her I need her help. I try to sound nice when I ask, "Where's the room you couldn't enter?"

I raise her chin so she'll look at me. "Is this it?"

Natalie nods. *The closet.*

It looks like a normal mirrored closet door, but it doesn't slide. Doesn't budge. It's a door, but there's no handle, no way for me to open it.

Becky thinks, *Right in front of you, above the door.*

The camera's small, but all we've got. I want him only seeing me so I direct Becky to my left. She guides Natalie by the neck up against the wall. I tell her, *You watch that door. See if you can block it.*

Natalie says, "I want to go home."

I shush her. "We know. This'll all be over soon."

The overhead speaker startles me, the general saying, "Now what?"

"This is Joe Nolan."

"Oh, I know who you are, Joe. I know all about you."

I can't think of anything to say with Becky grunting and shoving a waist-high dresser in front of the door, gunshots down below. I pretend this is some movie, and I'm the badass tough guy. "Heard you've been looking for me."

"You're a difficult man to get hold of." It sounds like he's enjoying this. "Must take after your father."

"Yeah, my mom wasn't so good at that, huh, you fuck."

"So what's the plan, Joe? Call to say goodbye to your father?" the general says, waiting to make sure I got it. "Planning on waiting us out?"

I keep cool, pretend I knew they had Dad. "Well, I was hoping you weren't going to be such a pussy. Is it everyone in the army, or just the generals who run when it comes time to battle. I hope you know I'm filming all this."

He doesn't call me on the lie, doesn't seem to care. "You guys were pretty good, but how could you not plan for a safe room?"

"No, we planned for it," Becky says. She leaves the door and joins my side, stares at the camera. "Took the necessary precautions, painful though they might be."

"You do understand the game is over," the general says. "Your time is up."

Becky says. "I accept that. You're totally right. But at least we're not going out alone." She grabs Natalie's wrist and pulls her between us, makes a show of sticking the barrel under her chin.

I say, "But enough about that. How about you open this door before we splatter your granddaughter's blood all over the ceiling. I've seen it done. It leaves quite an impression."

The delay says he's scared. "You're going to burn," he says.

"I don't want this to happen, General. I didn't want your grandsons killed either."

He's silent.

The voices are louder, might be on the staircase. "So, like I said, 'Open the fucking door.'"

"I'll kill your father."

Becky holds up a small black remote with a red button. "And I push this button, vaporize every inch of that room."

"He was pat down. It's a bluff."

Becky says, "Yeah, well, too bad you didn't check his wound."

The speaker buzzes and the general says, "Killing me won't do anything for you."

His tone says they've seen the lump pushing out Dad's incision, the one I knew nothing about until Becky filled me in. I tell the general, "Neither will letting you live."

There's no response, just more voices coming from the staircase.

I take Natalie and hold her in front of me, tell him, "You're running out of time."

He says, "I guess we both are."

I feel awful doing it, but pluck a handful of Natalie's hair, her shriek even worse than I hoped for. "Sacrificing your only remaining grandchild. How noble."

"Stop," he says, more of a plea than an order. "Okay," the general says. "We'll open up, exchange Natalie for your father."

I stick my gun under her chin; raise it until she's staring into the camera, tears falling. "We're not fucking idiots. We trade for you."

"Don't hurt her," he says. "I'll bring out your father."

Becky sets the shotgun down and tears a curtain from the window, ties Natalie's hands behind her back. She walks her to the dresser propped in front of the door and squeezes behind her so she can cover the safe room door and bedroom door at once. "You don't move until I say so," Becky tells Natalie like she's talking to a hardened criminal.

I take cover at the edge of the bed, my gun trained at the safe room door, a few feet too far to hear what the girls are thinking.

The general asks, "Are you ready for the exchange?"

There haven't been any more gunshots, no way for us to know what the general's been telling his men down the hall, their voices subdued.

Becky has a pistol in one hand, the remote in her other. She whispers, "They're waiting for the general's order. Can't see anyone through this, but I'm picking up their thoughts. Three or four of them."

A spasm shakes my failing body and I nearly drop my gun, time running out. I set the grenade on the bed a few inches from my face. "Go," I tell the general. "Exchange."

There's a low buzz and the mirrored door swings open slowly, the shoulder of someone pushing it the first thing to show.

Becky's got a clear shot of the safe room, but the half-opened door blocks everything but a sliver of light blue wall. I tell them, "Open it all the way."

My Dad walks out with the tall Boot that smacked him crouching behind, a big black gun driving into the back of Dad's head. Dad's in my range, the Boot just outside of it. Dad thinks, *It's time.*

I say, "That's not the deal."

From where we can't see him, the general says, "No, but this is the situation."

Dad thinks, *Press it!*

I've got no idea what kind of blast it'll be and clutch the bed as Becky holds up the remote. She steps in front of Natalie and says, "Goodbye."

The Boot pushes Dad right at me, fires as he backpedals toward the closing door, blam, blam, blam.

Dad slams face first into the foot of the bed and crumples to the floor. I pull the pin and leap to my right, pitch the grenade high and hard at the inside wall of the safe room.

The Boot in the doorway turns as it sails over his head and bounces off the back wall, but he's still firing blindly. Becky has her back to him, pressing Natalie against the wall.

I roll toward the bed as the general slams into the Boot's back, spinning him around so he's facing the grenade, the general controlling him by his jacket.

I bring up my gun, get the general in my sight, fumble with the trigger.

Then *boom!* A giant cloud of smoke, my hearing gone, blown onto my back.

Everything's ringing, and I'm staring at two visions of the ceiling until it blends into one. I roll over and get on all fours, grab the Glock.

No one else is moving, everyone on the ground, no thoughts close enough to hear. That's scary because Dad's in range, face down at the foot of the bed, fresh blood spreading across the back of his shirt.

The general's on his back halfway between Dad and the safe room, stuck under the Boot-turned-shield. The Boot's entire front is shredded, his face unrecognizable, a pool of red surrounding them. The general's eyes are open, but he's definitely stunned, blinking at me like what he sees make no sense.

Natalie's on the ground next to the dresser. Becky's piled on top of her, eyes closed, body limp.

I crawl to Dad's side, keep my gun aimed at the general's face.

The ringing's still loud, but I can make out Natalie's frantic screams, unable to get out from under Becky with her hands bound behind her back.

I say, "It'll be okay," but I can barely hear myself. I shake Dad, but there's nothing. I shake him harder, hate seeing how far the crimson puddle has spread.

Dad jerks his head off the ground, puts his face back down with a loud moan.

I touch his forehead, tell him, *We're almost done.*

He grimaces and pushes himself up so he's sitting against the foot of the bed.

The general's no threat so I check Becky. She doesn't respond to my touch so I circle to her side, slipping on the slick tile. The entire left side of her body is drenched in blood, a large piece of shrapnel sticking out of her neck.

I ease Becky off Natalie, hold my broken angel, her fight over so young. Her cheek is warm, her hair soft under my palm, no amount of my tears able to bring her back.

A week ago it was Rachel, now Sara and Becky, everyone who cares for me paying the price.

Natalie's petrified, eyes like a trapped deer's.

I say, "You're safe." *Thanks to Becky. Not your grandfather.*

She stays balled up, eyes on me, but no movement.

I think maybe she doesn't hear me, but it's probably just shock, her not trusting a bloodied killer. I back up and lay Becky down, pick up thoughts by the door.

I can't hear the man's whispering, but he's thinking it loud. *We go on three. Two.*

I stay crouched, aim at the hole.

*One!* The door bangs, the dresser barely moving. "It's blocked!"

I fire two rounds through the hole, hear him cry out, then yell, "Agent down!"

*Time to wrap it* up. Dad's thoughts are slow. *We gotta go.*

I peek over the top of the dresser, can't see anyone in the hallway. *There's nowhere to go.*

*This is it, son.* His face is drained of all color. He nods at Becky. *Let's finish the job.*

I'm afraid to leave the door but know I can't guard it forever. I crawl back to Becky. *What am I looking for?*

The general clears his throat, spits out a mouthful of blood, his eyes now clear. "What did you do?"

"Saved your granddaughter, you piece of shit."

The general rolls the Boot off his chest, his legs still stuck. "You broke into my house and killed my family."

There's no gun within his reach, so I turn back to Becky, wonder what Dad was talking about.

*The remote,* Dad thinks. *Check her hand.*

I open her fist, the tiny black box slick with sweat, the single red button.

The general's talking but I'm barely listening, something about him making the world a better place.

I'm confused and hold up the remote for Dad. *It's real? I thought you tricked them.*

"Becky didn't press it," Dad says with much effort. "Worried it'd kill the girl."

"What heroes," the general says. "This is the strongest our country has ever been. The most secure."

I check the door, don't see anyone, train the gun back on him to make him nervous. "Yeah, at what cost?"

He says, "A few meaningless lives for the greater good."

Dad's barely with us, Becky gone, no one around to guide me, say something smart. Mom always said look on the bright side, but you see even half the things I've seen, do half the things I've done, and even the brightest side is pretty fucking dark.

I peek through the hole in the door, see three Boots with rifles. They all fire and I collapse on the ground as their bullets blast by overhead.

With the remote in my left and gun in my right, I huddle next to Dad, his eyes half closed. I ask, *You ready?*

He nods.

The general begs for his life, doesn't say a word about Natalie.

I can't believe I'd almost forgotten about her. I say her name, but she doesn't respond. I shoot the general in his side to get her attention.

The general's screaming for help and I'm yelling at Natalie. "You got five seconds to get in that hot tub!"

The general's holding his side, can't move, but Natalie's on her feet, crouched over and hurrying to the other side of the room.

*Maybe that's it*, I tell Dad. *We did something good by saving her. We weren't all bad.*

Dad tries to smile. *Joe, please do me the honor.*

I want to shoot the general so he'll stop yelling, but I'd rather he watch. I drop the gun and take hold of Dad's shoulders, put my head against his.

He says, "You made me so proud."

I say, "I love you."

*I always loved you.*

There's gunfire and wood flying, shouts and screams, but it doesn't matter. The general doesn't matter. Becky doesn't matter.

I tell Dad, *All that's left is you and me.*

*This is it.*

*This is*


The End

# REVIEW

If you enjoyed this book, I hope you'll take a moment to write a quick review. As an independent author, word of mouth and reviews are incredibly helpful. Whether you leave one star or five, honest feedback is truly appreciated.

And if you're on Goodreads or BookBub please stalk me. I believe the technical term is follow, but I strive on anxiety and what better way to amp it up than thinking there are hundreds of strangers stalking me. Plus, you'll be alerted to all my new books and deals. Sounds like a win-win to me.

To leave a review on Amazon - https://amzn.to/32dAU87
To leave a review on Goodreads – https://bit.ly/2EDs2zV

Thank you!

# ACKNOWLEDGEMENTS

I would like to thank my editors, Mary Nyeholt and Michael Tullius, for all their help putting this book together and keeping it consistent with both *Brightside* and *Try Not to Die: In Brightside*. Being able to work with my sister and father has been a wonderful experience and I'm grateful they still talk to me despite all the disturbing scenes I force them to read.

I'd also like to thank Doctor Mike Simpson along with Jason and Suzie Velez for their help answering medical questions regarding Joe's injury. Any mistakes in the book are due to me not following their advice.

# OUT NOW

### *Brightside*

Across the nation, telepaths are rounded up and sent to the beautiful mountain town of Brightside. They're told it's just like everywhere else, probably even nicer. As long as they follow the rules and don't ever think about leaving. Joe Nolan is one of the accused, a man who spent his life hearing things people left unsaid. And now he's paying for it on his hundredth day in Brightside, fighting to keep hold of his secret in a town where no thought is safe.

### *Try Not to Die: In Brightside*

Mark and 10th Planet Jiu Jitsu teammate Dawna Gonzales continue the Brightside saga, bridging the gap between the first book and sequel, this time from the eyes of a female teenage telepath.

### *Try Not to Die: In the Pandemic*

Mark and John Palisano take readers on the most intense hour they will ever spend on a cruise ship in this non-stop interactive adventure.

### *Untold Mayhem*

24 unique stories of madman and monsters. Crime stories filled with suspense, horror, and mystery. Immerse yourself into the world of untold mayhem.

### *Ain't No Messiah*

The coming of age story of Joshua Campbell, a man of death-defying miracles, whose father proclaimed him the Second Coming of Christ.

This psychological thriller takes us through Joshua's childhood of physical and emotional abuse at the hands of his earthly father, and into adulthood as Joshua attempts to break away from his family and church in order to find happiness.

The entire world is watching as Joshua prepares to finally show the world who he really is.

### *Twisted Reunion*

"Time-honored frights with innovation infused throughout."- *Kirkus Reviews*

Plunge deep into darkness with 28 terrifying tales. Explore heartache, happiness, and horror in this collection of all the stories in *Each Dawn I Die*, *Every One's Lethal*, and *Repackaged Presents*, plus two bonus stories.

### *25 Perfect Days: Plus 5 More*

A totalitarian state doesn't just happen overnight. It's a slow, dangerous slide. *25 Perfect Days Plus 5 More* chronicles the path into a hellish future of food shortages, contaminated water, sweeping incarceration, an ultra-radical religion, and the extreme measures taken to reduce the population. Through 30 interlinked stories, each written from a different character's point of view, *25 Perfect Days* captures the sacrifice, courage, and love needed to survive and eventually overcome this dystopian nightmare.

Beyond Brightside

## *Try Not to Die: At Grandma's House*

It's Grandma's House – quiet, cozy, nestled on a little mountain in West Virginia. What could possibly go wrong? A lot, actually.

So watch your back. Choose wisely. One misstep will get you and your little sister killed.

To survive, you'll battle creatures, beasts, and even your grandparents as you unravel the mystery of your older brother's death in this interactive, graphic novel.

## *Unlocking the Cage*

For his first nonfiction project, Tullius spent 3 years traveling to 23 states and visiting 100 gyms where he interviewed 340 fighters in his search to understand who MMA fighters are and why they fight.

"The result is a surprisingly revealing read recommended not just for enthusiasts of boxing, fighting, and MMA in particular, but especially for outsiders who abhor the idea of such a sport without really understanding its players. This audience will find their eyes opened about many things, including evolving values and maturity processes in life, and will discover *Unlocking the Cage* also unlocks preconceived notions about a little-understood sport." - *D.Donovan, Senior Reviewer, Midwest Book Review*

# COMING SOON

### *Try Not to Die: Super High*

Mark and Steve Montgomery team up to bring the Try Not to Die series to Florida. Become a young competitive sharpshooter and enjoy a night out in Miami. Just don't get bit by any of the bath salt people.

### *The Bridge*

The second book in the Tales of the Blessed and Broken series scheduled for release late 2021.

### *TBI or CTE: What the Hell is Wrong with Me?*

A nonfiction book where Mark chronicles his attempts at rehabilitating his brain. Through fighting, football, accidents, Mark accumulated quite a few traumatic brain injuries and is paying the price for his actions. This book hopes to help others recognize their own problems and give them tools to overcome their obstacles.

# ABOUT THE AUTHOR

Mark Tullius is the author of *Unlocking the Cage, Ain't No Messiah, Twisted Reunion, 25 Perfect Days, Brightside,* and the creator of the *Try Not to Die* series. Mark resides in Southern California with his wife and two children.

Be the first to know when Mark's next book is available! Follow him at https://www.bookbub.com/authors/mark-tullius to get an alert whenever he has a new release, preorder, or discount!

To follow and connect with Mark you can check out https://youcanfollow.me/MarkTullius

To sign up for Mark's no-spam newsletter go to his website: https://www.marktullius.com/

Podcast - https://viciouswhispers.podbean.com
Instagram - @author_mark_tullius
Facebook – http://www.facebook.com/AuthorMarkTullius
Twitter - https://twitter.com/MarkTullius
YouTube – http://www.youtube.com/MarkTullius

To hear free audiobooks and listen to Mark's weekly rant, be sure to look for his new podcast, *Vicious Whispers with Mark Tullius* which you can find on YouTube, iTunes, iHeart radio, Spotify, Stitcher and other places podcasts are played.

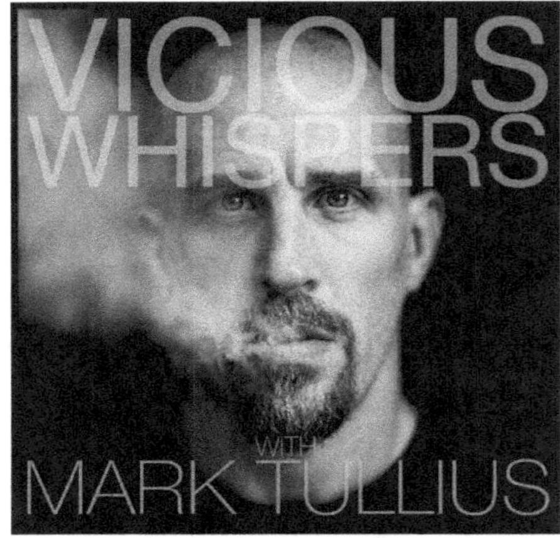


https://viciouswhispers.podbean.com